M3

Behind
the
Veil

Also in Large Print
by Linda Chaikin:

Swords and Scimitars

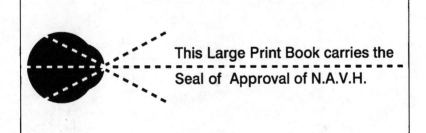

This Large Print Book carries the
Seal of Approval of N.A.V.H.

Behind
the
Veil

Linda Chaikin

F
Chai

Thorndike Press • Thorndike, Maine

10/98 Thorndike 22.95

Published in 1998 by arrangement with Bethany House Publishers.

Thorndike Large Print ® Christian Fiction Series.

The tree indicium is a trademark of Thorndike Press.

The text of this Large Print edition is unabridged.
Other aspects of the book may vary from the original edition.

Set in 16 pt. Plantin.

Printed in the United States on permanent paper.

Library of Congress Cataloging in Publication Data

Chaikin, L. L., 1943–
    Behind the veil / by Linda Chaikin.
       p. cm.
    ISBN 0-7862-1523-2 (lg. print : hc : alk. paper)
    1. Large type books. 2. Crusades — First, 1096–1099
— Fiction. I. Title.
[PS3553.H2427B44 1998]
813′.54—dc21   98-22308

Fictional Characters

Tancred Jehan Redwan, the hero, a Norman warrior, scholar, and seeker of Truth

Mosul, the Moor, and assassin; cousin to Tancred, and archenemy

Helena of the Nobility, Daughter of the Purple Belt, the beautiful Byzantine heroine

Nicholas, the maverick warrior-bishop, friend of Tancred, and Helena's uncle

Philip the Noble, Minister of War in Constantinople

Lady Irene, the aunt and enemy of Helena, the mother of Philip

Bishop Constantine in Constantinople, enemy of Nicholas

Bardas, the Greek eunuch slave belonging to Helena

Hakeem, the Moor from Palermo, and Tancred's faithful friend

al-Kareem, the Moorish grandfather of Tancred

Derek Redwan, deceased half brother of Tancred

Count Walter of Sicily, uncle of Tancred

Count Dreux Redwan, deceased father of Tancred

Count Rolf Redwan, uncle and adoptive father of Tancred

Prince Kalid, son of the emir of Antioch

Rufus, captain of Lady Irene's personal bodyguard

Adrianna, Helena's mother

Jamil, the Armenian slave boy serving Helena in Antioch

Aziza, Jamil's older sister and loyal maid to Helena and Tancred

Norris, one of Tancred's Norman cousins

Leif, another of Tancred's Norman cousins

Adele, niece of Bishop Adehemar and wife of Leif Redwan

Odo, the old Norman priest

Historical Characters

Alexius Comnenus, Emperor of Byzantium, A.D. 1081-1118

Bohemond I, Norman prince of Taranto

Count Raymond of Toulouse

Roger I, the Great Count of Norman Sicily

Godfrey of Bouillon, Duke of Lower Lorraine

Adehemar, Bishop of Le Puy, and official Papal Legate on the Crusade

Raymond of Aguilers, a chronicler of the First Crusade

Kerbogha, commander of Seljuk warriors

"The Red Lion of the Desert," Seljuk commander

Yaghi-Sian, Turkish commander at Antioch

Firouz, Christian Armenian in Antioch who delivered the city to the Norman Crusaders under Bohemond

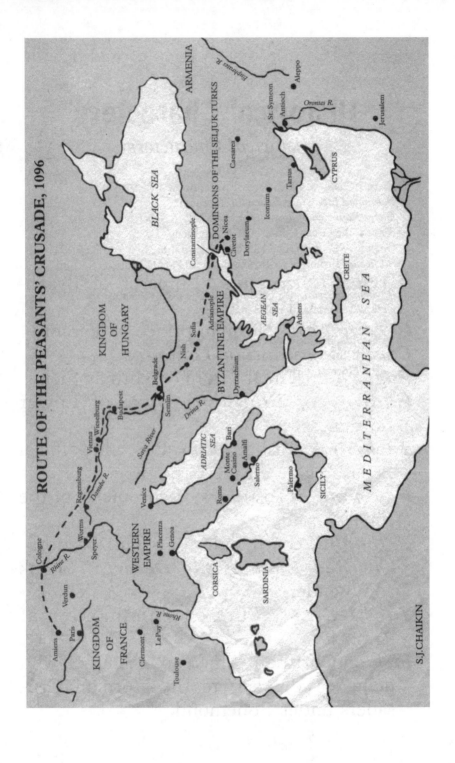

ROUTE OF THE PEASANTS' CRUSADE, 1096

S.J. CHAIKIN

PROLOGUE

What Has Gone Before

Count Tancred Redwan, a Norman knight from Sicily, has been wrongfully blamed for the assassination of his half brother, Derek. His Norman family is intent on making him stand trial for the murder. The only way to clear his name is to find the true murderer — his jealous Moslem cousin Mosul. In his search for Mosul, Tancred journeys to Constantinople, where he becomes involved with the beautiful Lady Helena of the royal house of Lysander. Helena's scheming aunt, Lady Irene, has arranged her niece's marriage to Kalid, a Moslem prince in Antioch, whom Helena detests.

After Helena and Tancred vow their loyalty and love to each other on the crusaders' battlefield, Tancred arranges for a military escort to take Helena and her mother, Adrianna, to the family castle. Confident that she is now protected from harm and saved from having to marry Prince Kalid, Tancred travels on to Antioch — to find the true assassin and avenge his brother's murder. He vows to return soon for Helena. . . .

PART ONE

Inside Constantinople

CHAPTER 1

In the Camp of the Red Lion

The crusaders camped that night among the spoils of the Red Lion of the Desert, whose tents and camels were sprawled along the desert plain between the flanking hills of Asia Minor. In the late hours of darkness, saturated with summer heat as the sky was throbbing with glittering stars, Tancred Redwan, exhausted from the day's battle, lounged near one of the tents on a red silk cushion left behind in the raid. Absently his strong fingers played with the gold silk fringe, his mind on Helena.

He had treated his own wounds received earlier in the day's battles and spread salve on his grazed side, binding himself with a clean cloth. His tunic was open to enjoy the faint breeze that stirred across the sand as he listened to the sound of a lute, remembering Helena's kiss while flickering fires wove through the night air like little gonfanons.

Silently, Bishop Nicholas Lysander, Helena's rugged warrior uncle from the west, squatted beside a small cooking fire, where a simmering stew bubbled in a blackened pot. From his moody expression, Tancred guessed that the warrior-bishop was worried over his sister, Adrianna. The child she was expecting by Prince Sinan, now dead, would be the grandson or granddaughter of the great Caliph of Baghdad. There would be trouble over who would rear the child.

Tancred remembered his own difficulties in Palermo, Sicily, and the conflict of faiths that had plagued him when growing up as the son of the great Norman Lord Dreux Redwan, who embraced Christianity, while his mother was from the Moslem family of al-Kareem. He'd been indoctrinated with both the Moslem religion and Christianity, and for a time he'd been obligated to memorize from both the Koran and the Bible, dividing his time, as well as his allegiance, between his teacher Nicholas at Monte Casino and his zealous grandfather in Palermo. Recently, Tancred had come to faith in Christ and carried a hand-bound New Testament that Nicholas had translated and presented to him as a gift when he arrived with the crusader knights.

He fingered the Scriptures, and although it

was too dark to read, he took satisfaction in feeling the pages and the leather that Nicholas had cut and trimmed to size. The New Testament was a precious and rare treasure. Except for the bishops in the great abbeys, there were few if any commoners outside the western and eastern branches of the Church who had access to the Word of God. He told himself he would live up to the privilege of his treasure by studying it daily. Recently, there had been little time. Battles surrounded him and loomed ever larger as the western lords and princes leading their armies made plans to capture Antioch from the Seljuk Turks, and finally, Jerusalem.

Seeing that Nicholas remained moody, Tancred attempted to dispel the dismal atmosphere. "Come, Nicholas, I am starving. Whatever concoction you have been brooding over for so long will not be made more digestible by your glowers. Surely it is edible by now; the dawn approaches."

Nicholas looked over at him grimly, and his robust black eyes glinted in the firelight. He dipped the ladle into the pot and filled a bowl with something thick and steaming.

Tancred took the bowl and gave a whiff. "What is it, decaying camel?"

"Saracen goat gruel — it will give you the courage to fight another hundred Moslems."

15

Tancred ignored the maliciously amused gaze; he was too hungry to refuse the food.

Somewhere in the distance, the lute player continued his heart-rending music. Despite Tancred's unspoken longing there came an inner peace. Helena and her mother were reunited; he knew that his cousin Mosul, the assassin who had murdered his brother, was in Antioch serving Prince Kalid as bodyguard, and his two Norman cousins Leif and Norris had come over to his side against their uncle Walter. All was not lost; there was some hope amid the spreading darkness and the tragedy of war and death.

Nicholas, too, stared off toward the stars as though remembering . . . or was it the future he wished to embrace?

Tancred set the empty bowl down and stirred restlessly. Tomorrow they would begin the march toward Antioch. He saw Nicholas stand, alert, looking into the near darkness. "Someone comes," said Nicholas.

Tancred's keen hearing had already picked up the sound of hesitant footsteps approaching. He reached for his weapons.

Nicholas drew his heavy blade. "Who goes there? Step into the firelight, lest we take you for the enemy."

A voice called hopefully at the sound of Nicholas's words. "I am no enemy, Master

Nicholas. I seek Count Redwan."

Tancred recognized the familiar voice of Bardas, the eunuch slave who served Helena. He pushed himself to his feet as the breeze tugged at his open tunic, and he held back the surge of anger. The last time he had seen Bardas was on the evening the eunuch had betrayed him to the enemy.

Bardas, wary, drew near the firelight, his marble eyes darting away from Nicholas to fix upon Tancred.

"Why have you come?" asked Nicholas sternly.

Bardas fell to one knee, keeping to the shadows that covered him. "I shall explain everything, Master Nicholas, but I must first beg the peace and forgiveness of Redwan — for the sake of your niece."

At the mention of Helena, Tancred's concerns stirred within his heart like embers jumping to flames. His fingers tightened about the handle of his sword. "Come forth, deceiver!"

Bardas cautiously drew near.

"That is close enough. If this is another of your ruses, you will surely die, Bardas."

"I come in peace, Redwan. Upon my oath of honor."

"Honor? You mock the word."

"I did not betray you that night in the

17

Court of the Oranges, Count Redwan. The enemy must have followed me. When I left you there and returned with your horse to bring you to Lady Helena as promised, Lady Irene's soldiers had already surrounded you. There was naught I could do. But that is all in the past, and I bring new information, most distressing."

Tancred walked up to him, looking down and holding his blade. His blue-gray eyes were hard, and his hair, the color of ripened wheat, glinted in the firelight. "What information? Speak!"

"The entourage you sent to bring Helena and her mother, Lady Adrianna, to the family castle was attacked and overcome by Bishop Constantine's men!"

Tancred held back his rush of anguish. Constantine had long been an enemy. He desired Adrianna for his own and, along with Lady Irene, had plotted the marriage of Helena to Prince Kalid. If both women were now under his greedy authority . . .

Nicholas stooped to the dust, grasping Bardas's shoulder. "Constantine holds them prisoner?"

Bardas struck his fist to his chest in despair. "He has your sister, Lady Adrianna, at the castle!"

"Who sent you to inform us?" demanded Tancred.

Bardas looked up, his marble brown eyes reflecting his own caution. "Captain Rufus," he admitted uneasily.

Tancred frowned. "So. You expect me to trust the bodyguard of Lady Irene?" He gave a laugh. "Rufus! The man who betrayed me! You must consider me an utter fool, Bardas."

"Nay, Redwan," he implored, "but for a warrior sworn to the safety of my mistress. Helena is not at the castle with her mother. She is being held in Constantinople."

"Where!" he gritted.

"A monastery dungeon. Rufus helped me escape prison to bring you word."

Tancred considered this. Did he believe him?

Nicholas turned gravely. "I think he speaks the truth. Constantine will not be stopped from executing his plans until I stop him myself."

"I should have escorted them to the castle," said Tancred, blaming himself for the foul turn of events.

"Neither of us could have known what Constantine had planned, but we must stop him now."

Bardas looked hopefully from one to the

other. "Rufus has a plan to help Helena," he insisted. "He desires to meet Tancred in the city."

Tancred looked at him sharply. "And walk into a trap? If I rescue your mistress from the dungeon, I will do so on my own."

"I tell you, I did not betray you," insisted Bardas. "And Rufus has a map of the dungeon area."

A map would help Tancred immensely. He met Bardas's gaze steadily, but the slave did not flinch, convincing Tancred he spoke the truth. Still, his anger burned that matters had turned out so wretchedly. Why had he not stopped to consider the whereabouts of Constantine before sending Helena and her mother to the castle?

"We've underestimated Constantine," he told Nicholas in a low voice.

"You are right. The battle here today so overwhelmed us that we unwisely believed Constantine's disappearance was inconsequential."

Tancred turned again to Bardas, who watched them anxiously. "You say Philip has returned to the palace and the emperor? Has he done nothing to aid Helena, or need I ask?"

Bardas's mouth twitched for the first time, showing his constrained resentment over any attack on the honor of the Noble. "Philip fought valiantly but was badly wounded in the skirmish at the olive tower. His recovery is slow. He is ill in spirit and in body."

"Ill?" mocked Tancred. "Do you not rather mean that he has again surrendered to the will of Irene? By now he should have recovered. Look about you! See the wounds of the knights who fought the Red Lion today? Are we moping about, expecting weeks of rest before we travel on to Antioch? But Philip, instead of seeking Helena, lolls about the imperial palace in purple silk."

Nicholas laid a restraining hand on Tancred's shoulder and looked down at Bardas. "When did Constantine's men attack the entourage?"

"Three days ago at least, Master Nicholas."

Three days, thought Tancred. By now Irene may have executed her plans to have Helena sent elsewhere.

Bardas pleaded, "There are few who can aid her now, except you, Redwan."

Tancred considered this, stirred more deeply than he wished to admit. "Perhaps this is another trap, set by my enemies, or perhaps Philip?"

Bardas snorted. "She did not ask for Philip. She asked for you. The guards say she cried out your name in her sleep."

Not wishing to display the depth of his feelings, Tancred remained silent. Nothing else seemed to matter; he must go. To find her again he would even scale the walls of the dungeon, though it could lead to his own arrest and death.

Tancred watched Bardas, veiling his feelings as the slave bowed before him. Moved by the genuineness of Bardas's words, he now pondered his own heart. The wind stirred the dried grasses about them. At the same moment a strange restless yearning pounded in his heart. *Helena* . . .

He saw Nicholas glance at him and there was no mistaking where Nicholas stood on the matter. Tancred masked his torment. He, too, must return. Could a trap be waiting for both him and Nicholas? After all, it was Nicholas whom Irene wanted.

"If you are lying, Bardas, I vow I'll live to see you die in the dust!"

"My face! My body! Do they not tell my truthful story? And I have jewels well worth your sacrifice. They belong to my mistress." He knelt and opened a satchel, removing a purple cloak — the same one Helena had worn when Tancred had last held her in his arms. Then it was true. She was a prisoner in the dungeon.

Bardas used his dagger to open a seam and collected several glittering gems. He stood, handing them to Tancred. "There is much more, Redwan. If you free her, much will be yours."

"Do you think I need gems to come to the aid of the woman who will be my bride? Put them away! Both her uncle and I are committed to her rescue, and Lady Adrianna's."

"Constantine holds the key to Adrianna's whereabouts," said Nicholas. "First, we will go to Constantinople. It is time I returned to pay Irene a visit. Though Constantine led the ambush, it is Irene who is behind the scheme."

Tancred believed he was right that Irene might be waiting for Nicholas to return, seeking Adrianna.

The wind stirred the dried grasses about the battlefield, whipping the fire and sending smoke to dim the light of the stars. Nothing mattered; he must go to her.

Nicholas watched him, and the flicker within his dark eyes seemed to read Tancred's soul. Nicholas laid a strong hand on his shoulder, the other on Bardas. "We will go together, and we will find her" — he looked toward the darkened east — "and the child Adrianna bears. He, too, is blood of my blood. I will not surrender the babe to any

23

false god. Should the Almighty help me find them again," he vowed quietly into the warm dark night, "I will, with Adrianna's agreement, see that the babe is raised to serve the one true and living God."

Tancred's two Norman cousins had walked up and must have overheard the dark news, for they did not look pleased. Leif Redwan spoke his concerns.

"This will all end badly enough, Tancred. Is it wise to trust the word of one man? Even now, Helena may have been sent to Antioch to marry Prince Kalid. Let us go on to take the city."

"He is right, cousin," said Norris, eyeing Bardas with dislike. "Never trust a Byzantine. Returning to the city of the Greeks is more dangerous than entering Antioch to seize her from Kalid."

Tancred turned and looked at the two blond warriors bronzed by the sun. A brief smile touched his mouth.

"You're both right," he admitted. "And your swords will join mine and Nicholas's to make certain of our success in Constantinople and" — he looked evenly at Bardas — "to make certain her bodyguard pays with his head if circumstances prove he lies. I will leave him in your care."

Bardas shifted uneasily and glanced at the

two Norman Redwan cousins.

"We will make certain," stated Leif. "He will walk barefoot on burning coals if either you or Nicholas are betrayed to a trap he is privy to."

Tancred snatched up his satchel and weapons and turned to Bardas. "Then bring us to meet Rufus."

CHAPTER 2

Rendezvous in the Byzantine Wineshop

At midnight in Constantinople, the famous Street Meese remained aglow with colored glass lanterns. The mile-long colonnade of a thousand shops and stalls was crowded with people from every land. There were wineshops and booksellers, vendors of hot Arabic coffee, and stands of rare perfumes and silk from Cathay.

Nicholas turned his horse to ride to the Sacred Palace with its numerous marble pavilions, porticoes, balconies, and gardens.

"I will meet with Irene alone, then if all goes well, rejoin you and Helena on the road to the Castle of Hohms," Nicholas explained.

Had Nicholas been any other bishop, Tancred would not have let him go alone, but he was a warrior, and Tancred pitied anyone who stood in his way. Constantine might be the one man who could prove a match for Nicholas in battle, but he was probably at the castle, not in the city.

When Nicholas had disappeared into the throng, Tancred turned to Leif and Norris. "Wait for me in front of the bookseller's stall." Then leaving a wary Bardas under their unfriendly eye, he walked across the cobbled street toward the fashionable wineshop constructed in spectacular Byzantine architecture. The shop was a favored meeting-house for the wealthy pleasure seekers of Constantinople, but hired bodyguards to the elite also claimed the place for off-hours relaxation. So also did men belonging to the emperor's famed Varangian Guard, and therefore Tancred must be careful to avoid recognition, even though he had friends among them. Loyalty in Constantinople was not established on affection for one's lord, however, but on either fear or high pay, and many could be bought. There was the chance that someone who served Philip would be present.

Irene was another enemy he would be foolish to underestimate. She was a woman equal to the most clever masculine mind on the throne of Byzantium, as he remembered from the last time she had held him prisoner.

Tancred entered the wineshop and saw soldiers and Greek nobles seated at the tables. Tonight he wore a coat of fine chain mesh under a light woolen tunic of black. He was duly belted with his weapons, and a dagger was within easy reach in a leather wrist sheath. Heads turned to look in his direction, but he didn't recognize any of the men present. Glancing about for Rufus, he saw nothing unusual among the soldiers that might alert him to a trap. He took a seat at a table near the back.

While he waited he ordered the celebrated Byzantium dish of shredded breast of chicken cooked in milk and sweetened.

He looked up. The door opened and Rufus walked in. At once, the young Byzantine aristocrats turned their heads in his direction, somewhat curious, and also a bit unnerved by his appearance. Rufus ignored the glances thrown his way and, seeing Tancred, crossed the room to his table. His eyes swept Tancred.

"I am sorry, my friend. I had to choose between delivering you to the bishop at the Court of the Oranges, or have my son Joseph sold as a slave."

Tancred used his boot to push a chair out for him. "Sit. I do not know what I would have done, but to betray a friend accomplishes nothing. Nevertheless, I am not one to carry grudges. They serve no usefulness and I have more than enough enemies. Only one man do I want, and he waits in Antioch."

Rufus sat down, a big man whose muscles rippled beneath his black-and-crimson Byzantine brocade. Tancred hated to see him this way, beaten by the stranglehold Irene had over his emotions.

"I knew you were a man to be reckoned with, Redwan. If anyone could have escaped the bishop's plans, you could. I believed all along you would manage to escape."

"Your confidence in me brings cheer," said Tancred dryly. He pushed the bottle across the table toward him. "For the moment, we will leave the past buried. What news do you bring of Helena Lysander?"

Rufus watched him for a moment in silence, then leaned closer, his face grave. "She asked me to get word to you of her situation."

"You have seen her?"

"No one is allowed to see her."

Tancred tapped the table. "Is escape possible?"

Rufus took a small map from his tunic and carefully pushed it across the table.

"I would not venture the task myself, yet she seemed to think you could do something. I do not question your willingness to face danger where she is concerned, but you must decide."

"You would not be following Irene's orders by setting another trap? If you are," warned Tancred, "I will show no mercy next time."

Rufus showed no emotion, but his eyes were cold. "My head will remain where it is, Norman. Pity any man who tries to remove it. I have sent for you because she wanted you, not because of Madame Irene. I would do nothing to hurt the girl. Irene? I despise her. If there is a trap, I would see her fall into it. I am but waiting the time, and it may be sooner than I had hoped."

"Where is your son Joseph?"

"She has him in the palace."

"The palace?"

Rufus grew sullen. "He despises her also. He is there because she insists. He will not stay if given an opportunity to escape."

Tancred knew that if Joseph were to turn against Irene, it would likely mean his death.

"There is," said Rufus, pointing to a spot on the drawing, "an underground passage here. It is unknown to many even in the monastery. It was constructed hundreds of years ago. If you follow it, you should come out about here." Again he pointed. "Here you will find a grove on the backside of the monastery wall."

Tancred studied the simple drawing. He had his doubts. "You do not speak with certainty."

"How can I? I have not been through the passage. There is a monk who serves Bishop Constantine. He knows the bishop is a pretender who holds no true faith, and this monk has no sympathy for him. He has promised to meet you in the meditation garden and lead you below to the dungeon."

"Do Constantine or Irene know of this passage?"

"The monks think not, but what can I say, Redwan? You risk your life. Yet should not a man risk his life for the woman with whom he is in love?"

Tancred arched a brow. "Then we understand each other."

Rufus handed him a leather satchel. His eyes were amused for the first time. "You will go there disguised as a monk. You will find everything you need in here. If anything goes wrong, I cannot be held accountable. I will deny ever aiding you."

"Understood. This underground passageway, what of light? Is the air breathable?"

"Our friend believes it is. He will have candles and some provisions of food and water."

Tancred folded the drawing and took the satchel. "What of monastery guards, how many?"

"There may be three, perhaps four."

As Tancred measured Rufus with a glance, he found the man's face unreadable.

Rufus stood. "I wish you well, Tancred."

"Before you go, what of Philip? How is he?"

A show of dislike reflected in Rufus's face. "Philip has returned to his position at the ministry of war. Do not underestimate him. He is not as subservient to Irene or Constantine as he pretends. His ego grows daily, and he believes he will one day be emperor. I've learned he has renewed contact with the Turkish commander at Antioch, Yaghi-Sian."

Tancred remembered the treachery of the Byzantine against the feudal princes over Nicaea. They had laid siege to the Turkish Citadel for weeks. Just when victory seemed assured, they awoke the next morning to find the flag of the emperor flying over the walls. During the night, the Turkish emir had surrendered to Philip rather than to the armies of the feudal princes.

The news that Philip had secretly contacted Antioch was not good. That meant he had not given up his first plan to negotiate the surrender of the city to the emperor. Nor would Irene have changed her plans to send Helena to Antioch.

"Has Philip asked for Helena's release from the dungeon?"

"I know nothing of his ambitions beyond outwardly pleasing the emperor," said Rufus. "He is injured and recuperating in the palace."

"Does Kalid know Helena is in confinement?"

"Kalid has been told nothing. He returned to Antioch to recruit soldiers to confront the western army."

Tancred stood and searched the man's face for truth, and it was there. "I will not rest," he vowed, "until I find Mosul and prove to Walter of Sicily that I am an innocent man. Irene has threatened me; she imprisoned me, as you know. She now has the woman I love, but once I have rescued Helena, I am willing to be about my own business if she lets me. But tell her this: if she insists on pursuing us, she will live to regret it. Meanwhile, I am your friend, Rufus."

Rufus held out his hand. "Farewell, then. May blessing anoint your sword."

Tancred watched him walk away and felt pity, but it was mingled with respect. Rufus was a true warrior. Tancred only hoped the hour would come when the man could rescue his son Joseph and himself from Irene's evil chains.

CHAPTER 3

The Dungeon

Tancred wore the customary dark habit and tall black hat as he walked sedately through the courts and gardens of the monastery, keeping his head somewhat lowered, his sword hidden. Bardas followed, dressed as a common slave in a tan hooded tunic. The monastery district of the green Vale of Lycus was built near the foot of the Great Wall; it greeted him with cloistered serenity. There were many buildings: libraries, guest houses for pilgrims, infirmaries for the ill, workshops, and wine cellars, all surrounded by the fragrant shade of gardens. He paused in the meditation garden, waiting for his contact, and leaned against a tree.

A monk crossed the grass and caught his eye, indicating he was to follow. He passed Tancred a leather bag. As he walked unhurriedly, it appeared that Rufus had arranged things well. They came to the other side of the monastery. A sullen, gray building stood shadowed by vines. Passing under a side arbor, a small door brought them into a quiet stone chamber.

At the end of a passage, an inner chamber with a steep flight of chiseled steps was illuminated by torches on the narrow walls. Bardas waited there while Tancred followed the monk down. Moving his hand cautiously through the opening in his robe, Tancred felt the handle of his sword.

The steps ended abruptly. They stood in an alcove. A lone guard lounged with a ring of keys on his belt. He eyed them.

"Why do you come?"

"To minister to Lady Helena," said the monk quietly. "Madame Irene is concerned about her illness. I have brought a physician."

The guard stood. He pointed to the leather bag and Tancred handed it over. The guard searched through the various medicinal herbs and wine. Apparently satisfied, he returned it, and at the same time took a key and dropped it into the monk's hand.

The hand had trembled. Had the guard noticed? Tancred glanced casually at the guard and saw his gaze abruptly measure them again, this time more carefully.

"Have you been here before?"

If the monk hesitated it could mean the end of their ruse.

"Yes."

"By whose orders?"

"Madame Irene's."

"And you?" he asked Tancred.

"I have not been here before, for I am newly arrived from Mount Athos."

The monk cast him a glance, but the guard hesitated, a slight frown between his brows.

"Come," said the monk to Tancred and turned toward a downward flight of steps. Tancred started to follow when the guard halted him.

"Wait, where did you say?"

Tancred kept his head lowered, now aware that he must have made a mistake. His hand tightened on his sword.

"Mount Athos?" the guard asked again.

The monk tried to answer for him, but the guard waved him to silence. "You, physician monk, answer for yourself."

Tancred paused. Why had Rufus told him to say Mount Athos? Something was wrong. The monk who had brought him seemed to understand, but Rufus had evidently missed something.

"I arrived last week," stated Tancred calmly, trying to bluff his way. "I have been trained as a physician. They sent for me when they discovered the woman was ill."

The guard's eyes grew hard. "The monks at Mount Athos are so rigid in their celibacy that not even a female beast is permitted there. You could not be called upon to treat a *woman*." He took a step toward him. "I suggest you are lying." He unleashed his sword. Tancred threw aside his cloak and whipped out his blade, parrying the guard's blow with the ring of steel. The guard lunged, but Tancred deflected his sword, and for an instant the guard was out of position. Tancred could have rammed him through, but instead merely pressed the point of his blade against his chest. Bardas came up stealthily and struck the guard from behind. As he collapsed to the steps, Bardas stepped over him, snatching up his sword.

"Quick, Redwan! Others are coming!"

They ran down the stone passageway, the monk in the lead. Torches flared above on the walls. They came to a dungeon and he quickly turned the key in the lock and swung it open with the creak of hinges. Tancred handed a torch from the wall to Bardas.

"Keep watch."

"Quickly!" whispered the monk.

Tancred entered the cell.

It was small, and it took a moment for his eyes to adjust well enough to see her. She was stretched out across some hay, and at first he thought she was asleep. "Bring the torch."

Tancred knelt beside her. Helena's long and wavy dark hair was tangled about her face, pale and drawn yet indescribably lovely. His heart contracted when he saw her. Her Byzantine tunic of purple-and-gold thread was torn and dirty, but it was not this that brought a leap of fire to his soul. There were bruises that showed on her throat and bare shoulder. Tancred gritted angrily and gently ran his finger over the mark on her shoulder.

Thumb prints. He guessed they had come from the guard trying to take advantage of her. In the struggle, her garment had torn.

"I should have rammed him through," he murmured.

"Yesterday she was ill, but there were no marks on her," the monk whispered. "I tended her myself, bringing her supper."

Had he come in time?

Bardas came running. "Some soldiers have discovered the guard!"

Helena's cloak was lying nearby and Tancred swiftly wrapped it about her. Lifting her, he handed her to Bardas. "Go! If needed I will hold them off!"

The monk rushed ahead with a torch and Bardas ran behind carrying Helena. Tancred

39

extinguished the wall torches, throwing the passageway behind them into darkness. He heard the clink of footsteps as he darted after Bardas.

At the end of the passage, the monk was struggling with a lever, and upon pulling it, a small opening emerged in what had appeared to be a solid rock wall. Short stone steps descended precariously into darkness.

"This way!" said the monk.

Tancred closed the opening in the wall, shutting them off from the soldiers.

The monk led the way down the steps, holding the torch. This new passage wound onward for some distance before Tancred felt a draft of fresh air from above. After a few minutes of brisk walking down the stone passage, he could see an exit.

"It opens beyond the monastery wall into a grove of fruit trees," the monk explained. "Do not stop until you get beyond the grove. Once there, you will find a high road that winds past large gardens. The road is not often used, but cross it with care. On the other side you will enter the gardens that belong to the private summer palaces of the nobility."

"What of you? How can you go back? The guard will inform your abbot that you helped us."

"The abbot was once a friend of Lady Adrianna. He will secure my safety once matters have quieted down. Go! Do not worry about me. And Christ aid you."

Once they were outside in the sunlight, the monk closed the exit and rearranged the vines to conceal the small opening, then slipped away silently into the garden trees of the monastery. Tancred led the way toward the road, and Bardas came behind carrying Helena.

They found a sheltered position near the road, and from there Tancred watched a group of soldiers pass on horseback. Their own horses waited with his cousins, but they were of no use now. In Helena's condition she would need to rest for several days. They all needed food, water, and a place to stay and keep the horses. He had to inform Leif and Norris. Perhaps by now Nicholas had returned from his mission and waited to hear from him.

Birds sang in the branches of the Judas trees, and sleepy flowers nodded their colorful heads in the soft breeze. The sun was still bright, but he dare not wait until dark. It would not take Irene long to marshal soldiers to begin a search of the city.

A path led through the grove, and Tancred followed it to a cutoff that brought him to a tangled slope where some horses munched on grass. Bardas stood holding Helena, who was yet unconscious.

"We need shelter," said Tancred.

"Shelter here? Impossible! Soon guards will be searching for us. They will swarm this area like hornets."

"Exactly, but if we continue on foot they will spot us sooner. They will expect us to make for the city gates to escape. We will hole up here for a few days, then make for the Castle of Hohms."

Tancred gestured across the road to where the domes of splendid houses shone like blue silver in the sunlight. "Those private palaces — are they all occupied?"

Bardas followed his gaze and frowned. "No . . . the nobility arrive at their leisure. Usually in spring when the entertainments are just beginning. Many have returned to their villas in Athens."

"You would know the nobles who own these houses better than I. Surely there is a vacant residence more isolated than the others. Find one."

Bardas sucked in his breath. "Are you suggesting —"

"You must. If need be, bribe someone. You have the jewels with you?"

He stiffened. "I have an emerald. That is

all. The rest . . ." He stopped and would say no more.

Bardas still did not completely trust him, and that both amused and irritated Tancred. He wondered what he would do if he knew his mistress had vowed her love to him — that she no longer desired to marry Philip. He could let him know that he and Helena might marry at the castle, but it would be more effective if Helena told him. Then again, even Nicholas did not know; nor had he as yet granted his blessing. Tancred assumed he would be pleased, but what if he were not?

"The emerald should suffice," he said sternly. "Go and look. Can you not see your mistress needs rest and care before we can travel to the castle?"

Bardas snorted, his old superior attitude descending upon him like a Byzantine garment. "And subject her to such scandalous behavior? Sneaking into some noble's abode in the stealthy company of a Norman warrior —"

Tancred took a step toward him, his eyes narrowing. "Eunuch, you weary me. I will delight to silence your whining once and for all if you do not do what is required of you. Place your mistress under that shade tree and trust me to protect her. Now go!"

Bardas hesitated, his nostrils flaring. He

was a muscled old warrior who could match most any opponent, but he finally relented. "As you wish."

Tancred watched as Bardas gently set Helena down on the grass, then disappeared among the trees. At least the eunuch had been wise enough to wear tan hose and a brown tunic instead of his crimson breeches and gold tunic. Tancred remembered with some respect how Bardas had once been a loyal fighting soldier, a bodyguard to Helena's father, General Lysander. He was more of a fighter and a soldier than the aristocratic Philip would ever be.

Philip — and where was he in all of this? Rufus had said there'd been correspondence between him and Antioch. The matter was of grave concern. What was Philip up to? Was he working alone behind the backs of Irene and Bishop Constantine, or was he doing this at their initiative?

And Constantine, where was he? Perhaps Nicholas would have the answers when he arrived back from a secret meeting with Irene. After he had Helena safely in a chamber and cared for, he would send a message through Bardas to Leif and Norris to come by night with the horses.

The private garden of a noble's summer

44

palace was walled and secluded. The birds chittered and cool water splashed invitingly in the Greek fountain. Helena lay on cushions in a room where dappled sunlight fell across the floor. Awakening, her feverish mind groped for understanding. Where was she? She was too drowsy to concentrate on finding the answers, and her thirst was excessive. There was someone with her. Her blurred vision could not see his face, yet she sensed his presence, and it was strong and comforting. She could reach and touch him, and when she did she thought it must be Philip . . . but no, that was impossible. Philip had been arrested, and she had been put in the dungeon — but then who was this silent stranger beside her, always there, yet so unreal? At night he stood at the window staring out, reminding her of a shadow. She would call, "Philip?" but he would not answer. Yet he always came. Sometimes he stood over her, and she feared the soldierlike presence; other times he bent over her and was so close she reached out and touched him. He was not a shadow; nor was he someone to fear. Rather he was a strong consolation whose arms lulled her to sleep, though he never spoke — he did not have to. His touch spoke clearly, and she did not awaken again until she made a desperate cry for water.

When she opened her eyes, morning light flooded the unfamiliar room; the next time they opened it was dark. She had a faint memory of quiet voices, candles, and the nauseating smell of food; then she was alone again with the stranger. The candle went out, and the shadow took his place at the open window. The next time she awoke he was gone! Panic seized her and she cried out, "Philip!" At once she felt his touch.

A vision of the dungeon tore at her mind. Rats! The guard coming to her, and when she screamed he grew angry and treated her roughly —

Helena awoke with a start, hearing her own muffled cry for help, and faced not the dungeon's dank, dark walls but the pale golden light of dawn.

She lay quite still, trying to understand where she was. Already the birds were chattering, and the fragrant air flooded the chamber through the open colonnade. Certainly she was not home. Had Irene taken her away? Her mother! Where was she!

It must have been a nightmare, she told herself. Her eyes now focused clearly, and while she felt weak, she was alert. This was no dungeon, but neither was it her chamber in the Sacred Palace. It was a lower chamber in a summer palace — but whose?

Everything came rushing back — the ambush by Constantine's soldiers . . . the wounding of Philip . . . the trip to the monastery dungeon . . . the bodyguard of Irene, Rufus, whom she had called out to for help, begging him to find Tancred —

Tancred!

It was *he* who had kept vigil during her illness, not Philip! She sat up, the sudden movement sending a wave of dizziness.

The chamber was empty, but outside in the warm garden she heard him moving about. How long had he been with her? Hours? Days? The last hour they had held each other, she had asked him if he would find her again. *"My dearest Helena, I vow it. I do not know the day or hour, but I shall return for you."*

That hour had come sooner than she had expected. But she could not face him yet. Her appearance must be dreadful! And she must digest what all this meant. How had he managed to get her out of the dungeon? Had he seen Philip? Obviously Philip had planned the escape and enabled Tancred to carry it out. She must see Philip as well.

She tossed the cover aside and staggered to her feet. Weakness enveloped her and she swayed, catching herself on the back of a table. There was a gilded mirror and she frowned. One glimpse of her reflection brought despair. Her ankle-length tunic was rumpled and in need of washing. She had grown thinner and paler. Her dark hair hung in tangles about her shoulders, giving her a childlike appearance. The bruise marks were fading but visible on her pale skin. Did Tancred guess the guard's attack?

At the moment it did not occur to her that she was blessed to be alive. She thought only of how dreadful she looked and that she did not want to face him, ignoring the obvious — that he had already seen her in this condition. There would be a bath somewhere in this great house, and a woman's summer wardrobe in the main chamber.

The marble steps took every ounce of strength she had; she rested several times before going on. Above, she came across a small room with rugs and a low table, and beyond, a round marble tub with a running fountain. There were sweet-smelling spices and oils, and she bathed, then washed her hair.

There was a sun garden past the alcove, and she went there to rest on the marble bench among the herbs and flowers. After weeks — or had it been months? — in the dungeon, the cleansing experience brought sighs of thankfulness. She drank in the quiet beauty and the feel of warmth upon her skin. Soon she thought of nothing but the peace of the moment and remained there until her hair was dry, giving thanks to God for sparing both her and Tancred, and interceding for the safety of her mother and the child she expected. The child was due to be born soon — what evil thing did Irene have in mind? She *must* talk to Philip to find out! He must do something to safeguard the baby, as well as her mother.

With her hair dried and in desperate need of brushing, she went off to find clean garments. The women's chamber was not hard to find. Carpets decorated the floor, rich Byzantine wall hangings depicted hunting scenes of embroidered animals, and there was a large bed with brocade coverings.

She found the wardrobe and donned a robe of dark blue silk and ivory. It was too large and she tied the waist with a gold-braided sash. She hoped the owner of this garment would not despise her for using it. A pearl-handled brush was on the table, and she began adorning her hair.

As she worked she thought of Tancred. Perhaps it had not been Rufus after all but Philip who had managed to send a messenger to locate Tancred.

Opening the chamber door, she stepped

into the passage, and beyond the stairs Bardas was setting a low table with fresh fruits, bread, and cheese. The sight of her faithful bodyguard brought joy to her heart.

"Bardas!" she cried. "Oh, I did not know you were here! You are safe! Thanks to God! I thought . . . thought you had been killed in the ambush."

A broad smile showed on his face. "They brought me back with Philip. He arranged for Rufus to help me escape."

It did not dawn on Helena to ask why he had not arranged for her own escape, nor did it seem to bother Bardas.

"Mistress — you must not tire yourself." He rushed to help her down the steps. "Mistress! You are looking better! This is a wonderful day!"

"What happened?" she cried, taking hold of his arm. "You must sit and explain everything! Where is Tancred?"

"He is with his two Norman cousins — both treacherous barbarians if you ask me. They are looking for Master Nicholas. He hasn't returned yet."

Immediately her concerns stole away the present joy as Bardas explained how her uncle had come to her aunt Irene to seek the whereabouts of her mother, Lady Adrianna.

"Do not worry so, mistress. We both know

Nicholas to be a man who can outwit your aunt, or the bishop if it comes to it. And he has only been gone three days."

"Three days!" Was that all? It seemed she had been struggling in and out of her fever for weeks, but Bardas told her they had arrived at the residence just a few days ago.

He talked while she ate, and Helena was amazed at how hungry she was. Her burdens were lighter now, and the smiling face of Bardas convinced her that the future would somehow brighten.

"So," Bardas concluded, "Rufus sent me to find Master Nicholas and the Norman."

Biting into a plump dried fig, she said nothing. Bardas was only a slave, but his opinions mattered dearly to her, and she refrained from telling him that she would marry Tancred one day. Still, her feelings for Philip went deep, and while she did not love him, she felt an emotional bond that could not easily be done away with. He had tried to save her from Kalid at the tower in their travels to Athens, and again, during the ambush. He was injured now and in disfavor with Irene and Constantine for coming bravely to her aid.

She frowned, pushing the plate of fruit aside.

"With Philip wounded, it is a blessing from

God we had Uncle Nicholas and Tancred to turn to again. Did you hear how they rescued my mother and me from Sinan and the Red Lion?"

"Surely it was Master Nicholas, little one. He is to be thanked."

Her eyes met his across the table. She reached for her glass. "You are still not convinced Tancred is trustworthy."

"What mercenary with his callous heritage is ever completely trustworthy? Yet he is a warrior, and he did rescue you from the dungeon."

During her fevered nights, or what had seemed to be many nights, when she had called out for someone, Tancred had been anything but callous. She looked at Bardas over her glass. One day Bardas would understand her deep love for Tancred, but not now.

"You still have the jewels I gave you? Did you sew them into the garment?"

"The garment is safe, mistress, but I did use an emerald to bribe the guards of the family who own this house. It was the Norman's idea," he suggested, a hint of disapproval in his voice.

She smiled. "It was a very wonderful idea. The perfect place to prepare for the journey to the castle once we discover where my mother is being held."

He brought his tunic to her. "Everything is still sewn in here as you requested."

Helena was pleased that her clever idea had worked. She had him remove a sizable gift, intending to give it to Tancred. "For the journey to the Castle of Hohms," she said. "We will need supplies for my mother and things for the baby. Did you say Tancred has gone into the city?"

"He ventured there, yes. For what reason, he did not explain." The tone of his voice hinted of suspicion.

"And the horses, and Apollo?" she asked of her prized stallion.

"Safe and waiting for your recovery. The Norman will be greatly pleased when he sees you well."

"Good." She hesitated, thinking of her mother and Constantine's obsession with her. Adrianna must be kept safe from him. "There is something you must do, Bardas. I must get a message to Philip to learn where my mother is being kept. No one must know, however. Disguise yourself in the monk's robe and go to Philip."

"Do you think it is wise? Suppose the enemy is watching him, expecting you to send word? They will follow Master Philip here."

"No. He must not come here; Tancred

will become upset. He trusts him not at all, and perhaps he has sound reason. But Philip has proven his abiding friendship with me. You saw how he fought for me at the ambush, and earlier at the tower he would have fought Kalid to try to save me if I hadn't intervened."

"Yea, mistress, did I not tell you he would one day become wise in his devotion to you? Yet you bade me always go to the Norman for help. A mistake! For even now —"

"Philip can help us, I'm sure of it. Is he strong enough to meet me at the Golden Horn?"

"Yes, but is it wise?"

"We will hire a Levantine's boat to bring us across the water to St. Symeon. From there we can travel to the castle in a short time. It will be much easier than a journey by horse or camel. We must reach the castle, Bardas. It is the one place where we can stay safely."

"I would not trust the Norman to take us there by ship. I saw Tancred studying a map last night. He would take you far from here to Sicily."

"Your suspicions are exaggerated. If he studies a map it is of the environs of Antioch, not his home in Sicily. He will never leave the east until he has the assassin and can prove his innocence."

"The Norman will not be pleased if you send me to Philip," Bardas warned.

"It is not a serious concern. Tancred understands perfectly about my feelings for Philip," she said, knowing that the true meaning of her words would be hidden from Bardas. Tancred now knew she did not love Philip, and he would not be jealous.

CHAPTER 4

Betrayal

An hour had passed before Bardas, dressed as a monk, left the house by the back garden route and reached the gate just as the sound of footsteps approached. Tancred, also dressed with a monk's cloak thrown over his shoulders to cover his weapons, stopped when he saw Bardas.

Tancred's anger mounted, for the slave was obviously going into the city with a disguise. "Did I not tell you to stay with your mistress? You are not to leave her unguarded even for an hour."

Bardas scowled defensively. "My first obligation is to obey the orders of my mistress. She is awake and recovering. She waits for you near the fountain."

Tancred was pleased but not satisfied with his answer. "You will go nowhere without my permission. It is too dangerous."

"My mistress intends to sail to St. Symeon

as soon as her mother is brought here by Nicholas. She sends me to make arrangements."

"You assume much. Nicholas has not returned from the Sacred Palace, and until he does, there is little hope of discovering Lady Adrianna's whereabouts. As for making arrangements on the wharf, I have already considered buying passage. But I will make the arrangements when the hour draws near. We must not move too soon. I do not trust those on the wharf to know our plans until the moment we depart. Spies are everywhere; so are men willing to betray for money."

"Then do you order me not to go?" Bardas inquired stiffly.

"I will speak with Helena. Wait here."

"As you wish."

Tancred left him there and walked toward the courtyard leading into the front salon. Something troubled him about the slave's actions. He glanced back, but Bardas was still there, sitting on a stone bench.

A moment later, Tancred came into the salon. Across the room a double door led out onto a tiered garden and he saw her there.

Jasmine and rose scented the air. He walked up and stood behind her, stopping for a minute to watch her, for she had not heard his steps. When he spoke, his voice was warm and tender. "The goddess of my dreams has at last awakened from her slumber."

Helena turned at once, a slight pause in her breath, expectation shining in her eyes. At the look in her gaze, his own heart paused, for that love was undeniable. Her dark lashes narrowed, and the smile he had been dreaming of touched the sweet curve of her mouth.

"Tancred . . ." she whispered and took a halting step toward him, hand outstretched, as though still unnerved and uncertain over the love that was between them, though spoken fully that night on the battlefield of the camp of the Red Lion.

He came toward her, tossing aside the cloak on the bench. At the same moment she approached him, her eyes warm. They met in an embrace, speaking their love.

"I was so afraid," she whispered, caressing him unashamedly. "I wanted you to come, but so deathly afraid you would and then be caught. And now you are here with me, safe, at least for the moment."

"I would come to you at any cost. Nothing could keep me from you, not death, not life. . . ."

"But how shall we escape?"

"I have plans, but they will take time to work out. I wait for Nicholas."

"What if something happens to him?"

"Do not think of that now." His lips found hers and he kissed her. "At this moment I want only to hear of your love."

"You know I love you," she whispered breathlessly. "I've thought of you constantly since we parted."

He buried his face in her hair, caressing her. "I want you more than life itself."

"I want you to feel that way. I want you to want me desperately."

They stood for a moment lost in their emotions, and she was limp within his embrace.

"You must let me go now," she breathed, but he bent slowly and lifted her chin tenderly.

"Know that I am very much in love with you."

They held each other as if afraid to let go, afraid the spell would be broken.

"I would do nothing to hurt you. Do you understand that?"

"Yes, yes. . . ."

"I have loved you from the moment I saw you, but there seemed no hope of winning your love in return, or even your respect."

"I was spoiled and foolish. About Philip, about you . . . I think I did love him once — in an immature way — but I never really loved him in the way I love you."

"Have you told Philip yet?"

"No. . . ."

"Forget him. You belong to me now. We belong to each other. It could end no other way. We will marry at the Castle of Hohms. Promise me."

"Yes. But I do not know what Philip will do. He will be angry."

"It is well you said nothing to him. I care not what he may think, but he would alert Irene. Too much depends on our reaching the castle. You will be safe there."

"And you? Will you go on to Antioch to find Mosul?"

"I must. How else can we ever be free? I will find him and bring him to Walter of Sicily. They search for me still. I put nothing past Philip when it comes to seeing to my demise, even betraying me to Walter if he could."

Her eyes were pained, and her fingers dug into his arms. "Do not blame Philip for everything. It is not all his fault, but Irene's. She has controlled him for years and filled his heart with deceit and pride."

"Had your kiss not convinced me of your love, I'd think once again that you would believe Philip over anything I said."

She smiled ruefully. "You no longer have

any reason for jealousy, my love. My heart has room for only you. But Philip —"

"Enough of Philip. I've returned from speaking with Leif and Norris. Nicholas has contacted them. He has learned where your mother is being kept."

She held to him tightly, her eyes searching his, as she must have read the quiet sobriety in his voice. He loathed to tell her the dark news.

"Where is she? Does Irene have her? Is she in a dungeon? The child she expects — is it well?"

"Perhaps you'd best sit down." He took her arm and led her toward the bench. She sank to it weakly, her eyes still holding to his, as though she knew.

"Constantine?" she whispered, her fingers clutching his hand.

He nodded. "I'm sorry, Helena."

Tears filled her eyes. "Where?"

"He did not bring her here to Constantinople when you were arrested and brought here. Irene told Nicholas she doesn't know where Adrianna is, but she suspects he went on with her and a handful of trusted soldiers to the castle."

"The Castle of Hohms? But why? That is where she wanted to go."

"You have one consolation. Constantine is

no enemy of your mother. He is passionately enamored with her and will do her no harm; at least he will guard her from Irene and a dungeon. He took her to the castle to protect her from your aunt. The baby will be born there. And if Adrianna is the wise and generous woman I think she is, she also realizes that as long as she cooperates with him and doesn't try to escape, he will treat her well."

Helena's breath escaped from her and she relaxed a little, then covered her face with her palms. "He will wish to marry her there."

"Yes" was all he said.

Helena fell into silence, then, "As you say, my mother is a wise woman. If anyone can reason with Constantine, she will be able to do so."

Tancred made no reply. He didn't think anyone could reason with him. He hoped he was wrong.

"At least he . . . he loves her and will not harm her," she said again, as though speaking the words to encourage herself. "And . . . and your uncle is there, Seigneur Rolf Redwan."

"He will do all he can to safeguard her, I am certain." Tancred didn't speak the obvious, that Constantine would have ambitious plans of his own concerning the castle and

62

Antioch. What those plans might be was anyone's guess.

"Then I will go to her," she said calmly. "When do we leave?"

"As soon as Nicholas arrives and safe and secret plans are made. We will journey by boat to St. Symeon, and if matters go as hoped, we will foil Constantine and Philip both."

She looked at him quickly. "Philip? But surely he has nothing to do with my mother being there."

"Perhaps not, but don't forget he and Irene have plans of their own when it comes to Antioch. You and the castle still play a role in that ambition. The sooner you are reunited with Adrianna and Constantine is dealt with, the sooner I can find Mosul and our own life can proceed."

She stood and came to his arms again. "Hold me. I'm afraid something dreadful will happen. If we lose each other now —"

"We won't lose each other," he said.

He touched the fading bruises on her throat, and his voice grew hard. "If he harmed you I will go back and —"

"No, he did not harm me," she said swiftly. "I screamed. It angered him, but he left."

He enfolded her within his arms and

smoothed her hair.

Bardas remained out of sight in the salon. His face showed disapproval, and as he looked at Tancred, his lips tightened. He had seen and heard everything. So he had been right about the Norman — he intended to take Helena from Master Philip. No doubt the barbarian was lying to her of his love and devotion. He would take advantage of her, then ride away. Had he not warned his mistress that this would happen? That Tancred was a dangerous man? He was not worthy of a woman of the Byzantine aristocracy. General Lysander would be much displeased if he knew the error his only daughter was about to make.

Bardas made up his mind; he would speak to Master Nicholas about this as soon as he returned. Surely Nicholas Lysander would not allow his mistress to marry the Norman warrior at the castle. Would not Philip have done what he could to release her from the dungeon except for his injury?

Bardas glowered. He must not stand idly by and allow his mistress to escape with the Norman.

When evening twilight darkened into purple and inky shadows, Bardas, donned in the monk's cowl, slipped silently away through the back garden gate.

Philip was pacing the marble floor before the open colonnade in his lavish chamber within the Sacred Palace. He stopped between the two white Corinthian columns where a scented garden stretched down to the seawall. In the distance he could see the familiar view of the Sea of Marmara, where caiques appeared as colorful winking lights on the waterway. Except for his arm, which remained for personal convenience in a sling, he had fully recovered from the injury he'd taken in the ambush, though his mother, Irene, had not guessed. His dark eyes, like flint smoldering with irrational temper, turned and fixed upon Bardas.

Bardas, dressed as a monk, had been ushered into the chamber secretly by way of the pavilions. Philip was ironically amused that his mother, who thought her intrigue so clever, had underestimated him. He had gained the loyalty of half the soldiers under her pay, even Rufus! Ah, the giant Nubian! He would turn against her, and like Queen Jezebel of the Old Testament, he would toss her down over the balcony to the dogs if it bought freedom for his son Joseph. Not that the use of dogs, or in this case hungry leopards, would be necessary, thought Philip.

Putting Irene on a restraining leash within the palace would be sufficient.

He turned to Bardas shortly and studied his sullen expression.

"So that is how she escaped the monastery dungeon. The Norman. Those serving Irene are in a stir over what's to become of her." He gave a short, humorless laugh. "So Tancred managed. I should have known he would. Well — it is good, then! It will spare me the risk and make my plans easier than I had anticipated. Where are they now?"

"At the summer palace of Senator Lucian. Lady Helena wishes to take a ship to St. Symeon to be reunited with her mother. Nicholas will go with her, and the Norman warrior. He is with her now making plans. She trusts him." Bardas walked forward, imploring him. "Master Philip, you must do something. They speak of love and marriage."

"Marriage?" Philip's smile of satisfaction turned poisonous. For a moment he did not reply but contemplated the consequences to his ambitions.

"The Norman cannot be trusted with such a woman as Helena, Master Philip. He lies to her. I have heard how he has loved many women, only to ride on. To which of them did he not vow marriage?"

Philip's dark eyes were cold. "So she loves the barbarian?"

"My mistress is a young girl," came the apologetic voice of Bardas. "She does not understand her folly. Do not be angry with her. She has been through so much. Once you speak with her she will see her error. It is the Norman you must stop. I have always said so."

"Yes . . . so you have, and so it has always been my plan to do so. The gods appear to favor his fortune," he remarked bitterly. "The only way I can destroy the Norman is to alert his enemies within the city. Judgment will best be executed at the hands of his blood relatives."

A flicker of alarm darkened the already troubled eyes of Bardas. "Betrayal, master? Would it not injure Helena and Master Nicholas?"

Philip glanced down the colonnade steps to the guards in the garden. "Search your conscience and see what it tells you. Who is better positioned to care for the future of Helena? Nicholas may be her uncle, but I fear he befriends the cause of Tancred and the western barbarians far more than he does the cause of the Lysander dynasty in Constantinople. He is a bitter man, seeking to reap vengeance on those whom he believes are responsible for his own past removal from the palace. He has no one to blame for his fall but himself."

He walked toward Bardas, who shifted his stance and glanced toward the guards below.

Philip poured wine into a goblet. "Even if he manages to bring down his enemies, he will not win good fortune with the emperor. He will march on with the barbarians to recapture territory belonging to Byzantium, only to put it into the hands of barbarians! Down in his heart he knows he can never return to his family position and rule for the emperor. It is too late for Nicholas. The hour has passed; the sun sets. But not for me, Bardas —" His hand tightened on the slave's shoulder. "Not for the three of us."

"I could wish it were so, but how?"

"After the fall of Antioch, I can bring Helena back to the Sacred Palace in peace, if you will help me with my plan."

Bardas watched him. "How can there ever be peace with Lady Irene and Bishop Constantine? Did they not throw her into a dungeon to die? And has not the bishop already gone to the Castle of Hohms with Lady Adrianna? Surely he has no plans to return with her, or to surrender the castle to Prince Kalid."

"Let me worry about that. My plans are

well laid. I have not been idle. But you can rest assured, my faithful friend, that there will be no future dungeons — not for Helena, nor for you — if you aid me now when I need you as my eyes, ears, and mouthpiece."

"I have always been loyal to your ambitions, Master Philip. For they do well for my mistress."

"Well said. And I shall make certain of it. As for the castle of Hohms, let Constantine keep it for now, along with Adrianna. It is Antioch we want as a gift for the emperor. Its price is above all the gold and jewels in Constantinople. Through its surrender I shall gain great respect and power. Upon our return, Antioch in hand, Helena and I will have proved our loyalty to the emperor. It will mean a new beginning for us. For all of us. Then I can move to thwart Irene, Constantine, and all others who oppose us."

Bardas stepped back, his eyes uncertain. "My mistress would rather die than see Lady Adrianna and Master Nicholas injured."

"Do not be a fool, Bardas. With my rise to favor with the emperor comes their liberty as well."

Bardas plucked at his walrus mustache, and Philip threw the goblet across the chamber. "Will you cooperate with *me,* or see Helena with the Norman warrior living in some barbarian hovel in Sicily?"

"Forbid!"

"Then you will cooperate with me for her sake. I have a plan. Our secret will die with us. Helena will never know either one of us was involved."

Philip took his ring from his hand. "Show this to the captain of the imperial cavalry. He will know what he is to do."

Bardas accepted the ring cautiously, a frown between his eyes. "And the Norman?"

Philip's eyes hardened. "It will be my pleasure to see his end."

CHAPTER 5

Treachery

Tancred had left the summer palace after midnight to keep a rendezvous with Nicholas in the Venetian quarter on the Golden Horn. Arrangements had been made to hire a Levantine to bring them by boat across the Bosporus into Anatolia and on to St. Symeon. He had left Helena under the guard of Bardas, and Norris and Leif were still on duty on the parklike grounds.

Daylight had not yet dappled the courtyard when Tancred returned quietly to the parlor, where he lay down on the divan. There was still time for a few hours of rest before Helena would awaken.

But he had hardly arranged himself on the cushions, fully dressed, when with drawn sword, he arose and looked toward the doorway leading into the outer hall. Always alert, he had responded even before he heard the footsteps on the other side of the chamber wall. A rustle of garments followed the footsteps.

Bardas appeared in the doorway, still shadowed in the early gray. "Is that you, Redwan?"

Irritably, Tancred lowered his blade. "Sneaking up on me like that is one way to find your life cut short, old friend. What is it?"

"I heard you return. And none too soon. Your cousin Leif left word last night that you are to be on guard."

"What were his concerns?"

"He saw a man snooping about the grounds after sunset. Perhaps a house slave, we are thinking. Sent to ready the abode for Senator Lucian. Lucian may return unexpectedly. But Leif worries the slave may have come upon the concealed horses. He trailed after him, but the slave disappeared through some small gate near the road."

Both of his cousins had been on watch during the night — Leif, near the garden gate; Norris, farther away toward the road in the direction of the monastery. Bardas had been guarding the back garden entrance nearest Helena's chamber. The news of a slave poking about was not good. Had the monk who aided them been forced to talk?

Tancred could not depart yet! Nicholas

was to arrive today, and they were to buy passage for St. Symeon and sail that night.

"Where is Leif now?" Tancred asked Bardas.

"Out searching, making certain there are not more slaves about —" He stopped and turned toward the door, drawing his sword. "Someone is coming."

Tancred held his blade, alert. Norris came in and said quickly, "Rufus waits for you. His son is injured. You know something of medicine, my cousin. Bring your satchel and come."

"Rufus? What happened?"

"His son who worked in the Royal Library escaped, Rufus with him, and two soldiers. The woman is out looking for them now. Joseph is bleeding badly."

"Rufus has long planned for this moment," said Bardas. "I will get your satchel, Redwan." He walked to his baggage beside the divan.

"Where are they?" Tancred asked.

"At the slave quarters in the olive grove, about five minutes from here among the trees."

Tancred took his medical satchel. "Guard your mistress. Nicholas will arrive soon."

"Should I not go with you?" asked Bardas. "Is it wise to go alone after Leif spotted the slave spying about?"

"A slave?" inquired Norris.

Tancred told him about the possibility of their horses being spotted.

He left Bardas guarding Helena and with Norris walked briskly toward a cottage farther back in the trees.

As he did so he became restless. Norris must have noticed and frowned. "Something troubles you?"

"Did you think the eunuch behaved oddly?"

"I have never fully trusted him. He is devoted to Helena. What do you suspect?"

"I am not certain. He has given me many reasons to doubt his fidelity." Tancred thought of the evening before when he had met with Helena in the garden and held her in his arms. But he'd left Bardas seated on the bench. "If it had been Bardas who told me of Rufus and his son instead of you, I'd have cause to wonder."

"About what? You think the Byzantine has reason to want Rufus and his son discovered by the woman's guards?"

"No, he would have nothing to gain. He has been friendly with Rufus. Perhaps it is only my unease. The sooner Nicholas arrives and we leave this place, the better."

Their boots crunched over the gravel walkway leading to the cottage. The sun was breaking through the morning mist.

A private mercenary soldier was waiting on guard some hundred feet from the house. Seeing them, he walked forward.

"Do you know him?" inquired Norris.

"I have seen him with Rufus at the armory."

Tancred was concerned about whether his medical supplies were adequate. "How badly are they wounded?"

"The guard did not say."

Tancred stopped and glanced about the trees. He tossed his satchel to the bushes and unleashed his sword.

Norris, looking confused, nevertheless followed suit. "What is it?" he breathed between his teeth, glancing about cautiously.

"You did not *see* Rufus and his son?" inquired Tancred.

"No —" Norris sucked in an incriminating breath.

Like a wolf smelling a trap, Tancred scanned the chinar trees. The guard walking toward them hesitated, as though he guessed their new caution.

They had a moment, but perhaps not time enough. Tancred touched his cousin's arm. "A trap. Quick! Away! Toward those trees —"

Their action forced the hand of the soldiers in hiding, who emerged from the trees on both sides of the path. Philip angrily pushed his way past. "Do not let them get away!"

The soldiers rushed the Normans. At once Tancred and Norris were fighting for their lives, dealing blow after blow to hold off the advancing soldiers. It was madness; they could not hope to survive. The fighting raged for a timeless period in which no sound captured the morning but the heavy blow of steel upon steel. He and Norris fought for a clearing in which to escape back to the house. Several soldiers lay dead or dying, strewn across the path, but Philip stalked at a safe distance. His voice was heard above the ringing steel and grunts of men: "Pursue them!"

One bold young Byzantine lunged with gritted teeth, but Tancred struck past his sword and smashed the side of his head.

The Byzantines far outnumbered them, and at last Philip's logic surfaced. "Circle behind them, you fools! Trap them like wolves in a pen!"

Norris was facing deadly trouble against three soldiers, and Tancred tried to help him, his blade exchanging furious blows. But he heard Norris gasp as a spear pierced his chest. Norris grasped it, still trying to fight. He fell.

"I want Tancred alive!" shouted Philip.

Tancred did not hear him. For the moment nothing mattered when he saw Norris dying on the dew-drenched flower bed into which he had tried to crawl. Tancred knelt beside him, wiping the sweat from his eyes in order to see, but Norris was already falling into unconsciousness, blood on his lips. A final gasp for air, then stillness, forever.

Tancred's fist clenched. He heard nothing but the thudding of his own heart in his ears.

Lord God, he prayed, broken in spirit, *Norris, my cousin . . .*

When he became aware again, soldiers surrounded him with pointed blades, their breathing coming hard, their sweating faces grim. Philip walked up and pushed his way through, his dark eyes cold and hard, refusing to glance at Norris's body.

"It is you, Tancred, who are to blame for his death, not I. You will taste the humility you have forced me to drink!"

From behind him there was a scuffle as soldiers were bringing someone from the cottage. Tancred heard Helena's muffled cry. His reason rushed back as he understood she had been imprisoned inside all along.

"Tancred!" She tried to break past Philip, but he blocked her.

Tancred stood. His emotions, having ebbed to the bottom in watching the death of his cousin, now returned with fury. His sword had been taken, but he struck Philip with a savage blow that toppled him backward into the soldiers. Blood streaked down Philip's cut mouth as he stared at Tancred with dazed eyes.

Helena was trying to break free from the grasp of two soldiers who held her arms, but seeing that Tancred was alive, she soon sank into hopeless silence, her eyes darting to Norris. She winced and turned her head away, and a sob came to her throat.

Philip recovered and stood glaring at Tancred. He took a clean white handkerchief from his purple vesture and blotted his lip. He managed a contemptuous smile. "I could kill you, but not before Helena. You will not die yet, Tancred. That would be too easy. And she would hate me for it."

"Let him go, Philip," she choked. "If you touch him further I will loathe you till the day I die."

"Let your boast of becoming emperor prove itself here and now with your sword," Tancred challenged. "If the stars are your trust to bring you to pride and glory, surely they will fight for you now. You put your trust in Zeus! Let him show himself on your behalf! Or are you afraid to show these soldiers that you are a miserable coward?"

Philip's hollow laughter drowned the unwitting song of a twittering bird, convincing many that looked on that the garden lurked with evil.

"I have nothing to prove, Norman. It is you who will prove what you are made of. Take him! Senator Lucian has more at his summer palace than fountains and roses. Take him to the dungeon! String him to the whipping post!"

Helena cried out, "Philip! You have gone mad!" She broke free of the guards and, before they could stop her, reached Tancred. He embraced her. "It's all right," he whispered. "Don't be afraid."

She trembled, her eyes wide with fear and tears. His touch tried to radiate courage and confidence.

"Take her away!" demanded the furious voice of Philip.

Tancred was looking into Helena's eyes. In spite of others about them, they saw only each other.

"I will live," he whispered for her alone.

"Whatever happens to you, I will come for you one day."

Tears ran down her cheeks. "I love you," her lips formed the words that would not come from her throat. Her eyes clung to Tancred's as the soldiers tore her away from him.

CHAPTER 6

Hope Deferred

Tancred concentrated on the narrow stream of light that trickled through the bars on the dungeon window. The guard lashed him again and the whip cracked. He gritted his pain into silence as Philip looked on with smug satisfaction. He had no idea what had befallen his cousin Leif. Had he been able to escape? Where was Nicholas? He assumed Philip had brought Helena back to the Sacred Palace, or perhaps to the family villa in Athens, but information was refused him.

"You might as well beg for my pity," said Philip. "If not, it shall go worse for you."

"If ever a doubt remained as to whose son you are, you have at long last crawled from your aristocratic den."

The remark increased Philip's temper, for he boasted himself to be wise.

"Where is Helena?" asked Tancred again.

"That is none of your concern."

The Byzantine commander stepped forward to delay a continuation of the whipping. "My advice, Noble Philip, is to spare his health. What good is a slave half dead? You would gain a goodly price for the barbarian."

Slave? Tancred looked at Philip.

"If you intend to sell him to the baron, he must be fit for the galley."

"Yes," said Philip as he smiled. "He must be able to pull an oar on the dromond."

Furious, Tancred avoided any reaction that would please his captor. "I will find you one day, Philip, no matter where you send me."

Philip gave him a measured glance, then tossing his purple cloak over his shoulder, strode away.

Later that day the baron arrived and was escorted to Tancred's cell by the Byzantine commander. The baron was a soft and colorful dandy, with a protruding stomach that appeared to accommodate a large appetite undaunted by the sight of unpleasant things. Garbed with a fine red cloak draped over his shoulders, he wore an embroidered white silk shirt and black leggings. A servant stood beside him with a bowl of fruit. The baron devoured the grapes, his bulging eyes measuring Tancred's worth as he lay on the hay.

The baron tossed the purple grapes back

into the bowl. "Did I pay Philip a good price for a skinned rabbit?"

"The muscle remains, baron," said the commander, "and he has a good wit. He is not your usual slave. He is a Norman, a warrior."

"I do not pay for a man's wit as long as he can row. It is less trouble if his tongue is cut out and he is blind."

"This one may prove of more value to you than a rower. He is learned in languages; he worked in the Royal Library translating Latin and Greek."

Tancred glanced at the commander. Why was he giving commendations?

"A Norman, you say?" The baron was interested. "The last Norman I bought has served me well for the past ten years. Zeus may pity the Turks if the Norman armies arrive at Antioch. Very well, I shall take him." He turned away. "When he recovers and grows some skin, deliver him to me in good condition. And tell Philip if he expects to sell any more slaves to me to keep his whip from their backs! A wise owner treats his beasts well. And do something with his wounds." He gestured. "I need a strong rower soon on one of the Venetian galleys."

The sun was setting and the cell grew dim

when a guard awakened Tancred, bringing him food. The guard spoke to a man accompanying him. "Be quick with your treatment. If you delay as long as you did yesterday, I will lock you up with him."

To Tancred's surprise, Bardas entered the dungeon and came and stooped beside him, bringing his medical satchel and a clean robe.

"Redwan," he whispered. "I can explain my treachery. I was ill put upon by Philip. I trusted him."

"I should kill you, Bardas," rasped Tancred, his throat raw.

Bardas quickly opened a skin of water and gave him a drink. "To die for what I have done would bring release to my soul."

Tancred managed to raise himself to his elbow, his hand grasping the front of the man's tunic. "Death will bring you to your just doom. You betrayed your mistress — and Nicholas! Many good men are dead this day!"

"I shall live to see you free, and my mistress with you. This, master, I vow!"

Tancred fell back weakly. His entire body was in pain, his vision dim. "I trusted you once too often. My cousin Norris is dead."

Bardas bowed his head, fist clenched in repentance. "I shall never forgive myself."

"Get out, Bardas."

"No, master. I will not leave you. Not this time. You are a far greater man than Philip. I see that now. I have been a fool. I can help Helena only by seeing that you escape this dungeon. I am searching for Master Nicholas and your other cousin, the one named Leif, but as yet I've learned nothing."

The guard heard them talking and walked up to the cell. Bardas grew silent. He worked to bathe Tancred's lacerations, cleaning them and using the medicines.

"We will talk again tomorrow," whispered Bardas. "By then I may have learned more."

The Byzantine commander had Tancred attended to daily, and slowly he began to recover. There was no doubt that Bardas was truly grieved for his deed. He attended him faithfully and always had some bit of information to pass on about Helena. She was well, he said, and kept under guard in the palace.

Weeks passed and Tancred was on his feet, able to wear his clothes in spite of the tenderness of his flesh.

"In a few days a garrison of men will bring you to the wharf. You will be placed under supervision of the baron's chief captain. A man named Hadrian," said Bardas.

"How many in the garrison?"

"Fifteen, maybe twenty. I have a plan. It might work."

Bardas glanced over his shoulder to see if they were being watched. The guard, apparently unconcerned, sat at a table, carving on a piece of wood. Bardas carefully opened his cloak to reveal the tunic he wore. There was nothing elaborate about it, a tunic any common citizen might wear. Then as Tancred watched, Bardas showed him the slight bulges in the seams. Helena's jewels? He was carrying a fortune.

"I have not been asleep many nights, master. I have found a guard who will help me escape. On the Street Meese there is a spy merchant, Ayub. For the right price an ambush can be staged along the route to the baron's fortress. Nicholas and Leif will be with them."

"The blood of Norris and the betrayal of Helena remain, though I escape. Think not that your debt is paid," said Tancred.

"Such a debt cannot be paid by mere mortals, master. Yet, by my life, I shall see you free."

He turned to go, and Tancred's hand rested briefly on his shoulder.

"Between us there is peace, but your mistress, I fear, will never forgive you."

Bardas was sober. "She will not. My relief comes not in her acceptance, but in knowing I have undone a small portion of my error . . . a small portion."

Lying awake in his cell that night, Tancred made plans. If Bardas could reach the merchant, and Nicholas and Leif form a band of brigands to waylay them on the road, he would somehow find Philip. And when he did . . . he would kill him. And Helena? He would find her again if it took the rest of his life.

The days passed restlessly. There was a delay in the trip to the wharf, and Bardas had not visited Tancred's cell for several days. When Tancred questioned the guard, sullen silence greeted him. Had Bardas been found out?

"I wish to see the commander," Tancred told the guard.

"He has no time for prisoners."

"Bardas, where is he?"

"You ask too many questions."

"When am I to be brought to the baron's captain?"

The guard did not answer, keeping his eyes on the wood carving in his hands.

Tancred wondered about Bardas. Had he managed to escape? Was he even now dead? He dare not press for information. The afternoon shadows fell across the cell window, darkening the dungeon. Soon the guard exchanged duty with yet another silent soldier. Then at evening, the door above the steps opened and the Byzantine captain came in with several guards.

"Am I free to go?" Tancred asked in sarcasm.

The commander's eyes searched Tancred as he spoke. "The eunuch slave has escaped."

"Ah! A smart man, Bardas. May he find a ship with wings!"

"The only ship for you, Norman, is the baron's galley. Bardas escaped with one of my guards. We trailed him toward Athens."

Athens? Had he tried to find Philip and Helena?

Tancred pretended innocence. "You caught the eunuch, no doubt."

The commander's eyes measured him. "We will. No rebel will get far for long. What do you know about this?"

"I? How could I know anything locked away for the last two months with rats? I will remember this ill treatment, Captain. I do not lightly waste so much of my life."

He smirked. "Do not complain. If you did not have the respect of men in the Varangian Guard, you would be dead by now. Rebels who displease Philip and Lady Irene are either hanged or thrown to the leopards."

"I am not a rebel to the Byzantine empire. I am a Norman. A captain and soldier in the service of Prince Bohemond."

The commander paused at the mention of Bohemond. "They say he and the crusaders are marching slowly toward Antioch. There is news that one named Baldwin has taken Edessa."

Baldwin was the brother of Duke Godfrey, and the news of a victory did not surprise Tancred.

"Bohemond will be insulted by the treatment I've received from the minister of war," warned Tancred, exaggerating the truth.

The commander grew more curious. "If you serve with the Normans, then why did you return to Constantinople to anger Philip?"

"For the love of a woman," said Tancred easily, "a mercenary soldier often finds himself involved in causes not his own. I speak the truth when I say I care not who sits warming the throne of your emperor, either Alexius or Philip."

"The beautiful woman you speak of is to marry Philip."

"Not by choice."

The commander studied him. "You might

be telling the truth. I wondered why Philip despised you so. Jealousy would be reason enough, but it matters not to me. I am to bring you to the baron later tonight. I will report to him what you have told me. Perhaps he will show you more consideration. He has no liking for Byzantium. He is a Roman."

If Bardas has done his work, thought Tancred, *I will never reach the baron's fortress.* Nicholas, Leif, and a band of mercenaries would be waiting in ambush on the road.

That night the Byzantine captain returned to his cell with five soldiers.

"Am I to be brought to the wharf?" Tancred asked.

"No, to the baron's fortress."

"Why? Am I not to sail as a galley slave?"

"Are you anxious?" the captain mocked.

"It is better than dining with rats."

"The order came to bring you to the baron's fortress. Captain Hadrian's new crew will wait there until the Venetian ship arrives."

Outside, horses awaited them, as well as a new group of men under the Roman captain Hadrian.

As they trotted forward, the gate opened, then shut firmly behind them. Tancred could only wonder how cousin Leif had escaped the garden alive. His memory called up the death of Norris. He turned in his saddle and looked back in a moment of tribute. *Farewell, Redwan cousin. Your friendship was short-lived but cherished.*

With the death of Norris Redwan, son of Walter of Sicily, came the certainty that his uncle would now hold Tancred responsible for more than the assassination of his half brother, Derek. His burdens were compounded, for Bardas and Helena were the only witnesses to what had happened. Leif would not know of Bardas's and Philip's treachery. Tancred would be blamed.

The horses' hooves broke the silence of the night, and the startled shriek of a nocturnal bird followed them as it soared across the grass into the chinar trees. After months in the dungeon, even the chill wind felt like a breath of spring to Tancred. The harvest moon was up, bright and bold.

Hope lived again. Had Bardas contacted Nicholas? Did a band of mercenaries wait down the road?

They were now miles from Constantinople and rounding a curve with a vineyard ahead. This, thought Tancred anxiously, would be the perfect place to set an ambush. The sounds of battle would not reach the Byzantine captain back at the summer palace, and they were still too far away from the baron's fortress to receive support from Captain Hadrian.

His eyes and ears sought some sign of movement ahead in the darkness of the vineyard, some sign that the plan had worked. The good omen did not come.

His hopes died with the first light in the eastern sky, revealing the dark walls of an ominous fortress. Captain Hadrian rode up to the gate and shouted orders to the sentry. The wooden gate opened and they rode through.

The ugly sight that greeted Tancred angered and repulsed him. There were two dead men left upon a gibbet in the outer courtyard. For a stark instant he saw Nicholas and Leif, but his mind had deceived him. One of the dead men, however, was familiar — Bardas!

Captain Hadrian drew his horse to a stop below the gibbet, and Tancred rode up beside him. Bardas had been hanged in his precious tunic, taking Helena's jewels to his death.

The rising fall wind carried the harbinger of a dark and bleak winter.

He felt Captain Hadrian's hard and curious gaze. "Do you know these men?" the captain demanded.

"That one is Bardas, the bodyguard of Lady Helena Lysander. I do not know the other," Tancred said, keeping his voice steady.

"They were caught hiring mercenaries to free you on the road. If you wish to know the fate of Bishop Nicholas Lysander and your Redwan cousin, Lady Irene has Nicholas imprisoned in Constantinople. And the Norman escaped to find his uncle Walter of Sicily. It is reported they ride with Bohemond."

Tancred's anger must have revealed itself in his face, for Hadrian said no more. The captain gestured for his troop to ride forward into the fortress.

As they rode through the inner gate, the baron came out of a doorway and stood there surrounded by his personal bodyguard of five burly-looking men. The baron measured Tancred with a keen eye, a pleased look on his round, sweating face.

"Ah! A Norman warrior indeed, Commander Hadrian! His skin and his strength have healed since the whipping, I see. Such a man is worth his price. See to it you put him to good use."

Hadrian did not smile. "A wild wolf is not easily tamed, Baron."

"But worth the effort. I wish to speak to

you about that lazy Venetian captain Rainald. Come inside. Bring the Norman with you." He turned and went back through the doorway.

Tancred judged from the scornful twitch of Hadrian's cheek that he did not like the baron. He would keep that information in mind for future use.

Inside the fortress hall, the baron was seated on a divan of comfortable cushions while silent slaves waited on him, bringing an assortment of meats and flagons of wine. The baron looked in good mood and motioned for Hadrian to sit and help himself to the delicacies.

Hadrian declined. "We ate on the march. I am anxious to put the Norman away. I shall have my men take down the body of my guard and be on my way."

"Ah yes, he was one of yours, wasn't he? A regret. There is no mercy for betrayers. He and the Byzantine would have brought mercenaries to attack me."

"So I have heard."

The baron turned a calculating look on Tancred. "The wolf has recovered from his ordeal. You are a strong one. I can use you well. There will be no whip if you cooperate. But first, you must prove your loyalty to me."

"It takes no loyalty to be chained to the oars of your galley."

The baron reached for his cup of wine. "The captain of my corsairs is looking for men willing to fight freely for a share in the bounty. Yet to be trusted with a sword or scimitar, a corsair must prove he will not turn and use it on his captain. Hadrian is particular about the men he sails with."

Tancred was thinking of the freedom that would come to him if he sailed a corsair. . . .

"He is not to be trusted," said Hadrian. "At the first chance he will jump ship to search for Lady Helena Lysander."

"He is in your hand, Hadrian. The decision is yours. Such can be your future, Norman, if you serve loyally. And if not, you shall find your new master grim indeed."

Tancred had no doubt. Without friends, the fortress would be impossible to escape.

Tancred was shown to a small chamber with a long table. He sat down and waited, with two guards at the door. An hour passed before the door opened and Hadrian stepped in. The guards left and Tancred stood.

"The baron is a greedy man," said Hadrian. "He sees in you a warrior to aid his ambitions. He will not free you."

"Did you ask him to?"

"I offered to buy you."

"I am moved," Tancred said wryly.

Hadrian's eyes were hard. "Only when you have my trust will I be able to help you. That may take a week, a month, or a year." He turned to walk out.

"Wait."

The captain looked at him, unmoved.

"I cannot squander such precious time. Help me escape now and I can see that you have a fortune without taking to the sea."

"I do not take bribes; I fight for a reason. The ships I prey upon are noted for carrying slaves and arrogant Byzantines."

"You do not approve of Byzantium, yet Rome once held more arrogance than even the Queen City of the East."

The captain shrugged. "Times change. Kingdoms fall. Only ideas live on."

"Truth lives forever."

"And what is truth?" he scorned.

"The question of another Roman who lived and basked in power. His name was Pilate. Truth stood before him in sinless flesh, and he compromised with a lie to retain a vain moment of political power. In fear of giving up his paltry throne, he gave the order to crucify the Son of God."

"Are you a bishop also?" Hadrian asked flippantly, then changed the subject with a brush of his hand.

"I am a free man, no citizen of Byzantium. What law, then, authorizes my being sold as a slave to the baron?"

Hadrian said distinctly, "The law of Philip Lysander. He makes his own."

"One day he will also die by his law."

"You shall see to that, I suppose? Listen to me, Norman. The baron also has vested authority."

"He is a pirate and a murderer. He did not have the authority to hang your soldier."

Hadrian grew quiet. "I cannot talk now. There will be other days."

"The fortune I promise depends on the burial of Bardas."

Hadrian looked impatient. "I intend to bury both men. Do you think I would leave them for the vultures?"

Tancred walked across the chamber until they stood eye to eye. "Then remove his tunic and keep it for me. It contains the jewels of Lady Helena."

A minute passed before Hadrian spoke. "What if I wished to keep it all?"

"What choice do I have but to trust you?"

Hadrian considered, then smiled reluctantly. "I see you are a gambler also." He walked out and the guard bolted the door after him.

CHAPTER 7

Hope Restored

A week had passed since Tancred had been brought to the guardhouse and kept in one of the cells. Nothing was resolved concerning Captain Hadrian. Perhaps even now he was planning to escape for some fair city where he could enjoy his good fortune. As for Tancred's lot, he worked in the baron's fortress under close supervision of sullen guards with a thirst for violence. Tancred had a good view of horsemen coming and going through the gate. Daily he rehearsed his escape, but the opportunity did not come. He had learned the names of others anxious for freedom who could handle a sword, if they could get their hands on one. And there were wretched women kept by the baron who dreamed of release and who eyed Tancred with hope. There was one problem. He could never get close enough to speak to them, and they were watched by the chief of the eunuchs.

Several more weeks passed, and his hope that the baron would place him on a ship failed to materialize. Guards were everywhere, watching his every move. The winter rains came. Far off, thunder rumbled, and the Mediterranean was rough.

Where was Helena? Had she become the wife of Philip?

One night some of the prisoners spoke in whispers of a ship from Genoa on its way to Constantinople that had taken harbor in rough weather at the local port. Tancred knew of the Genoese. They were a small but privileged colony of Italian merchants in Constantinople who were given special trading concessions by the emperor, and they had a reserved quarter at the Golden Horn where they lived and traded. They were a constant irritant to the Byzantine populace, who resented them, jealous of their prowess on the sea and in the guilds.

His opportunity came a few days later. Tancred and several other prisoners were needed to carry cargo from the Genoese galleon in trade with the baron. The ship's captain stood on the dock with several seamen, and Tancred could see that the captain was watching him. His name was Rainald, and he had the arrogance of an ostentatious monarch. He was handsome, dark haired, and boasted a fine-clipped mustache. His hat bore a plume, and his cape was decorated with gold brocade and gemstones.

The captain watched Tancred with intense black eyes, then turned and strutted away with his equally adorned men to meet with the baron and Hadrian.

In the ship's hold, Tancred's suspicions were aroused when he noticed that certain of the baron's barrels and crates were not unloaded but kept separate from the wine and silk. In a moment, while unguarded, he made certain of his suspicions. Grabbing a crowbar, he carefully pried open the lid on one of the crates and peered inside. They contained weapons! Stacks of them. This was no ordinary merchant ship. He reached his hand through the small opening and closed his fingers around a Toledo sword, glancing about to make sure no one could see him. But his desperate attempt was foiled.

"You!" the seaman called from the steps above Tancred's head. "Why do you linger? Get away from there!"

For the rest of the afternoon Tancred worked on the dock reloading the Genoese ship. If only he could get one of those swords.

By late afternoon the sky was changing, and lowering clouds and a damp wind promised rain. A drizzle soon turned into a heavy downpour.

"Move, animals!" shouted the baron's captain. Drenched and hungry, Tancred and the other slaves at last had the Genoese ship loaded. Hourly he fought his frustration as he was kept from the section of the hold where the weapons were stored. What was *he* doing as a slave to a foolish baron? Why could he not free himself? Why did his prayers appear to go unanswered? Where was his wit, his courage? Somehow there had to be an opening, if he only had the sense to see it!

The day ended with little hope. He'd not been permitted below deck again, and the guards had watched them too closely for Tancred to inform the others of the weapons. Most of the prisoners were defeated in spirit anyway and would have cowered from such a bold endeavor that held so little possibility of success.

I will not be beaten, he thought. *I will never give up.* He would live for another day, another opportunity. And there was still Hadrian and the tunic with Helena's jewels. While Hadrian had not mentioned it, Tancred continued to hope that he had not misread the character of the man. He was a soldier, and as such, he had detected an equal respect coming from Hadrian, who knew him to be a warrior.

After he and the other slaves were hauled back to the fortress, they lined up before the huge caldron of steaming broth to receive their portion of boiled mutton.

One of the guards appeared in the courtyard. "You, Norman, come!"

Tancred followed him through the bailey. He was tempted to jump him and take his weapons, but as usual two other guards appeared. Again he must wait.

The baron stood before a hearth. To Tancred's surprise, Captain Hadrian was also there, and next to him, the captain of the Genoese ship.

"Is this the man?" the baron inquired.

Captain Rainald looked at Tancred. "This is the one."

The baron scowled. "I have other slaves you could hire. The Norman is untrustworthy. He will jump ship."

"He is strong. I will guard him. How much?"

Still, the baron was reluctant. "For how long?"

"Two — three months."

The baron emptied his mug of wine. Captain Hadrian stepped beside him and spoke in a low voice. The baron's brows rushed together. "Very well. Take him. But I expect generous trade with the Genoese merchants for this favor," he warned Captain Rainald.

"Ah, you will surely get what you deserve," said Rainald.

"Then take him and go."

"In this rain!" said the Genoese captain indignantly. "I shall get my clothes ruined! I will wait until morning. Hadrian will take care of the Norman slave."

The baron gestured roughly for the guard to lead Rainald to a chamber for the night.

Outside in the mizzling rain, Tancred turned to Hadrian. "Have I you to thank for this?"

"Not now. There are spies everywhere."

Their horses were brought by a soldier, and Tancred and Hadrian mounted. The feel of the saddle brought a surge of freedom to Tancred, and he leaned over and gave the wet mane a pat, wondering about Apollo.

They rode from the fortress through the gate and raced along the wet road for perhaps a mile before Hadrian slowed. Tancred turned the horse to face him, the rain wetting their faces.

"Rainald has no intention of holding you. A word of advice: Do not return to Constantinople. I understand your desire to confront Philip Lysander, but he has the advantage of hundreds of soldiers and a city on his side. Ride on to find Bohemond."

"I owe you," said Tancred. "But I cannot take your advice. Philip has control of two people I care about deeply. And maybe a cousin as well. I must return."

"It is your neck." He reached into his saddlebag and pulled out the tunic once belonging to Bardas. It had been cut evenly in half. With a smile he held both sections out for Tancred to choose.

Tancred smiled and took one half of the garment. "And you, Hadrian? Where do you go?"

"Surely not to join the armies of the western princes. I am through with war, with corsairs, and men like the baron." He turned his horse and gestured to freedom. "If you ever come to Cordoba," he suggested with a slight smile, "you may find me relaxing in one of the famed coffee houses, studying poetry — or perhaps the words of Truth!"

Tancred folded the torn tunic and stuffed it inside his ragged garment. "A pleasant and prosperous future. Farewell."

They lifted their hands in salute and rode their separate ways through the wind-driven rain.

Tancred approached the Genoese ship expecting the men aboard to refuse him entry, but instead they brought him to the captain's cabin. A suit of clean clothing was waiting; a shirt of the finest smoke blue silk, black leggings, leather boots of the highest quality, and a mantle of the same fine wool as the suit, embroidered with silver. A bath in the cold water from the harbor came first, and Rainald's valet trimmed his shoulder-length hair, the rich color of ripened wheat tinged with dark auburn, to the masculine cut he preferred as a Norman warrior. The one thing missing was a good blade and dagger! He would not wait long to visit an armory and choose the finest that money could buy, now that he had jewels. One day he would repay Helena from his own resources as the true Redwan heir of the Sicilian dynasty — *if* he could capture Mosul.

It was early the next day when Captain Rainald boarded his ship, as elegant as ever. His dark eyes raked Tancred.

"The foul-smelling slave is now fit company for the honor of Rainald!" he stated vainly, his black eyes twinkling.

He pulled a flagon of wine from his drawer and two exquisite carved glasses from Venice.

Tancred imagined that the "fit company" of Rainald was not easy to endure, for he reeked with self-conceit.

Tancred offered a light bow, more in jest than sincerity. "Your generosity, my Captain, will be acclaimed throughout all the Norman camp!"

Rainald grinned. "My generosity, Norman, will be rewarded by means other than acclaim. The tunic of Bardas," he inquired smoothly. "You do have it with you?"

So he knew about the jewels. "Ah, the famous tunic. So Hadrian told you."

This time the captain gave a debonair bow. "Why else would I risk my handsome head, so remembered by charming ladies?"

"Why indeed?" Tancred smiled. He liked the conceited dandy. "I shall pay for your services. How much do I owe you?"

Rainald mused, pursing his lips. "The baron will be upset when he learns of your unfortunate escape — it may cost me future business in trade. And there are many dangers to my neck in bringing a man wanted by the Lysander family back to Constantinople."

Rainald was not only vain but a polished schemer.

"My generosity in buying your services for three months did not come cheaply to me," continued Rainald. "Therefore, my Norman friend," he gestured with his glass, "it seems but fair and equitable that the tunic should be divided — again."

"It seems I have no choice."

"We will divide now."

"So you can throw me over the ship and take it all? Not so, my fine Captain!"

"What! You would accuse Rainald of such vile treachery?"

"I am a man accustomed to treachery. I will also take one of your excellent swords." Tancred nodded in the direction of a cabinet where Toledo swords boasted their strength.

Rainald stood and spread his hands. "I am a generous man. Why not? Have your choice."

Tancred went to the cabinet and one by one tested their feel while Rainald watched, his expression showing that he knew Tancred to be no fool in bargaining.

Tancred chose the best, glanced at the captain to see his response, and Rainald sighed at the loss. Tancred smiled, belted on the scabbard, and slipped the sword into place.

"You know your weapons, Tancred."

"I would likely be dead by now if I did not." He then reached under his own cloak and pulled out the half tunic.

Rainald's teeth showed under his black mustache. He drew a Damascus dagger and cut the tunic in two. "Friend, my ship is yours, my wine, and my sword — but in Constantinople, the lovely ladies are mine."

"No contest, my Captain. There is but one for me."

Rainald refilled his glass and raised a brow at the wine left untouched by Tancred. He looked at him questioningly.

"I took a vow of restraint at Monte Casino when a boy. Have you any water?"

"Water!" he grimaced.

Tancred laughed and caught up a waterskin hanging on a hook on the cabin wall. "With enemies sniffing my trail, it is also wise to remain sober and alert."

"Ah, but you are safe aboard my ship."

"Am I?"

Rainald shrugged, sank into his captain's chair, and propped his boots on the desk. He grew serious, watching Tancred, who leaned into the wall drinking from the waterskin.

"When was the last time you changed this water?" Tancred mocked.

"So you are a Norman," stated Rainald reflectively. "We Venetians know about the Norman conquest into Italy. From what part do you come?"

"From Apulia, in Sicily."

"I know Sicily well. Count Roger rules."

"We are distantly related."

"Your father was a shipmaster?"

"Somewhat. Mainly, he was a warring lord in service to Count Roger."

"The brother of Bohemond."

"You know Bohemond?"

"Heard of him. He hopes to take Antioch, does he not?"

"As all the western princes do, including Count Raymond and Duke Godfrey."

"But Count Roger did not go on the expedition to take Jerusalem. That interests me. Why did he stay in Sicily?"

"He is not the restless adventurer that Bohemond is."

"And your father? Did he also remain in service to Count Roger?"

"My father is dead. I have an adoptive father — my uncle Rolf Redwan, Seigneur of the Castle of Hohms."

"And your journey now, where does it take you?"

Tancred explained about the assassin, how his other uncle Walter of Sicily sought him, and of the treachery of Philip and Lady Irene.

"And you?" Tancred asked.

"First, I go to the Genoese quarter of Constantinople," Rainald said. "I must deliver weapons to the Venetians."

"The weapons below?"

"You saw them?"

"I had hoped to *borrow* one. I couldn't get near them long enough."

"After delivery," Rainald went on, "I bring a report to the military in Constantinople."

Tancred told how he had once served in the imperial cavalry at the guard castle of Herion. "But you — you do not seem the military type."

"I cannot help my elegant flair," said Rainald vainly. "Have you been long a slave to the baron?"

"I have wasted months I could not lose."

Tancred pressed him for news of the western knights. "When I left, the princes had defeated the Red Lion outside Nicaea."

"They are journeying south across the Amanus Mountains of northern Syria toward Antioch."

Tancred knew just how treacherous the mountain pass was. His uncle Rolf had told him how he had crossed it, losing his horse and the guide. There were miles of nothing but rock, intolerable heat, and no water.

"They fall short of both food and water," said Rainald. "News has arrived that many died on the crossing, and mules and supplies are lost. If all goes with Christ's blessing, they should arrive at the walls of Antioch around October."

"A long siege will deplete their food supplies."

"That is where we noble Genoese come in. With the western knights threatened with famine, it is important to capture the small port of St. Symeon in order to bring in supplies. That, my friend, is left to me and others."

Tancred's estimation of the man climbed higher. The small but strategic port of St. Symeon was located near Antioch, and a main road led from the dock to the gates of the fortified city.

"That is my destination also," Tancred told him.

"A Genoese fleet will leave soon. And you? A man of your breeding will undoubtedly fare well. What do you seek at Constantinople?"

"Lady Helena Lysander. She may now be in the custody of Philip."

The smooth dark brow arched in wonder. Again he measured Tancred. "You play with very high stakes."

"The prize is well worth the risk."

"A man to admire sits before me. If I may be of help, you have only to ask."

"There is something," said Tancred. "I

111

have enemies in Constantinople. I do not want to be seen. I would take refuge in the Genoese quarter."

"Then you will be my guest," Rainald offered. "It will be some time before the fleet sets sail for St. Symeon. Philip will not find you there."

CHAPTER 8

Return to Constantinople

Alone in the fashionable room that Rainald had given him, Tancred opened the window, which looked directly onto the cloistered quarter of wealthy Genoese merchants. Beyond the walls that ran along the seaward side of the quarter, the wharves and quays were crowded with the houses of seamen, built on pilings over the water. The city within a city was located near a triangular point where the land opened onto the mouth of the Bosporus. Ships from all the known ports could be seen moving from the open sea and down the strait of the four-mile-long horn.

Across the Bosporus, dark under gathering clouds, lay the hills of Asia. Nicaea was there, now under Byzantine rule, and far beyond the mountains the great city of Antioch was under siege by the western lords.

The problem now facing Tancred was immense. To confront Philip in his own arena was to place himself at great risk. Philip was more dangerous than he had at first thought. His limitless ambitions had showed him a man ready to stoop to any level, however base, in order to strengthen his position.

Where was Helena? Months had slipped away. Anything might have happened to her in the interval. What if she were now the bride of Philip? Would Irene have allowed it for some devious reason of her own? She had been against the marriage of her son to Helena until now, but matters may have changed.

As for Tancred's love for Helena . . . its depths grew deeper with the absence between them and the threat of losing her. Since Philip did not know he had escaped the baron, he would have less reason to guard her every move. Was there opportunity to locate her and sweep her away aboard Rainald's ship for St. Symeon?

Then there was Irene. Did she have Nicholas her prisoner?

Rufus, the bodyguard to Irene, came to mind. He was the one source of information in the city. He must be reached with a message.

Rainald's unexpected return provided the opportunity Tancred was looking for. Emperor Alexius was to receive a group of Genoese to discuss the need to take the port of St. Symeon, opening up a supply route for the western armies.

"With a bribe I may somehow get word to this bodyguard friend of yours named Rufus," Rainald suggested.

During those days of waiting, Tancred moved about the city, cautious not to remain in one place for long. If only his faithful old Moorish friend Hakeem were here now! Tancred had not heard from him since he had ridden ahead to Antioch. What if either Kalid or Mosul had discovered his secret presence?

The streets were full of spies; he could trust no one. Even confiding in Rainald was a risk, but one he must take. So far the Genoese captain had done nothing to warrant suspicion. Tancred needed a friend, and why not Rainald?

Together, their masculine appearance was enough to turn the heads of many. Women treated them well; men were envious.

Tancred, however, thought of no other woman but Helena. He had excused himself from Rainald, who was having trouble remembering any woman but the one facing him, and stepped into the Byzantine garden of the exquisite wineshop.

A feminine voice spoke from the flowers. "What! You are alone? In Constantinople? What manner of visitor are you? Especially when the wealth of your dress and the arrogance in which you carry yourself demands a woman worthy of your attention!"

He turned slowly. The woman was quite attractive, painted, and boasting jewels from many pleased lovers of the past. Her eyes mocked him, and she tilted her head laden with adornments. "Do I not promise a worthy investment of your evening?"

He scanned her leisurely, deliberately remaining silent.

"Ah . . . ? Then there must be another woman on your mind," she said.

Still he said nothing and only watched her.

She arched a brow. "I envy her claim on you, stranger. Is she here in the city?"

When he remained unreadable, she smiled and walked up to him. "She is unwise to let you out of her sight."

Her perfume was strong with invitation, as were her eyes. "My slaves wait with my lift. I would be pleased if you would keep me company."

Tancred said, "At a young age, I learned the wisdom of choosing my own sword, my own breed of horse, and especially my own woman. I have vowed to keep my love for her alone. If I played with folly now, I would be like the young man King Solomon wrote about in his Proverbs. The way of the harlot leads to the abode of the dead. You will understand, madame, that I do not wish to treat you rudely, for Christ showed mercy and gentleness to such a woman as yourself; let it suffice to say that I await the perfumed sheets of another, whom I will take to be mine forever before God."

Her eyes hardened into narrow slits. She stood there a moment, then said viciously, "Arrogant pig!" and flounced away, with words of cursing on her lips, proving indeed that he had judged wisely.

Several more days had passed before Rainald met with the emperor. Tancred was waiting in the public stables, moving among the stalls of fine-blooded horses and examining the chariots. A worker led in an Arabian mare, sleek and magnificent.

"This afternoon in the armory," the voice barely whispered. The worker moved on with the spirited horse.

Rainald had been wise to not approach him with the news himself but to use an agreeable informant. Tancred's respect for the man grew.

CHAPTER 9

The Armory of the Varangian Guard

The armorer, a powerful man of Scandinavian ancestry, kept a courtyard where soldiers met to practice with all sorts of weapons. Hired Normans of Viking ancestry belonging to the emperor's Varangian guard were often present, as were other soldiers and bodyguards.

Rufus was there practicing scimitars with a Persian. Tancred was careful not to draw attention to himself as he merged among the others dressed as a common mercenary soldier.

Rufus saw him. Tancred pretended to prepare for sword practice, keeping his face averted. Rufus finished the practice with the Persian, then unhurriedly found his way over to Tancred.

"Try your hand at this, soldier." Rufus handed him the scimitar — that saber with a curved blade used so well by the Moors.

Tancred tried the balance of the menacing weapon. Swiftly he ran it through the various steps of style.

"Only a Seljuk prince could do better," said Rufus distinctly.

Their eyes met. Was the word choice deliberately chosen to convey a message? Who else could the prince be but Kalid?

Rufus spoke in a lower tone. "She was brought to the Castle of Hohms soon after you disappeared."

"I did not disappear willingly! I was sold as a slave!"

"Unfortunate. I searched for you to no avail. Your whereabouts was masterfully covered. Nevertheless, Redwan, I tell you the truth. She has been sent to Constantine at the Castle of Hohms. Undoubtedly, he will send her to Prince Kalid, unless his feelings for Adrianna influence him to spare her daughter. With Constantine one never knows, for he is unbalanced in mind."

Tancred's hopes revived. His uncle Rolf was there, and Adrianna knew he could be trusted as a friend. Could she have arranged to speak with him without Constantine knowing? If she had been able to tell him of her plight and Helena's — then Helena's arrival would not go unnoticed by Rolf, who might prevent her from being sent on to

Antioch. It was a hope, at least.

"And Lady Irene?" asked Tancred, always cautious of the golden goddess, the mistress of intrigue. He had come up against her in the palace of the Red Lion and nearly lost his head.

Rufus's lip curled with open contempt. "For now, Madame Irene is consumed with my son Joseph — and Nicholas, whom she has imprisoned."

I must find some way to free Nicholas before going on to the castle, Tancred thought. "Where is he held? In the Sacred Palace?"

"She moves him from place to place to make it impossible to know for certain where he is being held. She hopes to continue to hold him indefinitely and foil his allies who wish to free him. Yet," said Rufus cautiously, "there are ways. For I know her better than all others. It may be that we can do something, now that you are here. Joseph may be able to learn Nicholas's exact whereabouts. I will be allowed to see my son briefly tonight."

Hope lived on in Tancred's heart, but the news of Helena kept those fires from burning brightly. He stared moodily at the scimitar. A sense of doom threatened to leave him emotionally defeated. What if Helena had been sent to Kalid by now? What

120

if she were a married woman? Everything would change between them, and yet nothing in his heart had changed. He would always love her.

"What of Philip?" asked Tancred.

"His favor with the emperor has grown since the fall of Nicaea and the Citadel's return to Byzantine rule."

Tancred was already aware that Irene had arranged for the victory to be attributed to Philip's genius.

"He is now preoccupied with his advancement," said Rufus. "Philip remains careful to not compromise his ambitions for the sake of others, even Helena."

"Then he remains as vicious as I knew him to be since he abandoned his men to the Rhinelanders at the Danube."

"Yes," agreed Rufus, "but even more brutal. He no longer struggles with his conscience. For Philip, politics has always been his downfall. When he was a boy he had outstanding intellect; he was talented and even gracious. Had he married Helena long ago and left the power of the Sacred Palace, he might have become a man of history. Now . . ." Rufus paused, his face hard, "he is a typical Byzantine. Weak in character, greedy, but clever. Like Irene, he will one day stumble and never rise. Someday I will destroy her. It is the only reason I remain here. And that hour is fast approaching."

Tancred knew this. Only one question remained in his estimation of Philip: his treatment of Helena. "Who betrayed her to Constantine?"

"When Helena refused to show up for the wedding, Philip was enraged. He felt humiliated before the emperor. She despises him after his treachery to you and the death of your cousin Norris. She would have none of him. He knew she loved you — that there was no hope of regaining her devotion. In an act of revenge toward both of you, he delivered her to Bishop Constantine."

Tancred's heart boiled with anger. "Philip has sealed his doom this time. To betray me was one matter I might overlook, but I will not forget what he has done to Helena. I will see him before I leave Constantinople. Can you arrange it?"

Rufus mused, troubled. "Yes, I think it possible. Do you intend to go to the castle afterward?"

"I will go. I will find her, whatever the cost."

Rufus watched him alertly, as though he expected as much. He showed neither approval nor disapproval. "You will do what your convictions demand. If she has gone to

Antioch, you will face not only the sword of war but the scimitars of the prince's guard. They are a band of fanatical warriors who surround him constantly. They will risk death in order to protect him — Helena, as well."

Tancred returned the scimitar. "I am aware of the ways of Moslems. You forget my mother was a Moor. Sword or scimitar, I must find her. I have a vow to keep, whatever the outcome."

They left the armory together and stepped out onto the street to merge with the soldiers.

"If you kill Philip, you will have the emperor as an enemy," warned Rufus as they walked along. "I do not practice giving advice, yet do not seek him. The fate of Philip is bound up with Irene."

"And you intend to destroy her. Is that it?"

Rufus did not answer.

"Irene is your burden," said Tancred. "Philip is mine."

They came to a shop, where Rufus paused. "Do you insist on seeing Philip?"

"It is something I must do."

After a moment, Rufus spoke. "When a man becomes close to the emperor, his enemies increase. There is intrigue and discontent. Do you know what I'm saying?"

Tancred nodded. "Philip has enemies in the palace?"

Rufus glanced over his shoulder to make sure they were not being followed. "Among Philip's own bodyguard there are those no longer loyal. Certain men respected Lady Helena. They were not pleased with his action in sending her to Constantine. News has also circulated through one Captain Basil that Philip treated you unjustly. The soldiers respected your abilities when you served in the imperial cavalry. They know Philip pretends to be a soldier when he is not."

"That is just what I wanted to hear."

"I have a plan. I have learned intrigue and deception well from my Byzantine masters. Meet me here tonight."

Rainald was anxiously awaiting Tancred's return and jumped to his feet the moment the Norman came through the door. Rainald wore the uniform of an imposing Genoese naval captain, but neither of them yet mentioned what it meant — that he must soon leave for St. Symeon. Time was short to accomplish so much in Constantinople.

"I was beginning to fear this man Rufus had betrayed you," Rainald said. "Did you find out anything?"

Tancred told him the news.

Rainald measured him. "Your plans? Do you still wish to go to St. Symeon? I am under orders to sail no later than tomorrow night. We intend to seize the port. The crusaders under the princes will not be far away."

The news added to Tancred's restlessness. "I will not leave until I confront Philip and free Nicholas."

Rainald picked up his two bags and walked to the door. "We will sail after midnight tonight, friend. I will look for you, but I cannot wait long."

"Understood."

They parted, and Tancred paced the room. Tonight he would meet Rufus again. What news would he bring?

The sun seemed to take longer than usual to go down. He watched it set over the Asian mountains and thought of Helena. What was she doing now? Did she think of him? Did she pray for him as he prayed for her? Would Christ yet bring them together as one? Or was it forever too late?

CHAPTER 10

The Hippodrome

Alone, Tancred walked down the street to the wineshop where he would meet Rufus, his chain mesh concealed beneath dark clothing.

Rufus drove up in a chariot. His face was strained, and Tancred noted that he also appeared somewhat dazed.

"Did you locate Nicholas?" Tancred asked.

"He will meet you at the hippodrome. As will Philip," Rufus said, emotionless.

Tancred watched him, wondering. "Are you all right?"

"It no longer matters about me, Redwan. Get in," he said. "There is not much time. You and Nicholas must be aboard Rainald's ship tonight."

Did that mean Rufus and his son would not be coming?

Tancred jumped in beside him. The chariot turned onto a shadowed street and continued straight ahead.

"All is arranged where Philip is concerned," said Rufus. "The young rat was easier to bait than its mother."

Tancred studied the side of the bodyguard's hard face, his suspicions growing that matters with Irene had not gone well. Yet Nicholas was to meet him — and Philip. What had happened?

The tension showed on Rufus's dark face as he drove the chariot in dazed silence.

"What happened?" Tancred demanded.

"I told her Philip would be killed if she did not turn Nicholas free. She needed Philip to secure her own rise to the throne as empress. That was her dream."

Tancred looked at Rufus, amazed over the simplicity of the trap and wondering why the obvious had escaped him. Of course she would be forced to act to save Philip. But even if she let Nicholas go free, she would arrange an ambush to try to stop them from leaving.

The hippodrome came into view, empty and dark. It had been arranged for the gate to be left open, and they drove through and onto the track. The empty stands gazed down upon them, and Tancred imagined the seats to be filled with hysterical ghosts shouting their approval or hatred.

Why was Rufus bringing him here? A glance showed the ebony giant sitting immobile, his strong features displaying signs of resignation. Tancred reached under his cloak and felt the security of his sword.

They waited in the chariot at the far end of the race course without speaking. The minutes slipped past and there was no sound of Philip's chariot, nor of Irene.

What if Philip had been alerted?

Then another chariot could be heard coming through the gate, the prance of horse hooves and the rattle of wheels. Tancred stared ahead until he saw Philip's chariot advancing toward them, and as it neared, Rufus stepped down from the seat and walked forward into the darkness.

Except for the driver, Philip was alone. The driver produced a small caldron of coals and lit some torches. Soon an area of the hippodrome was ablaze with light, and Tancred could see Philip in his royal purple, woven with gold. His tanned lean face, handsome and aristocratic, showed disdain for Rufus, yet uncertainty. Why had Philip come alone? What had Rufus told him to lure him here?

Seated in the back of his own chariot, Philip leaned forward, abruptly questioning his personal bodyguard, Captain Basil — the one man with whom Philip trusted being alone, without other guards also present.

"There is no one here, Basil. Are you certain Constantine said to come?"

Constantine . . . his father! thought Tancred. So that was what Rufus and Basil had told him.

Captain Basil did not answer Philip and walked off into the darkness.

Philip, stunned, looked after him. "You fool! Get back here. Where are you going?"

No reply came. Philip's startled eyes darted about the hippodrome, then fixed upon the other chariot for the first time. Tancred knew he couldn't yet see who sat inside, for he and Rufus were in shadows.

"Father?" he called toward them, his voice showing bewilderment, then growing tension when no reply came. "Constantine! Is that you? Is it you, my father?"

Philip stood, looking about, clearly visible in the torchlight surrounding his chariot. Grave alarm showed on his face. "Basil! I'll have you strangled for this!" he shouted, and his words echoed about the stadium.

Rufus was about to climb down out of the chariot, but Tancred laid his hand on his arm, restraining him, and stepped onto the arena ground himself.

Appearing as a ghostly shadow, Tancred walked toward Philip's chariot.

Philip squinted to see who it was. He looked about wildly. "Guards!"

Tancred stepped into the torchlight.

Philip froze. "*You?* It cannot be. I thought you dead in slavery by now."

"The night is full of ghosts. Hear them, Philip? Look about you and see the cheering crowds."

"You are mad!"

"Do you not hear the mob acclaiming your greatness? Philip the Byzantine, Emperor!" he mocked.

Sweat beaded Philip's brow. His eyes darted to the stands as if he could hear voices.

"How soon the cheering spectators turn into a mob," said Tancred. "The ghosts are now those of good and valorous men you deserted in battle. Remember them? The blood of men far more noble than you cry out — my cousin Norris Redwan, for one."

Philip lunged and crawled over the seat, snatching the horse's reins, but Tancred was swiftly beside him, jerking the reins from his grip and hauling him down from the chariot. Philip fell back against the side of the chariot, his breath coming rapidly. "I should have killed you at the palace," he spat the words.

Tancred unsheathed his sword. "Now is your opportunity. I give you more chance than you gave to either Norris or me. You have betrayed Helena — to me an unforgivable deed. A duel, Philip," he stated flatly. "I insist."

Philip's eyes narrowed. He glanced at the faint glimmer of steel in the torchlight. "Guards!" he shouted. "Basil!"

"The silence mocks you, Philip. You are alone this time. There are no pawns to carry out your murderous deeds. You must stand on your own feet and prove yourself a man. You will fight for your life. It is you and I. We have much to settle."

"Betrayal!" he shouted into the darkness at Basil. "I will have you executed for this!"

"First you must execute me," said Tancred. "Did you think I would not find you? You played the fool, Philip."

"You think I am a fool? I will not fight you! Why should I? Soon there will be a hundred soldiers out looking for me. When they come, they will kill you."

"Not this time. For once in your life you must answer for yourself. Did you have the courage to face Helena with the truth about holding Nicholas before sending her to Kalid?"

"Helena chose her future when she chose

you instead of me. Everything I've done, I did with her in mind. The struggle for power was to be shared with her, but she rejected me — for you, Norman," he said bitterly. "You were a curse from the time I first laid eyes on you at the Danube. I should have had you eliminated then."

"You left her little choice. Did you think she would marry the man who betrayed her mother to Constantine and her uncle to Irene?"

"Neither will you have her, Norman! The Turkish prince has her now! I have taken her from you."

"We both lose, Philip. Our meeting can end no other way but in your death."

"It will mean yours also," Philip scoffed. "You think I am a coward? You will see differently. You wish a duel, you will have one! And if you kill me, you will never leave Constantinople alive. You will never escape the edict of the emperor."

"So be it." Tancred drew his blade, coming swiftly to meet Philip's thrust, turning it aside. Philip came at him with more determination than Tancred thought him capable of. He fought off his rush, but Philip's sword made brief contact, bringing blood to his arm. Tancred beat back his blade with several powerful blows that drove Philip backward onto the arena floor.

In the torchlight the sweat could be seen beading Philip's brow as they fought back and forth, the sounds of clashing metal echoing off the walls, filling the night with the sureness of death.

Tancred shouted contemptuously, "For once, Philip, I commend you. At least you are fighting your own battle! How does it feel to be alone with nothing but your abilities?" Tancred leaped his blade past and nicked Philip on the neck. "This is how the soldiers always live! While you sit back and send them to face death!"

Philip cursed him and swung his sword, but Tancred beat it down, his blade sliding off. Their swords smashed, and disengaging, Tancred jabbed swiftly, unexpectedly. He felt the purple cloth give under the point, but Philip's sword leaped to cut his shoulder.

Philip laughed. Rushing at him recklessly, he struck again viciously and Tancred parried the blow. Philip kicked his kneecap and Tancred retreated, going down on his one good knee. It seemed a tremendous shout from the empty stands went up, and Philip laughed again. "I have no need to play by the rules." He came at Tancred yet hoping to kick him in the face, but the strong Norman caught his foot and twisted until Philip, off balance, went down clumsily on his side. Tancred stood.

"Then neither will I." He grabbed him by the front of his tunic and pulled him to his feet, smashing one fist into his belly. As he doubled, Tancred landed a second blow. Philip sank to the dust, doubled over, groaning.

Tancred wiped the sweat from his face, and snatching up their swords, he tossed Philip's beside him and waited.

"Get up," demanded Tancred. "I've not finished with you yet."

Philip struggled to his feet, hissing a curse at him under his breath, and came at him with an angry swing of his blade.

They circled. Philip feinted, then lunged. Tancred deflected the blade, then, lowering his sword, stepped back and moved in again, narrowly missing Philip's throat.

They circled again, Philip already growing exhausted. While Tancred was far stronger and battle continued, he wished for the ugly moment to be over.

Philip, desperate now, sprang at him. Tancred warded off the attack. Turning Philip's blade aside and moving in, he delivered a swift and final plunge through his heart. Philip gave a choking curse, his teeth bared, and Tancred jerked his weapon free and stepped back, leaving Philip to fall forward. His sword clattered from his hand onto the arena floor — the same floor that had received the fallen dead from hundreds of Roman-style games.

Tancred looked down upon him, then slowly turned and walked back toward the chariot. Rufus and Captain Basil strode over to meet him.

"It was fairly fought," said Captain Basil, handing him a skin of water.

Rufus looked at Tancred, who was catching his breath as he leaned against the side of the chariot, quenching his thirst.

"Nicholas comes. You best leave at once. Madame Irene will soon learn of this," warned Basil. "Few escape her wrath. She has a thousand spies!"

"Irene already knows," came the dull voice of Rufus.

Both Tancred and Basil turned their heads to look in his direction.

"She was at the Lysander summer palace when I arrived and told her you were here with Redwan," explained Rufus. "You need fear her no longer."

The waterskin stilled at Tancred's lips.

"Like Jezebel, she is dead. I threw her over the terrace tonight. Unlike the high priestess of Baal, Irene, the queen of astrology, was not eaten by dogs but by her own leopards — the same fate she heaped upon my beloved Joseph."

Stunned silence gripped Tancred and Captain Basil. They looked at him. Joseph? Thrown to the leopards?

"You?" Basil whispered, amazed. "You had the courage to kill her?"

"I have long intended to do so. Only her threats against Joseph prevented me. But she learned that he helped Nicholas escape and had him killed and thrown to the leopards. She was most unwise," said Rufus in a too-calm voice. "His life was her only safeguard."

Rufus turned and walked away.

At the gate of the hippodrome came the rush of horse hooves. The men scattered, swords drawn, but it was Nicholas who came bounding up, his robust and handsome face alert and sober in the torchlight. Tancred walked out to meet him, and Nicholas slowly relaxed astride the horse, the breeze touching his cloak. His black eyes were quick to see, by the stain of blood on Tancred's sleeve, that he had done battle.

Nicholas's jaw flexed. "He is dead?"

Tancred remained silent. Captain Basil gestured to the track. "Over there."

Nicholas swung himself down and walked to the place, gazing down. Tancred turned and walked away.

Rufus had loosened the horses from the chariots and tossed Tancred the reins while he and Basil mounted.

Nicholas returned and mounted, then looked over at Tancred. "Under Irene's influence, Philip's false trust in his future being written in the stars actually directed his own sad epitaph. It is well. He is responsible for many deaths and much suffering. But now we must hurry; it is nearing midnight and the ship may sail without us."

When they arrived at the wharf, the Genoese ship was preparing to leave the Golden Horn for the port of St. Symeon. They ran past the darkened hulls of many ships, past the crewmen and lone guards, who paid them no heed.

Rainald was on deck when Tancred shouted for his attention.

Rainald leaned over the ship's side and, seeing who it was, gave command to those about him. He tossed the rope, and Tancred grabbed hold and climbed up onto the solid deck, Nicholas, Rufus, and Basil coming behind.

Rainald stood there, grinning, a picture of elegance, his black hat sporting gems.

"You had me worried, Norman. Welcome aboard!"

As the ship left the Golden Horn, Tancred looked back, his face grave. Constantinople, the Queen City, was forever behind him. But what did the future hold for him and Nicholas?

CHAPTER 11

Outside Antioch

Captain Rainald was indignant. "What is this? You will not fight with us to take St. Symeon?"

They were nearing the port when Tancred explained that his destiny did not lie with the Genoese. "I will not yet join Bohemond in the siege of Antioch."

Rainald did not bother to hide his displeasure. "You and I," he said, "I thought we would fight together."

"We may yet join swords, my friend, but now, I must go directly to the Castle of Hohms."

"Perhaps it is best. The crusading armies will soon starve," cautioned Rainald.

"Not if you Genoese take the port. Then supplies can be brought in from Cyprus."

"Even if we could take the port tomorrow, it will take time to bring in food."

"I have every confidence in you and your

Italian friends. We will meet again."

The appeal to his ego encouraged Rainald's cooperation. In the captain's cabin, Tancred and Nicholas studied the map of the environs of Antioch that Tancred had drawn when in the Royal Library. The lantern hanging above the wooden table cast a glow.

"It is best to go ashore late at night on a small boat," suggested Nicholas. "Can you bring us close to the shore at St. Symeon?"

"Slipping past the Turks will be difficult, but being the most excellent captain that I am, it can be done," agreed Rainald. "I shall bring you to a point farther south."

Tancred exchanged smiles with Nicholas.

Late that night the ship lowered its anchor a mile offshore from a deserted stretch of beach. The weather was poor. The wind had picked up, and clouds blotted out the light of the moon. No word was spoken as a rowboat was lowered into the dark swells. Tancred picked up his two bags, tossed them down to a crewman, then grabbed the rope and descended, followed by Nicholas, Rufus, and Basil.

The small boat pulled away from the ship's hull toward the distant shoreline, the oars manned by two Genoese. At last the beach became discernible. Tancred listened to the boom of the waves crashing against the not-too-distant sand. It was raining when they neared the beach. Without a word the crewmen left them and rowed back toward the ship. The four men climbed a hill and found themselves on a small coastal mound above the main port of St. Symeon, now dark and quiet. Rain wet Tancred's face as the frontal wind blew against him. He was far from being disillusioned. In a few days he would be at the castle. Helena waited, and also his adoptive father, whom he had not seen in six years. He was, at last, coming to his destination. What lay ahead? The arms of Helena, or treachery?

He would not be defeated. Somehow he would reach her.

They took the path to the harbor. The drenching rain and the late hour kept dock-side activity to a minimum. The shores were crowded with merchandise to be loaded or unloaded with the light of dawn. Camels slept, and the guards had taken shelter. They needed horses — well fed, sleek, and anxious for battle.

Ahead were several caravans from the southern regions of Aleppo and Damascus.

"Turks?" whispered Nicholas.

"Arabs is my guess."

"We are in good fortune."

"Maybe. There is no love between the Arabs and their Turkish overlords, but Arab princes are inclined to commit their desert warriors to the cause of Islam rather than Christendom. We must remain cautious."

The drivers were up early and a fire burned. Tancred smelled the delightful aroma of the small round Arab breads, chunks of goat, and hot bean curry.

Leaving Rufus and Basil on guard, Tancred and Nicholas approached three men sitting about a fire, their heads covered. At the sound of footsteps, the men turned and measured the newcomers' appearance.

"We are looking to buy horses," called Nicholas.

One of the men stood and beckoned them to enter the goatskin shelter.

"You come from Cyprus?" the graybeard inquired, scanning first Nicholas, then Tancred.

Tancred avoided a direct reply, as did Nicholas, whose cleric outfit had been carefully concealed beneath a peasant's rough tunic. Tancred's armor was not of any particular uniform, but a mixture of the best.

"We are from many places," said Nicholas. "And your caravan? Does it come from far?"

"Aleppo."

While Tancred deliberately remained in the background, Nicholas gestured to the pen of horses. "They look to be good animals. Are you willing to sell?"

The Arab's alert gaze studied them. "If it is Allah's good pleasure to see them with another," he said evasively. "We were bringing them to Antioch to be sold to Prince Kalid, but the way grows dangerous to travel."

Tancred affected indifference and Nicholas inquired, "How goes the preparations of siege against the barbarians? Have they arrived yet?"

The keen dark eyes of the Arab were equally cautious. "News from Armenian shepherds tells us they have crossed the mountains. In Antioch the great Yaghi-Sian prepares for battle. His Seljuk commander Kerbogha expects more soldiers from the sultan at Aleppo to ride to their defense."

We dare not ask too many questions, Tancred thought.

"Kerbogha rules your city of Aleppo?" asked Tancred, knowing, in fact, that he did and that the Arabs were not pleased. Arabs looked upon Turks as being little better than Byzantines.

"You have heard of Kerbogha?" the Arab asked.

Nicholas turned to Tancred, his black eyes

gleaming in the firelight. "Have you heard of him, my son?"

"Who has not?" said Tancred. "He is much feared. A ferocious fighter."

The eyes of the Arab trader seemed to question Tancred's weaponry. "You also look like a warrior." He went on: "There is talk that the barbarians from the West are fighting equals. They defeated the Red Lion near Nicaea. There is news that one of their chief princes has taken Edessa. He married an Armenian princess. Kerbogha rode with his Turks to free Edessa — but failed."

Was the Arab measuring his response? Tancred showed none, and instead gestured the second time toward the horses. "Prince Kalid collects horses?" He thought of Alzira.

"He races them. There are none to best these."

"We will pay handsomely to own four of them," said Nicholas. He reached beneath his tunic and produced a leather pouch. "We will reward you well for your trouble."

The bartering continued until Tancred began to fear the light of dawn. At last Nicholas paid the Arab, and bidding them peace, they went to get the horses.

The Arab led them to the pen. The rain had ceased. "If you ride to Antioch, you may see the father of this mare."

He had cunningly guessed their destination in spite of their caution. "The stallion belongs to Prince Kalid. It is said that he will give it to his bride for a wedding gift."

Tancred struggled to keep his voice calm and uninterested. "When is the marriage to be?"

"Who knows?"

"I will be sure to ask of his horse and of his princess when I see him," said Tancred.

Nicholas cleared his throat. "Come," he said to Tancred. "The dawn will soon break. We have troubled our Arab friend long enough."

They saluted the Arabs and mounted two of the horses, leading the other two back to where Rufus and Basil awaited them. The four rode from St. Symeon while it was still dark. Before them lay the road to Antioch and the castle, behind them St. Symeon, asleep. Besides owning a good horse again, Tancred was well supplied. He carried his Toledo sword, his Damascus dagger, and a quiver of arrows. In his bag were the maps that he had secured while in Constantinople, one of them detailing the environs of Antioch and its twelve gates; the other was a drawing he had made of the Castle of Hohms. Inside his inner garment the remaining jewels belonging to Helena were sewn securely. He had an advantage the western princes did not have; he had the location of the emir's palace where Mosul served as chief bodyguard, and a detailed layout of the chambers, including the *zenanna* — the women's area, or harem, and the eunuchs' quarters.

It was about twenty miles from the sea to Antioch, which lay on the banks of the Orontes River. They followed the river where possible, with the mountainous country of Syria to the south, then they traveled eastward toward the ancient city boasting twelve gates in its massive walls.

The Orontes ran along the far side of the plain, and behind it rose the city's great front wall, which ran for several miles along the gray river. Tancred studied the impressive fortification as it rambled steeply upward over the hills to disappear, then emerge again among laurel trees, olive vineyards, and sesame plantations. The impregnable wall of gray stone looked to him to be at least thirty feet high, and he had read that it was wide enough across its top to ride four horses abreast. The tower-studded walls then climbed even farther up to the shoulder of Mount Silpius, where he recognized a huge tower-citadel a thousand feet above the plain.

He had learned from his studies in the Royal Library that Antioch would be unassailable to the crusaders' attack. In addition to the great wall surrounding the city, a half wall stood below the hills, its five main gates staring down as though mocking the advancing army. Each of these gates was flanked strategically by a massive sixty-foot tower, guarded by Seljuk Turks carrying their deadly short bows and scimitars. Tancred suspected they watched them now as the caravan approached the gate that opened toward the east and the road leading to Aleppo.

Tancred held his mount. The siege lines of the feudal lords lay before him. His heart lifted. Many may have perished on the journey across the bleak and barren mountains of Anatolia, where its sparse summer grasslands were scorched with heat and the dry volcanic plains were lifeless. The knights had lost precious supplies and some of their Great Horses, but the bulk of the fighting men under the various princes and nobles had arrived and were camped as far as the eye could see outside the great thick walls of the city.

Nicholas looked proud. "It is a tribute to their courage that the majority of the men have survived. The knights and barons of Western Europe are a force the Turks will find difficult to defeat. Already Nicaea has fallen, followed by Iconium, Heraclea, Capadocia, Tarsus on the coast, and Edessa."

What of Antioch? wondered Tancred, thinking not of the victory of the princes but of Helena. How could he get inside the city to find her?

"Though the knights and fighting men number over a hundred thousand," Nicholas continued, "they cannot breach those walls, and little remains of their food supplies."

Nicholas fell silent. Both men knew that famine stalked the crusaders. When Tancred had ridden aside into the smaller districts and wealthy villas looking for food for themselves and provision for the horses, the Armenians and Arabs informed him they had long ago been looted of poultry, sheep, wine, and clothing. The country was stripped bare.

"I will ride into the Norman camp to locate Adehemar," Nicholas told him, speaking of his old bishop friend who was Pope Urban's official church legate on the expedition. "He is a friend of Rolf and may have earlier ridden to the Castle of Hohms to visit him. It may be he knows something of the news of Helena and Adrianna and whether both women are captive within Antioch. I put nothing past the schemes of Constantine. He may be in the city as well, dining on a fatted calf with Yaghi-Sian."

As Nicholas rode toward the Norman camp where Prince Bohemond's blue-and-crimson gonfanon stood like a sentinel in the hot morning, Tancred sat resting astride his horse, brooding to himself as he contemplated the walls and gates. Somehow he would get inside. He would wait for the opportunity to break.

"Someone comes riding to meet us," said Rufus.

"And he looks Moslem," added Basil.

The man rode not from the direction of the camp but from some distant cypress trees on a ridge. Tancred watched the lone figure, who wore a faded blue Arab headscarf, until the rider drew closer.

"Caution, he carries a bow and scimitar," warned Rufus.

Tancred smiled and spurred his horse forward on the sun-bleached plain.

They met alone, their Arab horses whinnying and touching noses as though they knew each other, and Tancred reached to grasp the wily old warrior's arm. It was Hakeem, the Moor from Palermo, Tancred's faithful friend. He'd not seen him since Hakeem had ridden from the guard castle of Herion to remain a spy in Antioch. Hakeem was thinner, yet if possible, no worse for it. Lean and tough, he wore the scars of battle well.

"So, you come at the last, master, but only when victory is in the wind! What spoils in the city do you think to take?" Hakeem said, referring to Helena. "Perhaps the true booty waits at the Castle of Hohms."

"It is good to see you, conniving old spy! But where have you been these months when I needed you? Enjoying the favors of Antioch, I suppose. And while I've wasted two months being a slave to a mentally inferior baron!"

Hakeem's hard eyes laughed. "Ah, Jehan, I knew if I prowled the Moslem streets long enough you would escape to come here. And see! My confidence in you is unshaken. I bring news of the assassin!"

"Is Mosul in the city?"

"He serves as captain of the guard to the royal family of the emir. He is now with Kalid's uncle, Ma'sud Khan."

Tancred had heard of Ma'sud but had never met Kalid's uncle. "And Kalid?"

"Away from the city. I trailed him and Commander Kerbogha from Antioch to Aleppo. They seek from the sultan more warriors to come to the aid of the city."

Tancred steeled himself against the next possible dark answer. "And Helena?"

Hakeem's rough brown face, lined with wrinkles, sobered. "I have not been able to hear anything of her, master. The last piece of news insists she is under the guardianship of Constantine inside the city. I cannot say for certain. I was attacked near Aleppo by Kalid's men and received a wound." He lifted his tunic and proudly showed his dagger scar. "It heals. But two weeks were lost."

"At least you are alive. You've done well, Hakeem. We will yet find her."

"Ha! That treacherous old wolf Constantine. He has perhaps thirty men loyal to him. He makes plans since Philip sent Helena to him."

"Philip is dead," said Tancred bluntly, feeling no sorrow when he remembered how Philip had turned Helena over to Constantine against her will. "Bardas is dead also."

Hakeem's rough brows lifted. "You have been busy."

"Bardas died by the hands of a wealthy baron's men, but no doubt with Philip's consent." His heart turned toward Helena. "If she is in the city, I must find a way inside."

"An impossible feat, but if any warrior can do it, you can, Jehan. I have found a secret route through the hills." He gestured. "But

151

the Turks set a guard at the postern gate once the princes arrived."

"Come! We'll take refuge in the Norman camp until my plans are secure."

"Ah, but it is my infidel head I wish to keep secure, master. You forget that in asking me to enter the crusaders' camp, you invite the rooster into the fox's den!"

Tancred laughed. He *had* forgotten. "Where will I find you when I need you?"

Hakeem gestured back toward the trees. "An abandoned village." Then reaching over to his shoulder, Hakeem took the falcon, which had traveled with him all the way from Palermo, and handed the bird to Tancred. "Take Othello with you. He will find me with your message."

Tancred accepted the fowl, who came willingly to the saddle bar. "Othello, eh? I shall look after him well. Thank you, my friend, and take care!"

Riding inside the Norman camp, Tancred soon discovered that Nicholas had come upon his Norman cousin.

"Leif!" Tancred's spirits rose. His cousin was alive. He'd all but given up hope. It was unfortunate he must give him news of Norris's death.

Upon entering his Norman cousin's tent, Tancred was surprised to find Adele, the niece of Bishop Adehemar. "This is my wife," announced Leif, and his eyes glimmered like pale blue stone in his handsome sun-bronzed face. His long golden hair was drawn back with a leather thong.

"You work fast," said Tancred, taunting him, and turned with a smile as Adele rushed to greet him with joy. She was representative of all the women who had joined the expedition to free Jerusalem from the infidel.

"Your cousin Erich died as a brave knight for our Lord," she said. "Then I met your other cousin Leif, and I knew my future was blessed of God to join his. He, too, is a great warrior. We will both fight for our Lord to take Jerusalem!"

After she brought them what refreshments she had in her meager store, Leif explained how he had searched for Tancred and Norris after the attack at the summer palace.

"Philip's guards surrounded the palace, and after several days when I could do nothing, I went into the city hoping I could learn something more and gain the help of warrior friends. When we returned, you were gone, the palace deserted. We searched on but discovered nothing. At last we gave up and rode to join Bohemond."

Tancred was satisfied. He had worried more about Leif also being dead or taken prisoner than he had about whether he had tried to help him escape. Leif was a warrior of honor, and Tancred knew he had gone the full measure.

"Walter has not been seen," Nicholas told Tancred later. "Bohemond has not heard from him since Constantinople."

"None of the clan is here," Leif assured him. "I sought for them as soon as I arrived."

"Strange," said Nicholas, frowning. He looked at Tancred. "I am not comfortable with their silence. If Constantine has made contact with Walter, hoping to trap you to stand trial, they may be at the Castle of Hohms expecting you to come that way."

"But why would they think so?" asked Leif. "Is not the Byzantine woman Helena inside Antioch?"

Nicholas stroked his black mustache, and his lively black eyes reflected his deep musings. "Did Hakeem have any word of her or Adrianna's whereabouts?"

Tancred explained the difficulty Hakeem had undergone near Aleppo.

"Then we do not know for certain," said Nicholas, leaning back on his elbow as he chomped on a roasted leg of lamb. "Adehemar is also uncertain. When he arrived at the Castle of Hohms, Rolf was not there but out on a patrol. The guards left in charge knew nothing."

Neither did Tancred like the uncertain news. Helena could be anywhere — the castle, Antioch, or even Aleppo.

"My instincts tell me she is within Antioch," said Tancred.

"Never trust your instincts," said Nicholas wryly, tossing aside the bone.

"Nevertheless, I must get inside the city."

"And I will send spies to search out the castle," stated Nicholas.

"In the meantime, the common soldiers are going without food," said Leif. "What news do you have from Constantinople, Nicholas? Does the emperor send us provisions, or has he abandoned us again?"

Tancred suspected that the emperor had long ago abandoned them, withholding the delivery of necessary provisions because the princes and nobles had refused to surrender the villages conquered along the way since Nicaea.

"Do you blame them for not yielding the booty to him?" complained Leif. "They remember the treachery done them at Nicaea. And there will be treachery anew over Antioch. General Taticus is here as legate of the emperor. Again, he wishes to secretly negotiate the surrender of Antioch to Byzantium before any of the princes take the city.

But Bohemond has plans to thwart General Taticus."

The news was not surprising to either Tancred or Nicholas. Tancred told him of the Genoese fleet. "By now St. Symeon is in the hands of the Byzantines. Captain Rainald will waste no time in setting a course for Cyprus, but the arrival of the Genoese to reinforce the knights here will do you little good. The problem of food will only mount. The princes will have even more soldiers to feed."

"Rumors abound of hope," complained Leif. "By summer, there will be food."

"In three more weeks we will be in Jerusalem." Tancred gestured his impatience. "The words of hope circle like falcons but never land. Rumors also persist that the emperor will send his engineers with siege weapons as he did at Nicaea. Whether anyone truly believes it is doubtful. Bohemond wishes to take Antioch and become its seigneur."

"So does Count Raymond," said Nicholas. "There is misunderstanding and bickering. Duke Godfrey, however, seems to have mellowed. He speaks more of the glory of God than his own. That is a miracle!"

The pride, arrogance, and bold ruthless courage of the western lords were well known to Tancred and the others. If there were a breed of warriors who could take Antioch and Jerusalem from the well-armored Moslem Turks, it would be these men, he thought.

Leif seemed to become aware of something he had not noticed at first when he rejoiced to see Tancred. "Where is our cousin Norris? Did he not escape the baron with you?"

Nicholas looked up from his cup to meet Tancred's gaze. "We bring you dark news," Nicholas told him and went on to explain Philip's treachery. "He and Tancred went to the bungalow thinking to aid Rufus and his son Joseph and were met by arrows and swords from Philip's soldiers."

Leif's sense of loss was great, for he and Norris had grown as close as brothers.

CHAPTER 12

Kerbogha's Cavalry

As the famine worsened, poorer bands of ribald French vagabonds began to feast upon dead Turks outside the walls of Antioch. They would disperse and hunt out several bodies, then bring them back to their encampment to pound them with flails and skin them. The vagrants would then boil the meat in caldrons over their cooking fires. The stench of simmering human flesh wafted to the tops of the walls, where Turkish soldiers looked on in disgust.

When the news of the "feast" reached Bohemond, he and several lords went to investigate. Tancred, Nicholas, and Leif walked with them to the ragged encampment of vagabonds.

They came upon the ribald King Tafur and his followers seated on the ground, who mockingly complained in French, "But there is no bread!"

Others laughed, "*Voici mardi gras!* This is a party!"

The feudal lords, wearing their fur mantles, watched them in silence.

"How do you feel?" Bohemond inquired after a long silence.

Tafur responded, "I feel revived. If only I had something in the way of wine to go with this!"

A lord laughed. "Sir King, you shall have it." He sent his servant at once to fetch a jar of his own good wine for the rabble monarch.

Tancred caught the eye of Nicholas and gestured to the summit of the gray wall of Antioch where the Turkish sentries stood watching the blasphemous cannibalism. They shouted down in anger.

"What do they say?" asked King Tafur.

"They say your fine taste in food compels them to show you a kindness," interpreted Tancred.

"A kindness?"

"They will execute all barbarian prisoners tomorrow and catapult their heads over the wall for you to eat as well."

In the days ahead a decision was made to travel farther from Antioch in search of food. Nearly twenty thousand knights gathered to ride with Bohemond and Robert of Flanders on a desperate foraging expedition. Tancred chose to ride ahead of the army to scout, believing that Hakeem would find it safe enough to join him. He was right; Hakeem rode from some rocks to meet him.

"Hakeem, there may be trouble at the Castle of Hohms. Rolf Redwan has not been seen since Constantine came from Constantinople with Adrianna."

"I will go and spy it out."

"You know well enough to search out her possible presence there," Tancred said of Helena. "Here, take Othello. Send me word if it is so. I will come."

Hakeem took his falcon and was about to turn and ride when they saw a massive army of Seljuk Turks proceeding toward them.

"I have never seen so many Turks," whispered Hakeem.

Was this the army led by Kerbogha for the relief of Antioch? wondered Tancred, his adrenaline rising as he speculated whether Kalid were with them.

They turned to leave when Hakeem shouted, "Bohemond has ridden ahead!"

Robert of Flanders also rode forward, oblivious to the danger. Tancred and Hakeem drove hard toward the knights.

"Escape!" Tancred shouted at Hakeem

over the wind. "They will take you for one of them!"

"I will not desert you, Jehan!"

"Depart, friend! Ride to the castle! It is there I need you!"

Hakeem hesitated, riding on beside him, then lifted a salute and headed left toward the distant rocks from which he had come. The falcon soared after him.

Did Bohemond see the Seljuks coming? wondered Tancred.

They came as if from a desert mirage. They were a force composed entirely of horsemen, carrying strong short bows and scimitars, and the curved stabbing knives — *yataghans*. Each of them handled his mount with the ease of a master horseman. They weaved back and forth as if to music, moving in formations that were strange to the skills of the western knights. A charge by Robert's men was impossible, and they were engulfed, taken completely by surprise. A barrage of arrows struck, followed by a charge. Tancred's sword smashed into a rider who leaped past him. The Seljuks kept coming, pressing them, dividing their ranks, and in the distance the drums beat and the high weird shout of "Allah! Allah!" rang through the hills. Robert's knights of Flanders were falling, yet they fought on tenaciously, in spite of overwhelming odds. As men were struck from their mounts, they grabbed fallen weapons and swung them savagely into the Turkish charge. Tancred's sword struck again and again, and still the Seljuks sent fresh cavalrymen into the battle. The men of Flanders held. How long could the charge last? The minutes stretched. The Turks came and came again, and Tancred was caught up in an endless struggle with his blade to stay alive. Arrows whizzed; knights fell only to pass on their weapons to the foot soldiers, and they fought on madly, but still the Turkish cavalry came. Tancred was knocked from his horse and fought on foot. Men died beside him, and then as if in an unreal dream, he heard distant shouts as Bohemond's Normans rushed to the foray.

Kerbogha's cavalry saw them coming and the attack broke. The Turks withdrew, but only for the moment.

Bohemond's crimson standard was raised. The shout of the Normans grimly challenged the Moslems: "God wills it!" With this, Bohemond led the charge into the shouting masses, their great swords swinging above their heads and scattering the Turks in the push forward. Like thunder the impact sent a breach into the Moslem cavalry, now falling over the heaped-up bodies of the knights of

Flanders. But from the foothills on both flanks, Tancred saw new groups of Turks. The wave of bowmen galloped toward them, their arrows striking with deadly accuracy, followed by riders swinging scimitars. The two forces collided in bloody hand-to-hand fighting. The Normans fought savagely, like wounded wolves cornered and determined to break free. The long swords of the knights struck, smashing bones; the scimitars slashed heads from bodies. Neither side would yield, nor consider running. They persisted stubbornly. Seeing a riderless horse, Tancred swung himself up and rode to the side of Bohemond, and as he did, his own scimitar removed the head of a Turk who had leaped past the baron, expecting a famous kill. The fighting line of Bohemond held, and because of it, the onslaught reaped a devastating harvest of Kerbogha's cavalry. The grim leader, far too wise and clever to lose any more of his men, was now quick to command a retreat, and the attack broke as they fled back toward the hills.

The men of Flanders were exhausted. Robert, somber and silent, rode past his knights in wordless tribute to their stand. Leif rode up to Tancred; both were too weary to speak. They joined Bohemond and rode back toward Antioch.

The foraging expedition had been a failure, and good knights and horses were lost. The Seljuks from Aleppo had been beaten back and lost many men, but Kerbogha was not ready to give up. Tancred knew he would return with even more soldiers to relieve Antioch. A far greater and more bloody battle only awaited another day.

That night he and Nicholas rode through the camp when a commotion near the tent of Count Raymond of Toulouse drew them aside. They had a prisoner from Antioch. At once Tancred recognized that the Turk was no ordinary soldier. He rode to Raymond. "That man may be of use to us. He is an emir. If I were you, I would bring him to your tent."

Count Raymond ordered him brought inside and motioned for Tancred to follow. The emir's black eyes moved from Count Raymond to Tancred.

"Who is your commander?" Tancred asked.

"Yaghi-Sian."

"A strong leader. And Prince Kalid?"

"He is with Kerbogha at Aleppo."

"Was it not Kerbogha's soldiers we fought?"

"You fought with a contingent of his cavalry from Aleppo under Ma'sud Khan. But

Ma'sud came not to fight you. He waits for a million Moslems from the East! He was riding to the Castle of Hohms to bring his nephew's bride to Aleppo when you came upon him."

Ma'sud Khan, Kalid's uncle. Tancred knew of him, though they had not met. He had heard Ma'sud was a more honorable man than Kalid.

"Ma'sud Khan turned back. The losses were heavy on both sides. How long has Prince Kalid been in Aleppo?"

"Since before the siege began."

"Are you saying the marriage to the woman of Byzantine nobility has not yet happened?"

"It has not yet happened."

Only Nicholas understood the intensity of emotion behind Tancred's pause.

Count Raymond looked curiously at Tancred. "You know this Prince Kalid?"

"He is my cousin."

Raymond appeared shocked. He looked over at Nicholas, who lifted both brows. "Tancred is a Christian. The son of Count Dreux Redwan. But his mother was a Moor from Palermo. I thought you knew this."

The emir scanned Tancred. "You are Jehan, grandson of al-Kareem?"

"I am. And I seek Kalid and his bodyguard

Mosul, the assassin of my brother Derek."

The emir made no reply but watched him.

"How did you find this man?" Tancred asked Count Raymond.

One of Raymond's captains explained. "The Turkish commander, the one you called Yaghi-Sian, slipped through the gate and launched a night attack against my men who were north of here near the Orontes. They had intended to ambush us, but the night watch alerted Count Raymond, who reacted with great courage and speed. He came out of the darkness, taking these wretched Turks by surprise instead. We routed them in no time and chased them back across the river to Antioch. We nearly succeeded in storming the gate into the city!"

"We would have entered the city," said the captain bitterly, "if this miserable emir had not been thrown by his bolting horse! The incident threw our small group of knights into confusion."

"The grand moment," sighed Count Raymond, "was lost."

Nicholas drew Tancred aside, his hand on his shoulder. "If Ma'sud rides to the castle to bring Helena, it is likely Constantine is there with Adrianna."

"I intend to leave tonight," said Tancred.

"I will go with you. See if the emir knows

of your uncle. We must not ride into a trap."

Tancred had been so enamored with the news that Helena had not yet been given to Kalid that he'd forgotten all about the danger of Walter and his Redwan cousins. He spoke again to the emir, but he denied knowing anything about them.

"Are not this Bohemond and his barbarians from the Norman kingdom in the West enough?" the emir inquired with contempt. "You encamp about our city like starving locusts. Do you need this Walter also?"

CHAPTER 13

Good-bye . . . My Love

The afternoon sun grew glaringly hot in the azure sky, beating down on the rugged and barren countryside. With the oncoming evening, the sky became an awesome stage displaying the handiwork of the Creator, its stars and planets burning white. A rush of wind tore mightily through the hills and swept clean the valley floor.

With the golden dawn the restless winds ceased, and on the ridge of rocky gray slopes stood the Castle of Hohms — solitary, formidable, with arched windows, battlements, and bulwarks carved from the naked rock, which formed many of its chamber walls. A long flight of steps bounded upward to the main bulk of the castle, where its roof touched the brightening sky of hard Arabian blue.

Tancred and Nicholas drew rein, with Leif, Rufus, and Basil holding their mounts.

In the vast expanse of the plain rimmed with mor.

"Soldiers," warned Tancredmountains came the undeniable glint of ar. "They ride toward the castle."

His gaze riveted on the main gate. It stood ajar!

A group of Byzantine horsemen, perhaps twenty, emerged through the gate, and the man in the lead carried a white flag with a crimson cross.

"They surrender?" scoffed Basil with disgust. "Is this the great Seigneur Rolf Redwan I have heard you boast of, Tancred? Do you not say that fifty men serve him? Why, then, are they not on the bulwarks? If they hold out, Bohemond may arrive in time —"

"That man who rides is not our uncle," said Leif. "Rolf would rather die than surrender without a battle."

"I have served under Seigneur Redwan," added Rufus. "There is none better than he, or more courageous."

"Who then?" Basil's impatience for soldiers who would not stand and fight, though outnumbered, flared.

Tancred's blue-gray eyes glittered in silence.

"The man in the lead wears the garb of a

bishop. Who else but my enemy?" declared Nicholas.

"And is that not a woman who rides guarded?" asked Basil.

When Tancred did not respond, Basil turned in his saddle to look at him, understanding dawning. "Lady Helena?"

"Yes."

A rider came galloping toward them, but not from the gate. He came from the hills and brush near the castle.

It was Hakeem. He rode up to them and announced, "Constantine rides with the entourage to bring Helena to the Seljuks. They come through the gate now! I could not get near her, master."

Tancred swerved his horse to look toward the plain.

"What of Adrianna?" asked Nicholas.

"She remains behind. Nor could I locate Seigneur Rolf, but Walter is there and others from the Redwan clan."

Nicholas turned toward Tancred, but his attention was riveted upon the entourage under Constantine.

"Look how many Seljuks came to receive her," breathed Basil, awed. "Five hundred? A thousand! We are but six men!"

Nicholas was deadly silent, the wind touching his black hair sprinkled with gray.

"We are worth thirty Seljuks," said Rufus, his dark face contemptuous. His powerful arm flexed with muscle as he reached toward his sword.

"But not even we could survive this onslaught," countered Basil.

"You, who just scorned Seigneur Redwan for surrender without a battle, now retreats behind his words," goaded Leif.

Hakeem was watching Tancred knowingly. "What will you do, Jehan?"

Tancred could think of nothing but Helena. "I will not allow Constantine to betray her to Kalid," he gritted. "I will kill him first."

Nicholas laid a firm brown hand on his arm. "He is my enemy, son. He always has been, from the day he arranged to have me banished from Constantinople to the West. It is I who must deal with the bishop."

"What do you have in mind?" asked Leif.

Tancred shaded his eyes, looking far off into the distance toward the Turks, then back to Constantine's entourage riding to meet them on the plain. "Attack the bishop's entourage, then make for the castle gate. There may be just enough time, but it will be six against twenty. As you say, I do not see my father among them, which tells me he is either being held captive or unaware of what is actually happening."

"You cannot ride into the castle with Walter there," said Nicholas.

"The gate to the castle is closing," warned Hakeem.

"What if they do not open it again to receive us?" Basil asked dryly.

Tancred turned in his saddle and looked back toward the road leading to St. Symeon. Twenty miles was too far to hope to stay ahead of the Seljuks.

Hakeem gestured toward the rocky hills behind the castle. "I know the area. There are hiding places. The Turks will not follow; it is too steep."

He was right. The only recourse was a swift flight toward the hills. "It may be that not all who ride with Constantine are loyal to him."

Rufus was immutable. "As a Nubian, my sword can take five of the enemy! What of you, Basil? Can a Byzantine rise to the moment?"

Basil fingered the Viking sword, which he had gotten from Ordic in the Varangian Guard. It was of the long, slashing variety that could cut through bone. "I shall go for three!"

"That leaves twelve," said Tancred, looking at Nicholas, whose finger stroked his mustache.

"First, I take Constantine," Nicholas said.

"The rest are mine," boasted Leif.

"Do not be overly brave," Tancred warned them. "See if you can divert the soldiers and scatter their formation. Get them away from Constantine. Nicholas will try to thwart him while I escape with Helena and ride toward the hills with Hakeem. Once she is safely away, I will come back to help you in the battle."

"By then they will all be dead," said Leif.

"If anything goes wrong," warned Tancred soberly, "make for the hills. Save your own lives, understood?"

They said nothing and glanced at one another.

"We will meet up again outside the walls of Antioch," said Tancred.

He strapped on his helmet, as did the others. There followed the clink of metal, the neighing of the horses as they sensed battle in the wind. Tancred turned to Nicholas and waited.

Nicholas reached under his warrior-bishop tunic, produced a small silver cross, and raised it with benediction. "You, O Lord, are a shield about us, the defender of our heads! The Lord be with us and scatter our enemies! The Lord's will be done!"

"So be it," said Tancred, and touching his stallion lightly with his heel, he was the first to ride down the sandy mound in the direction of the castle and plain, Hakeem on his right and Nicholas toward his left hand. Leif, Rufus, and Basil each rode their chosen position, their weapons drawn.

Rufus let go with a Nubian war cry, and swooping up his great hacking blade in his fist, he surged out ahead, his dark face deadly and determined. Basil was swinging his Viking blade above his head, racing for the entourage. "Ai-yeee!" screeched Hakeem, his scimitar lifted proudly.

The Arabian racing horses sped, their dainty nostrils flaring, their eyes wide and excited, manes flying.

Tancred eased out ahead, followed by Nicholas; Hakeem held close, low in the saddle. Tancred's gaze was fixed upon Helena riding just ahead of Bishop Constantine.

"Constantine! Thou diabolic enemy!" shouted Nicholas, his teeth clenching white and hard against his tanned rugged face. "Come forth and fight, thou false bishop of Christ!"

Tancred was silent, racing toward Helena's mare. *Beloved!* he thought.

★ ★ ★

Helena had only a moment to glimpse the warriors riding toward her and Constantine. The armor they wore was unfamiliar. Protective nosepieces projected from their helmets so that their faces could not be seen. Like warrior phantoms out of the morning dawn with blades glinting, the men came thundering over the plain.

"Brigands from the hills!" shouted the captain to Bishop Constantine, who rode beside Helena. "Quick! Back to the castle gate!"

"No! Too late. Stop them at any cost!" Constantine ordered the soldiers. "I will ride forward with Helena! We may be able to outrun them. Prince Kalid is coming now." He turned to Helena. "Forward! Forward!"

Brigands! she thought, terrified, remembering the Rhinelanders near the Danube.

Constantine gave a yelp fit to stir any attacking tribal warrior, and with a lash sent Helena's mare lunging forward.

Who were enemies, who were friends? Helena wondered. She despised them all — Turks, Constantine's mercenaries, and brigands from the hills. Was she yet to be conquered by some ruthless murderer who would carry her off to add to his harem in the hills? Even Kalid did not seem as dreadful as a wild leader of brigands.

She urged her mare forward toward the Seljuk cavalry, Constantine just behind her, the sunlight falling on his black-and-crimson garb.

Rufus and Basil clashed with the soldiers outside the castle of Hohms, steel against steel, but Tancred and Nicholas pursued Constantine and Helena. A soldier rushed Tancred's horse to block him, but Tancred hacked a blow. The soldier fell toward him, but another warrior coming down onto his helmet sent him clumsily from the saddle.

Before Tancred could race his stallion forward in pursuit of Helena, he had to defend himself again, and the wall of fighting men began to close in, holding him back, while Constantine and Helena surged ahead. Where was Nicholas? Had he gotten past to pursue Constantine?

Tancred's blade struck — whacking, hacking, thrusting, parrying. He fought on, trying desperately to break through. Rufus and Basil were holding their own. Hakeem appeared from the dust and came up beside Tancred, his scimitar swinging, allowing Tancred to surge ahead.

But the Seljuks under Ma'sud were now aware of the fighting, and a number of them broke formation to ride toward the castle to secure Helena and Constantine.

Nicholas rode up, his halberd clearing a moment of escape. Seizing the opening, Tancred leaped his stallion over the dead and wounded to race ahead. He was dimly aware that Nicholas had caught up and was turning toward Constantine's horse.

The desert sand and rock flew past, the rugged brown hills looming large against the morning sky. The wind was picking up speed and battering against him. "Helena!" he shouted, but the wind hurled her name back in his face, and she rushed ahead, Constantine just behind her. Tancred's sword was drawn now as he glanced back over his shoulder to see Constantine bearing down on him like some grim reaper of death.

They raced. The Seljuk armor glinted, drawing closer, their sleek light thoroughbreds charging, the wind at their backs. He was a fool. He felt the sand rising in the wind and beginning to blow into his face shield.

Helena glanced back at him. Her hood had blown off, and her thick dark hair was whipping about her. She saw he was gaining and clutched at her mare's mane, her body stretched low to give the horse more speed.

Tancred murmured wrathfully under his

breath. Her experience with horses taught her to ride to its best advantage.

Constantine was falling behind; Nicholas was gaining!

Tancred spurred his stallion forward, lashing him furiously as he left Constantine behind to face Nicholas. Tancred blessed the Arab trader who had sold them the racing horses, for while Helena's mare grew winded, the stallion had gained fiery determination and had picked up speed. Tancred rode low in the saddle to try to come up alongside her.

Furiously Helena lashed her mare, then kept her face close to its sweating neck. "Faster, girl, faster, faster!"

"Helena!"

The Seljuks were nearing from the opposite direction. Now Tancred could see their small painted breastplates more clearly. The horse hooves thundered across the sand — or was it real thunder?

"Helena!" he shouted again. "You infuriating woman — it's *me!*"

The sky rapidly grew darker. The warm wind swirled the sand along the desert floor. As the blowing sand increased, Helena began to lose firm control of the mare.

Tancred's face shield offered him some protection from the stinging sand, but he saw

Helena reaching for her cloak, and the moment of confusion broke the onward thrust of her reins so he could gain a length of distance. He was coming up beside her now.

"Helena! My love! Turn aside!"

She looked at him wildly. He leaned over and grabbed the reins, slowing the horse, until he could turn them both back in the direction of the Castle of Hohms.

She struck him with her whip, but he jerked it from her hand and grasped her wrist mercilessly, swiftly turning their neighing horses in the opposite direction. Still she fought him, trying to beat him with her free hand. Tancred suddenly realized that his face shield was still in place and she did not understand who he was, that his words had been garbled. With one quick lift of his hand he threw back his shield.

With a stunned gasp Helena stared into the face of Tancred.

Nicholas measured the distance between him and Constantine, noting the oncoming Turks serving Prince Kalid. He knew Constantine would not surrender his dreams now, not when Kalid was so near to claiming Helena, and Adrianna might be his. He was right, for Constantine turned his horse around to confront Nicholas and whipped out his sword.

"At last, Nicholas," he shouted above the wind. "It is you and I now! You will not leave here alive!"

Nicholas gripped his blade and they rode toward each other, the sand swirling about the legs of the horses.

The horses gathered speed. Charging, they swept past and Nicholas hacked a savage blow against Constantine's sword. Wheeling his horse, Nicholas lunged at him, but Constantine had turned, too, and parried, deflecting the full force of his attack.

Nicholas circled his horse, hearing his own breathing with the snorting of the animals.

"Too late, Nicholas," mocked Constantine, his eyes flashing in hate. "In another minute you will fall under fifty scimitars."

"Alas, you will not be here to enjoy it. It is your end too, Constantine! Taste your defeat. It is the bitter cup of your unrepentant transgression."

The two swords clashed with ringing steel, thrust, and hacked. The two riders, each in bishop's garb, circled, looking for an advantage. Nicholas saw his. At once he attacked, thrusting the heavy Norman blade, which cut savagely into his enemy's collarbone.

Constantine cursed him. His blade smashed a blow against the side of Nicholas's helmet, leaving a dent and his brain dazed.

"The worm dieth not where you will spend eternity, Nicholas!"

Nicholas was off balance in the saddle. Constantine gleefully rushed his horse, raising his sword arm to hack another blow into his skull, but Nicholas was able to halt the blow, and their swords crossed and held for a second.

"Lying prophet!" said Nicholas. "Thou corrupter of the Church!" With relentless calm he hammered another blow that shook Constantine's arm, loosening his grip on his weapon and sending it into the sand.

Nicholas drew back, lowering the point of his blade.

"How does it feel to know you have come to your just end?" Nicholas jeered. "The wind and sand mock you! The Seljuks will forget you in a moment of time, and who will mourn your passing? How fleeting life, how sour the fruit of your ambitions. Irene is dead. Philip is dead. You, too, die alone! You have mocked Christianity. You have defamed the cross you wore so carelessly! Who now will save you? You have rejected the only Savior!"

Constantine hissed another dark curse. He drew the gold chain and Byzantine cross from over his head and hurled them at Nicholas with contempt. He then unleashed his morning star, a deadly round steel ball with protruding spikes and attached to a handle with a chain. "This is my weapon."

Nicholas sheathed his blade and removed his mace, the favorite weapon of the warrior priests. The significance was not lost on Constantine; the weapon was sanctified and carried in ceremonial processions before battle. Slung on a loop on the right wrist, its quatrefoil-shaped head could smash a skull.

They circled, each looking for opportunity. It came for Nicholas, who was far more adept with the weapons he had trained to master so long and hard when at Monte Casino. He swung the mace and it gathered deadly speed. He released it and the ball smashed into Constantine's forehead.

Constantine's crumpled body lay sprawled on the ground, and the blowing sands began to cover over his scarlet-and-black tunic.

Gravely, Nicholas looked down at him.

The riderless horse, with its religious crimson saddle cloth, trotted away, shaking its sweating black mane.

Tancred had lost Hakeem somewhere in

the battle. He looked behind but could not see him.

"Ride back!" Tancred was shouting above the wind at Helena, but her heart was in her throat and weakness left her trembling. The pursuer had been her beloved and she had thought him a brigand. It was too late to ride back to the castle, for they could not escape together, and she would not leave without him. The Seljuks were upon them.

Tancred cast a swift glance at the approaching warriors, then rode up to her, sword in hand. The blue-gray eyes under dark lashes melted her heart. The stormy and passionate gaze seemed unaware of anything else but her face, her eyes welling now with tears, the dark strands of hair sticking to her ivory skin.

He stared at her, as though wanting to brand this last moment on his mind before facing certain death. The wind whipped against them.

Helena's gaze was riveting. One look between them had wiped everything from her mind but this fleeting final moment. Nothing mattered now, only their being together.

"I love you," she choked.

Even as the thud of horse hooves neared, Tancred reached out an arm to grasp her waist, and Helena leaned across the saddle to reach him, tilting her face toward his to meet his kiss, her hand slipping around his neck. Her lips trembled beneath his, her fingers desperately trying to hold on to a dying dream.

The violent moment might have brought a savage kiss, unfulfilled with longing, but the kiss was tender, poignant with love.

The shouts of the Seljuks could be heard, and in the distance the beating drums and the high weird shout of "Allah! Allah!" rang out. Tancred forced himself to release her.

"I love you," he whispered.

Her hand slipped away and he turned to face the oncoming enemy, lifting his blade as he rode forward.

Helena bit back a heartbreaking sob and dropped her head, her hand clutching at her heart. "Christ, Thou blessed Son of God, Thou precious Redeemer, help us now! Oh, help us!" she wept.

The disciplined cavalry of Seljuks that approached wore wide-sleeved *khalats* lined with padded cloth and Persian chain mail, and high damascened helmets. Their horses were swift and light thoroughbreds, with high-peaked saddles. In their hands the horsemen carried small painted shields and scimitars, and their short bows were strapped to their backs. With frightening speed they reached Helena and Tancred and moved to surround them. Helena screamed as she was swept from her saddle by several Seljuks and was hauled, kicking and struggling, to another horse.

Tancred's sword brought the first rider down, but another emerged, then two, three more, and in the wild abandon of the struggle to stay alive, he soon lost reality and simply fought. Blood was running into his eyes. His head throbbed from a severe blow. He wrenched an arrow from his chest and fought on. Then stunned by a blow from behind him, his awareness narrowed into a sucking pool of blackness. . . .

"No!" Helena screamed as Tancred was knocked from the stallion. Oblivious to her own danger, she tried to break free from the two Seljuks, but they held her fast. She thought she would faint as she stared at Tancred's empty saddle. Any moment now they would trample him to death or use the scimitar to make sure he was dead, and she began to scream, "No, no, no. . . ."

A voice commanded, "Release her at once!"

She turned her head to see who it was, and

her gaze fell upon an older man, the age of her uncle Nicholas, a man of dignified manner, with a neatly trimmed Moslem beard and mustache. He was of warrior bearing and carried weapons, including the curved scimitar. He had ridden up with some inner guardsmen who were sworn to die for his safety. Silver ornaments jingled on his royal Arabian horse.

"See if he yet breathes!" he commanded.

The order was swiftly carried out, and one called back to him, "He breathes, Eminence."

She felt the Seljuk commander staring at her as though measuring the relief she felt. Who was he? Yaghi-Sian? Kerbogha? Some other captain who served the emir and his son Prince Kalid?

"The warrior," he inquired abruptly, "who is he?"

Helena could not speak at first. The sun beat upon her, and she felt the sharp eyes of the Seljuk soldiers watching her with immobile faces that showed no kindness. What could she say? What could she do? They would surely kill him here and now if they knew it was Tancred Jehan Redwan, a distant cousin of Kalid himself, for the two men were enemies.

"A mercenary soldier in service to . . . to

Emperor Alexius Comnenus." It was true — at least it had been so until recently. "Please! Do something to help him! Do not let him bleed to death!"

"And if he is a spy, Eminence? What if he has been sent ahead by the one named Bohemond? This Byzantine is not worth the bother to save, Your Highness. Let them strike him dead. Why waste time?"

Helena's eyes darted toward a younger man beside the commander who may have been a captain of his guard. He carried several weapons, and the horse he rode caught her attention. Knowing her breeds, she believed it to be a mare of famous breeding. The man was sullen and haughty looking, wearing a short clipped beard and a thin mustache. There was a glimmer of ruthlessness in his eyes, and a mark on his cheek just below his left eye that was healing. His tight lips showed he was not a man of contentment. At once, she did not like him.

The commander appeared to consider the wisdom of his warning. Taut with fear, she wondered how to respond. If she begged or showed too much concern, they would know at once that Tancred meant more to her than a guard. Yet, if he was a favorite guard?

"He is no spy, Eminence," she announced, relieved her voice did not tremble. "He is a friend and bodyguard." *Lord, forgive me —* "I . . . I have had him in my service since I was a young girl. His name is . . . Bardas."

"I have heard of him," said the younger man. "He is a eunuch. Your Eminence, I think your nephew will have no reason for concern."

Nephew? Then was this commander the uncle of Prince Kalid?

Without a word the older man lifted his hand toward his soldiers, showing a reprieve for Tancred. Gold rings and rubies flashed in the morning sunlight. "Bring the body-guard."

At once several Seljuks went to the spot where she had seen him fall. She watched, trying to keep a calm demeanor. It would never do to show too much excitement.

Her spine stiffened. She had forgotten! Some of the soldiers who had arrived first must have seen her and Tancred kissing! They would know he was not her guard, nor a eunuch.

Her wary gaze shifted toward the com-mander. He had ridden up later and had not seen their good-bye, neither had the haughty captain of his guard, but some of the others must have! What if they said something?

She glanced about at the faces of the hard-ened warriors, but they all might as well have worn iron masks, so hidden were their emotions. Then she realized the reason for their silence. The verbal exchange between her and the commander and his captain of the guard had transpired in Latin, and evidently they had not understood the meaning. What if someone mentioned later that they had seen them in an embrace?

The wind was picking up again and the sand was blowing. She turned her face from the wind to guard her eyes, feeling the grit between her teeth.

"Mosul, bring Prince Kalid's bride to the caravan," ordered the commander.

Mosul!

The haughty and ruthless-looking guard rode up beside her, and others under him followed suit. She was escorted away toward the main body of the Seljuk army on the plain. She wisely showed no emotion. So this man was the assassin Tancred had been searching for. Her eyes came back to the scar. Tancred had placed it there in the fighting in the camp of the Red Lion when her mother had been rescued. Fear gripped her. Mosul would recognize him! How could he not? Thus far he had not seen his face, but could she manage to keep Tancred disguised until he was strong enough to ride from Antioch?

Helena turned briefly in her saddle to look back. She could see Tancred now. He was unconscious and bleeding as they secured him to the back of his horse. The sight wrenched at her heart. Only the mercies of Christ could aid them. She found herself praying desperately for His protection and a way of escape.

Tancred would be helpless inside Antioch. What could she do? What could either of them do now? Kalid, too, would recognize him. Tancred was trapped between Kalid and Mosul. And she had not seen the real Bardas since Philip betrayed them at the summer palace. She was without a friend.

They rode toward the city, fighting the wind and sand. The rest of the cavalry passed on through the Gate of St. Paul.

PART
TWO

Inside Antioch

CHAPTER 14

The House of Khan

Helena's eyes were busy seeking to place in memory any means of escape, although it seemed an impossible task. Still, Tancred would wish to know everything when she could speak with him alone. Could she manage to have him brought to her chamber? Wherever there were women kept, there were eunuchs who had charge over them, so a request to have her own eunuch bodyguard close by would be deemed normal.

Despondency swept over her as she gazed upon the thick walls. How would the feudal lords be able to take the city? Until now, she had not concerned herself with the Western Crusade. The expedition to take Jerusalem back from the Moslems had been simply an ambition of the western branch of the church in Rome and a political concern of the Emperor Alexius, who saw his Byzantine Empire shrinking. Now, however, her own future was involved, and freedom for her and Tancred was bound up in the victory of the crusaders. She despised the idea of being married to the Seljuk prince. Their liberty would come with the fall of Antioch and the arrival of Bohemond.

Tancred! The very thought of him brought a fresh wave of regret. Even if he recovered from the wounds inflicted in battle, how could he ever escape the notice of his enemies? She must somehow escape marriage to Prince Kalid, but how?

They neared the Gate of St. Paul, and it swung open to admit the caravan to pass through. As a matter of choice she veiled herself to keep away prying and curious eyes, though unlike Arab women, Turkish women did not always, as a matter of edict, veil themselves.

Although far from the splendors of Constantinople, Antioch, under favorable circumstances, would have proven to be a pleasant city. Here, during the iron rule of ancient Rome, Caesar had once sat in its theater. Herod, in the days of Christ, had sections paved with marble for his enjoyment. Titus, the general who destroyed Jerusalem and the Jewish temple in A.D. 70, had watched the chariot races here. And the Byzantines, from the time of Justinian in the sixth century, had created the beautiful hanging gardens among the myrtle trees and the running fountains.

Her eyes passed over the disciplined Seljuk cavalry lining the route to the palace. As the caravan wound its way down the stone street in the direction of the Moslem palace, the Seljuks fell in around her. *Lord, I'm afraid,* she prayed. *Help me to be brave.*

At the palace, their horses were led away by slaves, and Helena was delivered to more Turkish guards. She wanted to avoid speaking to Mosul, and her eyes sought for the uncle of Kalid. At first she thought he had left, but he reappeared now, followed by Mosul and another guard.

"You will be taken to my father, the emir. He wishes to see you first to see if you are worthy of his grandson."

"And my bodyguard?"

He turned indifferently and spoke in his own language to the other soldiers. "He will be brought later."

Later? What did they expect to do with him? Would they tend his wounds? She would have protested but feared it would alert them to suspicion.

"Kalid has arranged for your comfort. His servants will see to your every need. I am his uncle Ma'sud Khan."

She wondered where Kalid might be, but she was not anxious to see him. Still, it was strange that he had not come himself to meet Constantine's entourage and escort her back to Antioch. Thinking of Constantine, she wondered how the battle had gone. Now that she knew the marauders who had come sweeping down from the hills had not been brigands as he had said, she wondered if Constantine had escaped. Had Uncle Nicholas been with Tancred?

She blinked back tears as she thought of her uncle. Oh, if only Nicholas were here with her now instead of this man, Ma'sud Kahn, the uncle of Kalid! Yet she believed Ma'sud was a warrior of honor, else he would not have spared the wounded man he thought to be Bardas.

"If you need me, you may send Captain Mosul with a message, or one of the other palace guards. As Kalid's proud uncle, I wish you peace and prosperity among us."

She did not forget her upbringing and lowered her head in a gesture of gratitude. He strode away with Mosul and the guards, and Helena was turned over to slaves. They bowed and gestured a wide arm toward a shadowed colonnade bordering a fragrant court.

She followed through the court, then

across exquisite rugs, soft and thick under her feet. They were not of the celebrated Persian design, she noted, but of Turkish knot, tufted, with floral design and colors ranging from sapphire blue to yellow. They looked to be made not only from wool but also silk. There was a glitter of gold and marble everywhere, the sound of a splashing fountain, and the fragrance of flowers.

Ahead, the slaves paused, their backs toward her. They were bowing in the direction of an elderly man who was seated on cushions on a dais in the far corner of a splendid chamber.

Helena found herself before the emir, one ruler among others who held authority in Antioch. His name was Oman, and he was the grandfather of Kalid. His brown wrinkled face was contemplative, his slanting black eyes vigilant.

Helena stood in silence, waiting. At last he lifted a jeweled hand toward a muscled slave, and the man came toward her.

"He will see you closer now. Come forward."

She approached and bowed in respect, not forgetting her manners in the hour of captivity. "Greetings, Your Excellency. The most noble emperor of Byzantium sends his wishes of favor and peace."

Emir Oman was helped to his feet. "Welcome! Lady Helena Lysander of the Nobility. Welcome to Antioch, and to the house of Khan. It is with regret my grandson Kalid could not ride to meet you and the Byzantine entourage, but I trust my son Ma'sud has made your arrival one of welcome."

Then he did not know yet about the fighting. Helena lowered her head and said nothing.

"Kalid will soon arrive to greet you. He has ridden to Aleppo to meet with the sultan. The great locust-army of the West has been sighted."

"I know of them, Your Excellency," she responded.

"It is said that soon they will be here at Antioch, beneath our walls. It is unfortunate your arrival has come at this time. Prince Kalid will meet with the sultan and the other emirs to form a relief army to aid us, should there be a siege."

Her own relief was veiled. Kalid was not in Antioch. His departure meant a postponement in the expected marriage ceremony.

As their eyes met she hoped the emir did not see her glee.

"He will return in a few weeks," the emir went on. "Until then, you will refresh yourself. Your slaves will see to your wishes."

At his handclap the slippered slave re-appeared and led her away and across the palace to a far assemblage of chambers that she knew to be the women's section.

Here the floor was also veined marble, with magnificent rugs, and in the marble arches there were gold mosaics from a far earlier time in Byzantine history.

The voice of the chief eunuch could be heard shouting his dissatisfaction over some failure of the slaves, and a moment later she had her first look at Asad, a Turk who was as round in the middle as he was tall. He ushered three girls forward to meet her and a young boy of perhaps fourteen.

"Your slaves, Princess Helena!" he announced breathlessly. "A gift from the wise and noble Prince Kalid!"

The girls were dressed in tight-fitting silk that covered them from ankle to shoulder, then sheer pantaloons that billowed out about their legs and arms. They bowed low while the chief eunuch, Asad, looked on with hawkeye, judging their performance. He seemed pleased, then turned with a scowl to the boy, ushering him forward as though he expected him to blunder.

The handsome boy had mischievous brown eyes and olive skin polished with oil. He came forward on sandaled feet and, with enlarged fanfare, bowed deeply. "Welcome, O most lovely among women!"

Helena smiled, and Asad, too, appeared relieved and pleasantly surprised. "Quickly, Jamil, my boy, quickly!"

The boy proceeded to bring her an armful of costly and colorful silk garments.

"From Prince Kalid," he said. "Greatest of all living warriors."

"I am sure," she said innocently.

The three young girls came forward one by one, bowed, and extended lavish gifts of jewels, gold bangles, and carved ivory containers of perfumes: musk, ambergris, and spikenard. There followed other rare gifts, even animals: a large cat, black with white paws, and a bird of red-and-green plumage, but the gift that caused her heart to skip was the promise of a thoroughbred horse.

"Ah, princess," crooned Asad. "Most noble Kalid had hoped to present the stallion to you, but business has interfered. The horse is magnificent and has won all the races in the last year!"

When she thought of a sleek racing horse, she thought of speed and . . . freedom.

"I am pleased, Asad. You have made my coming indeed welcome . . . um, and when may I see my horse?"

"Tomorrow, if you wish."

"Tomorrow pleases me well."

Asad turned to the boy. "This should make you most happy, Jamil. You will go with your new mistress."

The boy's eyes glittered like ripe brown plums as they focused on Helena. "He is a most wondrous horse, Your Loveliness! I helped train him myself."

"Then he will be fine indeed."

The pride and excitement showed in his winsome smile. She already knew she was going to become attached to the boy.

He bowed a second time. "I will prepare him well, mistress. Perhaps you will wish to ride him tomorrow? He is the most beautiful of the prince's thoroughbreds. I am sure you will like him. I was given the honor of naming him, but you may change the name if you wish."

She smiled at him, her mind racing. Would it be possible to escape with Tancred while Kalid was away? Would the boy know of some secret route to take them from Antioch? What eager young boy did not know of such things? And one glimpse of Jamil said he was full of adventure.

"I am sure I will like his name. Jamil, you must show me everything in Antioch."

He beamed. "I know every trail, every tree, every gate, mistress."

"You and I will become good friends, Jamil."

"Then can we not go early and spend the entire day?"

Helena thought of Tancred. She expected him to be brought to her the next morning.

"If not tomorrow, soon."

Jamil showed his disappointment but wiped his face clear of expression when Asad scolded him with his eyes. Jamil bowed.

"When you would see your horse, mistress, you have but to speak the word. I will never be far away."

CHAPTER 15

Valley of the Shadow

It was the evening of Helena's arrival in Antioch. Her ten-course meal, delivered by Jamil, sat untouched on the long, low table. Helena paced in her chambers — a grouping of four elaborately decorated rooms. Her stomach remained tense and her hands clammy. Her fears raced mindlessly out of control. What if Mosul discovered who Tancred was and put a dagger through his heart while he slept? If all was well, then where was he? Why had he not been brought to her as Ma'sud Khan had promised?

She opened the door of her outer chamber and found Jamil perched like a pet bird on the top of the latticed terrace, munching from a bowl of purple grapes and figs she herself had refused.

"Is there any sign of the physician yet?" she demanded, as she had several times earlier.

"No, mistress, but I shall go again and see, if you so desire."

"Yes. And send, too, for Asad," she said of the chief of eunuchs. "Tell him I do not care if it means my own head; I shall go in search for Bardas if I must."

Jamil's winsome brown eyes widened. He swallowed a lump of fig with difficulty. "Mistress — you would show *disobedience?*" He added with horror, "In *public?*"

Helena's eyes narrowed under dark lashes. "If my bodyguard is not brought to me this night, I shall make a scene the emir will long remember. Go!"

Jamil tossed the remaining fruit aside and disappeared in flight. She heard his bare feet slapping down the stairs and his shout echoing in the corridor: "Asad! Asad! It is true what they say about Byzantine women!"

Within minutes, Jamil came racing back up the outer steps, followed by Asad, who labored with heavy tread, puffing his indignation all the way up. When he saw Helena he shouted and blustered his horror.

"You cannot behave this way! Perish the thought! You must never go out without proper chaperon. You *must* show grave honor to Prince Kalid." He waved his finger under her nose. "Obedience, obedience!"

Helena pretended indifference. "Nay! Unless the Byzantine is brought to me this night, I shall take to the armory myself to find him."

"*What?*" he nearly shouted. "And disgrace the son of the emir? The greatest of warriors? The auspicious prince?"

"I wish to speak to Ma'sud Khan."

"He cannot come at this time!"

"Then I will see the physician who has attended my bodyguard. I want the Byzantine brought to me now!"

"The Byzantine cannot be moved! It is the wise physician's orders —"

"Then my guard is alive?" she interrupted. "He is being attended, safely? Where?"

"In the military quarters, but —"

Asad could be intimidated, she could see as much. He was constantly upset, caught between pleasing her and offending the customs he must uphold. She didn't wish to upset him further, but she felt it was imperative that Tancred be brought to her.

"Then I will go there at once," she said, and her own determination nearly convinced her.

"Your Loveliness, I beg of you —"

"Jamil! Bring me to the bunkhouse."

Jamil appeared enthralled with the scandalous situation. "Yes, mistress. I will get your cloak."

"Wait, Your Loveliness, wait," Asad said

with a sigh. He sat down hard on the seat, one hand at his heart.

Jamil quickly produced a feathered fan and with a deep bow cooled him, enjoying the scene. Asad mopped his brow.

"May Allah see my burdens," he groaned.

"Allah already has many burdens of his own," said Jamil. "Master Asad, shall I hasten to the wise physician and bid that he bring her bodyguard here?"

"Yes, yes! Go, Jamil!"

Jamil glanced at Helena and smiled. She covered her smile and turned away, folding her arms.

"Wait, Jamil!" cried Asad, evidently changing his mind. "You should not go alone. I will come with you."

Some time later she heard them coming. The chief eunuch was trying to explain his ordeal to the pompous physician as he rushed along beside him, his short legs at disadvantage to keep up with the doctor's long stride.

"He should not be moved!" the physician was saying. "If he bleeds to death, I will be held responsible!"

The physician swept into the room with brows furrowed, his eyes seeking the woman who dared interfere with his medical practice. When they collided with Helena's determined gaze, his lips tightened into a grim line above the neatly trimmed Moslem beard. He was extremely tall and slim, wearing a smoke blue turban and a knee-length embroidered tunic tied with a fringed silk sash. In his long, thin hand he carried a satchel.

"Lady Helena, such behavior is unheard of. What will Prince Kalid say to your actions?"

Helena's gaze swerved to Tancred stretched out on a palanquin carried by two slaves. "Bring him into the next chamber." She led the way into a room where Jamil rushed to throw back the silken bedcovers.

"Lay him here," she ordered.

"Your Loveliness," cried the chief eunuch, exasperated, "is it wise to have so ill a man here in your chambers? True, we all can see he is your favored slave, but —"

Helena turned to Jamil. "Make a fire in the hearth. And bring me curdled wine and all the herbs you have in the culinary."

The physician gripped his satchel. "Your Highness, I am the physician — am I not?"

Helena looked at him. "Fear not, I intend to do as you bid. How serious are his wounds?"

"Quite serious. I do not know if the lung was punctured or not. I had no time to examine him closely. The bleeding had to be stopped. He has lost much. He is strong, a warrior, and so . . ." His voice trailed off as his mind turned in another direction.

". . . and another wound in his shoulder, but it is not as serious, and he has a concussion." His pointed beard quivered again with insulted rage. "I might add, he behaves with arrogance. Before he lapsed into unconsciousness, he dared tell me how to treat him. You are both entitled to each other's company. Good evening." He bowed and started to leave.

"Wait — will he live?"

"He should not have been moved. The bleeding could start again. If you keep him quiet and the wounds do not fester, he should improve."

The physician swept out of the chamber, and she was left alone with Jamil and the chief eunuch, who stood in the doorway to Tancred's chamber, wringing his hands.

"You may go now, Asad."

"Yes, Highness, as you wish, but please do not leave your chambers."

He went out, following after the physician. Helena, disoriented, stood staring at the closed door, then turned and rushed into the smaller chamber.

Tancred was asleep, or unconscious; she

was not sure which. She hovered anxiously near his bed for a few minutes and then rushed back into the main chamber to make sure Jamil had the fire going. He did, and a vessel of water was slung from a winch above the flames. She heard a groan and hurried back into Tancred's chamber to find him struggling to rise from the bed.

He still wore his trousers and boots, though his blood-soaked shirt was gone, and she saw with horror that fresh blood had begun to seep through the bandages on his chest as the physician had warned.

With a start she rushed to the bed and tried to push him back to the pillows. "Tancred, you must lie still."

He looked at her, startled at her presence, then suddenly caught her, drawing her toward him. "Helena . . ." he said with feverish confusion, "are you unhurt?"

"Yes," she whispered and kissed him. "Yes, I am well, my darling."

"What are you doing here . . ." he said, somewhat dazed, "in the armory?"

She soothed his brow. "Hush, my darling, you are in my quarters," she whispered, trying to explain. "I am going to look after you until —"

His hand closed tightly about her arm. He could summon more strength than she had thought possible. He blinked, coming momentarily alert. "*Your* chamber? I cannot stay here . . . for your sake —"

"Hush, it's all right."

He thrashed about in search of his scabbard, and in his struggle knocked over a small marble table. "My sword — where is it?"

She grappled with him, trying to push him back to the bed, but even in his weakened condition, she found his strength could not be mastered.

"Be still, darling," she gasped. "Your thrashing about will harm you — your wounds will open again. And if Kalid learns —" She caught herself in time. How much *dare* she tell him?

Tancred noted the change in her voice. "Kalid, where is he?"

"Away, at Aleppo, trying to raise an army to come to the aid of Antioch. We are in good fortune for a time. You must get well. You must escape. I will seek to find some way out and divert them while you do."

His eyes burned into hers. "And leave you here? No. Facing fifty Seljuks was not enough to convince you of my dedication?"

She smiled sadly, laying her palm against his face. "You have convinced me," she whispered. "And now, I must convince you how much I love you."

"We escape together or not at all. You must know I will not leave you here."

His words hurt all the more because of his terrible wounds. Yet she, too, felt wounded. They were helplessly trapped. She might warn him of Mosul, but he was in no condition.

"You must rest and sleep," she whispered.

"There is no time to waste. I must think, must learn the layout of the palace —"

"There is nothing you can do now. Be reasonable, Tancred. You are delirious."

The blue of his irises glittered. "What happened to Nicholas, Rufus, the others?"

She tried to soothe him. "Surely they have survived and made it back through the gate. There is no talk of them being prisoners."

"Whatever Philip and Constantine told you about me is a lie. . . ."

"Yes, my darling, I know."

"They are dead," he murmured in a feverish sleep. "Dead. . . ."

She stiffened. *Philip, dead?*

He must be wrong. She would wait until he was recovering to ask him. But that Constantine may be dead did not surprise her, not if he had confronted Nicholas.

"Bardas also misled you. Dead too. . . ."

She wanted to wince. Bardas? Oh no, not

her faithful Bardas — he must be wrong. He had to be wrong.

"It does not matter now," she soothed.

She thought he was falling asleep, but when she began to pull away from his grip, his eyes opened and he pulled her down to him. His eyes searched hers. Her lashes faltered under his gaze.

"How is it that Kalid has allowed me to stay here alive? Why did he not kill me?"

"I told you, Kalid is not here. It was his uncle who came for me."

"Ma'sud Khan?"

Then Tancred knew of him, Helena thought. "Yes, he treated me well. I requested he spare your life. We have much reason to thank God."

"Ma'sud has no pity for enemies. Why would he spare me?"

It was time to confess. "I did the only thing I could think of. I convinced them you were a favored slave. My personal bodyguard, Bardas."

His eyes, alert now, grew speculative and drifted across her face. A brow shot up, and his mouth turned. "A eunuch. That accounts for it. And besides Ma'sud, who else believes this?"

"Mosul," she whispered.

His grip tightened. "He knows I am here,

with you? Neither of us will escape easily, regardless of Kalid's absence. Mosul will soon know who I am, if he does not know already."

Tancred suddenly grimaced. He fell back weakly, paling, but gritted his teeth, trying to still a short, dry cough.

Seeing him in pain crumbled her determination to show bravery. At once she felt a surge of contrition. She had been unwise to tell him now; this was not the time!

He was beginning to perspire. Her eyes darted back to his wounds. She knelt quickly beside the bed, watching him anxiously. She whispered calmly, "Mosul will not discover the truth. I will manage to keep your identity hidden until you are strong. Then . . . then we will both escape together," she said, stroking his feverish brow. "We must not talk now. It will wait. You must rest."

His gaze showed frustration over his inability to help her, to help them both.

"Who else knows I'm here?"

"Asad, the chief eunuch, and the physician. And my servants, but they are already supportive. You are safe, at least until Kalid returns. And I will not let him into my chamber. He knows the name of Bardas and will think nothing of it. Mosul has also heard of him, and he was not suspicious."

"He will grow suspicious. My sword, hand it to me. Find me some kind of tunic."

She was becoming alarmed. He had no sword. Everything had been taken from him, but she feared to tell him. And his pain could no longer be disguised. His skin was hot to her touch, and though he was sweating profusely, he had begun to shiver.

"Do not be difficult, Tancred, please. You have no place to go. If you try to walk, you will collapse. At the moment I am the only one who can help you. You will never get down the hall in your condition."

"Nevertheless . . . I will not stay here. My presence only endangers you."

Her heart ached. Even now, he was concerned for her protection. The truth was, they were both trapped.

"Do stop thrashing. Did I not tell you Ma'sud Khan knows you are here? He will let you recover in peace. Now please! Stop squirming. And if you toss the covers off one more time —"

His breathing became more labored, and Helena felt a growing fear over what the physician had said about possible damage to the lung.

"Rest," she pleaded, but his fingers closed painfully about her wrist. She was surprised at his determination as he flung aside the covers and struggled to his feet. Helena sprang to stop him, clutching him frantically.

"Tancred, no —"

The exertion brought pain that swiftly contorted his face. Frightened, she grabbed him, trying to hold his balance. "Darling! Please! You're in no condition."

He was streaming with sweat and turning pale. She felt him shake with sudden chills, despite the heat of his flesh.

In a frenzy Helena held to him, staring up at him wildly. "Darling, *please!* You must stay out of sight. You must behave as though you are Bardas —" her voice caught.

His eyes were sick now and his speech slurred, and he was clinging to her to stand up straight, but his weight was great and she felt she was beginning to fall.

He was choked to silence by a retching cough that promised to erupt into new bleeding. He collapsed to the bed, Helena still holding him.

She could see he was struggling to think clearly, as though he wanted to speak but was growing faint. Frustration marked his face, and his present agony seemed to be more demanding on him than the confrontations of battle. He was a prisoner to helplessness, and it tortured him. Was he dying? Her panic set in. She stared down at him, unable to move. Then she grabbed him tightly until her knuckles went white.

"No!" she cried. "Tancred, oh, my beloved!"

She leaned over him as he coughed and saw blood on the corner of his mouth.

Her eyes fell to his chest, where the golden candlelight reflected, and the strong muscles now were still and useless. The white bandages were turning red before her eyes, the size of the circle increasing until it became shiny and started dripping to the white silk coverlet.

She wanted to scream, but no sound would come through her parched throat. Horror, then guilt and shame rocked her soul. He was going to die! And she was behaving like a coward. She must do something. She began to pray, but the words came out as sobs through her lips.

Her fist went to her mouth, her eyes wide, and her heart seemed to constrict. "Tancred!" she rasped. Then more demandingly, "Tancred! No! Hear me! Live! Live!"

He was unconscious. *Dear God . . .* she prayed again.

A dart of sanity came to her. She grabbed the clean white cover from a pillow and pressed it against his chest, holding with steady pressure.

"Do not die! I love you, I love you!"

The slip was turning wet and sticky. "Lord in heaven! Please forgive my sin! Have mercy on me! I need him. Oh, do not take him from me." Tears ran streaming down her face, splashing against his chest. She clung to him, burying her face against him, repeating his name over and over with vows of love, her nails digging into his shoulder. She was in a nightmare, a terrible dark nightmare where there was no light. Then his voice, slurred and very weak, came to her as if a faint glimmer of light sprang up. It brought her to her senses at once. She raised her head and wiped her face with both hands.

"Sphagnum . . ." he uttered, the word barely audible.

"Tancred, do you hear me?"

He scowled with his last effort, as though trying to think, to speak to her.

"Sphagnum . . ."

"W-what?"

"Sphag . . . num . . ."

Her frantic mind grasped the word. Sphagnum. Sphagnum. What was sphagnum?

She bolted upright. Moss! Sphagnum moss! She tumbled from the bed and ran toward the other chamber. "Jamil! Jamil!"

The boy was already there. He had evidently been hovering in the archway since her first scream of despair, like some restless little bird that didn't know where to land.

"The physician, hurry! Tell him to bring sphagnum moss!"

He turned and fled.

She ran into a third chamber and found her knees so weak she thought they would buckle. Her fingers were cold and clumsy as she snatched another coverlet. She hurried back to Tancred and began pressing the cloth to his chest. How much blood could he lose and live?

The moments seemed endless. She glanced at his face; it was pale under the bronzed skin. His breath was slow and ragged.

"Lord," she kept praying, "do not take him from me. Please, not yet. . . ."

Her heart pounding, Helena continued to press steadily on the chest wound. His eyes were slightly open, but she knew he was not aware of her presence.

Her ears strained for the sound of running feet. Where was Jamil? Why did the physician delay? Her eyes left Tancred to gaze longingly toward the door. Suppose there was no sphagnum?

At last she heard them. The physician rushed in with Jamil at his heels.

He took one look at Tancred's soaked bandages, then began to cut them away. His brows came together, but quickly his features were wiped clean of emotion. From his open bag he took out some strange-looking spongy material and soaked it with wine, then pressed it into the wounds. He left it in place as he applied new bandages.

As he was finishing, he seemed satisfied. "It should work. There is something about the sphagnum that stops the bleeding, but none of the wisest physicians understand it. Your Highness, how did you know of this? I have once read that this remedy was used in ancient battles. I did not think it was known to the Byzantines. You have become learned in medicine?"

Helena was too emotionally depleted to answer.

"You have my humble apology. I believe that your marriage to His Eminence will bring benefit to many in Antioch."

With that, he proceeded to mix equal amounts of two types of powder onto a leaf.

Gaining a little strength, Helena thought she recognized the same drugs used by Lady Irene in Constantinople, but for less noble purposes than to help the dying.

"Will the sphagnum work?" her teeth chattered.

"It *is* working. But there is another problem. I suggest that poisons are forming in his body."

"Poisons?"

"He is hot with fever. He will go into delirium. Keep this chamber as warm as you can bear it. Mix this powder into a brew. See that he drinks it through the night. I can promise you nothing. By tomorrow, if the fever cools, he will live."

For Helena, the darkness of the night made the trials more painful, and hopes seemed to wane with the shadows. Trapped in an unfamiliar Moslem palace, the ordeal could not have been more frightening. As Tancred lay near death, his delirium made it more heart wrenching, for she could not commune with him.

He thrashed about, muttering words she could not understand. When he did speak, the words were sometimes in Greek, sometimes in Arabic. This surprised her, but she realized that it shouldn't have. There were many Moors in Sicily, and had he not said his father had married a Moorish woman?

He spoke of Palermo, mumbling the names of the Redwan family, of the sea and galleons . . . then, without any reason, of a falcon named Othello. A boyhood pet, she thought. How strange to imagine Tancred a boy on the sun-drenched wharves of Palermo, hanging about ships or training falcons. Once, the name of a girl was mentioned. Kamila, he called her.

She felt an emptiness. He did not call her own name. . . .

Through the long, pain-wracked night, Tancred fought for survival, and Helena fought with him, rarely leaving his side except to attend to her personal needs, and even with Jamil beside his bed, her ears were busy to hear any sound that might come from Tancred. Finally she insisted that Jamil get some sleep.

"I am not sleepy, mistress. I will sit with you," Jamil whispered, and his hand went up to his mouth to hide a yawn.

"To bed at once. I will call you when I need you."

Reluctantly he left Tancred's chamber and curled up on the Persian rug before the glowing hearth. In a moment he was in a deep slumber.

It was now late, but she was too troubled to feel the need of sleep. She arose to add more wood to the hearth. It was so hot that her clothing clung to her skin. Restless, Tancred tossed the covers from his sweating body. Helena dried him with towels and then drew the covers back up, pausing to touch his damp tendrils with affection. Despite the heat and the extra covers, he would sometimes shiver as if very cold. Not wanting to leave him even for a moment, she grabbed the Persian cover from off the table and used it as another blanket.

He grew still, and she went back to the hearth to stir the medicinal brew. The water had boiled down, and she ladled another mug of the brew to bring him. But how was it possible to get him to drink? She heard him moving restlessly again. She set the cup down to cool and held the candle down close beside him to check the bandage, fearing the worst in the darkness of night. He was sweating profusely, but there was no fresh blood. She heaved a sigh. Touching him, his flesh burned. She wiped him with the cloth and tossed it aside with the others. He murmured and she bent her face closer, hoping he was conscious.

"Tancred?"

". . . water!"

Helena scowled to herself. She would have given him all the water he wanted, but the physician said for him to drink the brew first.

She brought the cup to his mouth, and he reached for it thirstily, only to push it away impatiently, spilling some on his chest. She wiped him quickly, but he only groaned for water until she could hardly stand to hear him.

Tancred hallucinated that he was chained to a torturous rack while the haunting voice of a beautiful woman tormented him. She mocked his love; her fragrance drugged his senses into confusion. He tried to see, to think, and could not.

Someone hovered over him with a candle, and his eyes suddenly opened, blinking at the light as if it were the glaring sun. He tried to focus on the face above him, to make out the voice that spoke.

"Tancred, it's me, Helena."

Her voice penetrated his semidarkened consciousness, and he tried to speak to her, but he could only close his eyes again. This was not the woman he wanted so desperately at this moment of death. "Helena . . . where are you?" he whispered.

A cool palm caressed his forehead. "I am right here, darling. I will never leave you."

Tancred agonized for water. His lips were dry and his tongue so swollen he could hardly swallow. Like a deceptive witch she lied to him! She was prolonging his suffering. Pain stabbed at his body; his thirst was unquenchable! She deliberately denied him.

His mind swam in darkness, and the cloak of her intoxicating perfume brushed his skin. "Helena . . ."

Her fingers caressed him, a low voice soothing in his ears promised endearments. It could not be Helena who hovered near his bed, beguiling him with her potions and insisting he remain enslaved. If he could just once get his hands on her . . . but each time she drew near — so near that he was sure he felt her heartbeat pulsating in time with his own — he could not lift his hands to grab her. His arms felt weighted down, and she escaped as he sank back into hot, painful darkness. . . .

Then . . . he saw his brother, Derek, lying in a pool of blood, but it was Tancred's dagger protruding from his chest. Mosul came from behind a drape to mock, and when he tried to get up off the bed to reach him, the woman would hold him back while her tormenting voice bid him suffer.

"— water!"

Helena could stand his pleas no longer. The dark and loathsome brew! It was doing nothing to help him. The physician was wrong. Even when it came to the sphagnum moss, it had been Tancred who thought of it. She left him and ran swiftly into the next chamber, where her supper remained untouched on the low table. She grabbed the water vessel and brought it to the other chamber.

"Tancred, here . . . water, my love. Drink as much as you want."

He seemed to hear her and struggled as she slipped her arm under his damp head to raise him. He drank avidly as she tipped the vessel to his mouth, spilling some on him. She continued to give him all that he wanted. The cool water brought a sigh of contentment.

As the dawn broke, he began to rest calmly, and in the candlelight she saw that he was not sweating as much, and his brow felt cooler to her touch. The fever was breaking. She wrung out the cool, wet cloths and bathed his face.

He was no longer groaning in his sleep, and his hands were not clenched. She removed his boots, and as she pulled she discovered a dagger concealed in one of them. It was like Tancred to keep a hidden weapon. The handle was studded with jewels, and holding it to the candle flame she read the inscription on the blade written in Norman: *Justice.*

She drew the covers about him and started to turn away, exhausted, when to her surprise she felt his hand close about her wrist, but the touch was different. He was alert.

She looked down at him and his eyes were slightly open. "Angel . . ." he whispered meaningfully.

Helena felt a glowing sense of satisfaction to know she had eased his suffering. She managed a slight, weary smile and leaned toward him with a whisper. "No longer a witch?"

"Angel. . . ."

His hand, weak, still persisted in holding hers.

She kissed his forehead. "Rest now."

He gave a deep sigh, then lay still, falling back into a deep sleep.

Helena, too, sighed, for she believed the worst was over and that he would live. Exhausted, her eyes felt pained with the need for sleep. She went to the divan and lowered herself into it wearily, allowing her eyes to shut. "Just a little rest," she thought. Darkness came. This time she welcomed it, for it held not terror but welcome relief. "Thank you, merciful God," she prayed.

CHAPTER 16

Hidden Paths

The fragrance of boiling meat simmering overnight in broth permeated the chamber as Helena awoke with a groan. Her head was dull and aching, and the smell of food was offensive, despite the fact that she had not eaten a full meal in several days.

As she came through the doorway of Tancred's chamber, she saw Jamil on his haunches before the hearth, where the kettle was strung across hot coals. At first she thought he was stirring the broth. Then her eyes fell on the object he held in both hands. He stared at it with awe.

Helena came softly up behind him. Tancred's sword and sheath! The heraldic of the Norman House of Redwan was engraved on the handle. It was the same familiar falcon, but this time she saw not only the name *Redwan,* but also the formidable title of *William the Conqueror.*

Her first reaction was to grab the scabbard, but she bit back her impulse. It would only alert him to the importance of his discovery and make him more suspicious. Would he understand the implications pointing to "Bardas" being of Norman blood rather than Byzantine? What of the name Redwan?

Jamil was young but extremely clever. If he decided to mention the heraldic to the chief eunuch, Asad, it would not take long before the news reached Mosul.

"You may put the sword in a safe place, Jamil."

The calmness of her voice satisfied her, but Jamil jumped to his feet, and holding the heavy scabbard clumsily, he managed a bow. "Good morning, mistress."

She watched him trot across the room and place the sword behind the tapestry drape. The boy obviously understood that it was to be concealed. *Who else may have seen the engraving?* she wondered.

"Bardas will be pleased to get his weapon back," she told him when Jamil returned. "Where did you find it?"

"Oh, it was leaning against the wall in the armory when Asad and the physician had the slaves carry him from the barracks, mistress. I knew he would want it when he awoke."

She felt her way cautiously. Had he mentioned the sword to anyone?

"I am surprised the soldiers did not stop you. Did they see you take the sword?"

"None of the soldiers noticed, mistress." His head lifted proudly. "I waited until they were busy."

She dared to breathe a little easier. "You did well. My bodyguard will be pleased with your loyalty." He avoided her eyes and went at once to the kettle and dipped a mug of broth. He brought it to her.

"Careful, mistress, it is hot."

The sight of the broth caused her stomach to churn. "Thank you, but I am not able to eat this early in the morning. Perhaps some grapes or a melon."

"Yes, mistress, but the broth can give you strength, and your Byzantine bodyguard, too, when he awakes."

At once she caught the deliberate reference to "Byzantine" and scanned his face. From his expression she could tell nothing. She decided to test him, proceeding cautiously after he returned with a bowl of fruit.

"Do you handle a sword yet, Jamil?"

"Oh yes, mistress." His shoulders straightened proudly. "I study all arts of warfare. I had hoped one day to be a soldier."

For the first time he showed disappointment. "Now that I belong to you, it will be your decision."

She smiled. "I have no reason to make you less than what you wish to be."

Jamil brightened. Then he looked toward the chamber where Tancred slept. "But you have a bodyguard. He will be better soon. He is strong."

"He does look much better today."

"The sword I can handle," Jamil went on, "but I handle the scimitar far better. A dagger?" he shrugged his small shoulders. "I need much practice to become accurate. I cannot throw strongly yet and I miss the mark."

"You seemed to like the sword belonging to my servant Bardas."

Jamil's black lashes fluttered. He started to say something, then stopped. His eyes drifted away from her to Tancred's chamber. "I have not seen a finer one," he said simply.

Her fear that Tancred's identity might soon be discovered reminded her of the need to find an escape route from Antioch. As she ate the sweet fruit and sipped strong Arabic coffee, she remembered Prince Kalid's gift of the stallion. She arose from the cushions and walked to the terrace.

"It looks to be a fine day, Jamil. Now that my guard is improving, perhaps we can ride the stallion into the hills today."

"I would like nothing better, mistress!"

"Good. Then go to the stables and prepare the horse. I will join you as soon as the physician comes and looks at the Byzantine."

"Yes, mistress, at once!" And he ran out.

Over an hour had passed before Helena arrived at the stables, led there by one of the many slaves. She had not informed Tancred of her plans and had waited until the physician left and Tancred was in a deep sleep. She had left word with a door slave to permit no one to go inside her chambers.

Jamil waited impatiently. "He is ready and saddled, mistress. And Haroun has let me ride one of the common horses."

The day was warm and clear as they set out. Helena rode the fine Arabian horse, and Jamil led the way on the brown war horse.

The boy was pleased to show her everything. She viewed the gates and walls, but her interest was in the trails winding through the upper portion of the city into the hills. Was there a less-guarded section somewhere in the city walls from which an escape was possible? For security reasons, the family of Emir Khan, as well as the Turkish commander Kerbogha, should have some secret passage between Antioch and the mountains. She thought that there must be some kind of escape route for them in case of attack — a hidden exit somewhere in the mound of the city past the walls and before the barren brown hills.

"I suppose, Jamil," she said, baiting him, "that Yaghi-Sian and the other nobles have a route of escape prepared for them and their families should the crusaders be able to conquer the city?" She gestured toward the hills. "Surely they would have constructed a back postern gate, or have had slaves dig a tunnel."

Jamil leaned forward in his saddle and patted the strong neck of the horse, avoiding her gaze. For a moment he was silent.

"What makes you think so, mistress?"

She smiled. "I was born and raised amid intrigue. It is said that none know the art as well as a Byzantine." She could see the interest in his face. "Did you know the marriage to Prince Kalid was arranged by my enemies in Constantinople? They are also giving him the Castle of Hohms."

"I have heard," he admitted. "It is the way of great families, they say. For Aziza, it is even worse. She is to be given to a man she hates."

Helena looked at him. "Aziza? I do not know her."

His eyes turned sullen. "She is my sister, mistress. She is a slave to the Armenian wife of Master Firouz, who serves Yaghi-Sian."

"I am sorry for your sister."

"She loves the son of the physician. But Habib is to be given to the daughter of the stable master. And —"

"Yes, I see it is sad and complicated." She directed the topic back to the hills. "Does the Commander Yaghi-Sian often ride into the hills?"

He shrugged again, as though he guessed the reason for her question.

"I suppose all rulers have escape routes," she said.

"They would be foolish if they did not. The Seljuk army in the city must have one, as well as Emir Khan. And Prince Kalid would know of it. It is said, 'a fox has his small den, but he is crafty enough to have another exit.' "

She looked at him now, and the strained silence was broken by a rush of wind in the olive trees above.

Jamil watched a falcon soaring. "Someone is out hunting," he suggested. "I will be in trouble if I bring you into forbidden territory, mistress. Sometimes I go that direction, but only alone when no one knows. I like to watch the falcons with the wind freely in their wings."

"I suppose," she said, "that not even you could get through one of the gates without being caught."

"If I were going to have my head struck off for some crime? Then I could get out!"

"Oh?" she asked artfully.

He pointed toward the paths leaving the postern gates. "The smaller gates open onto seldom-used trails leading into Syrian villages."

"You must show me sometime."

"It is dangerous to go near there. His Eminence will hear of it."

"I suppose a clever young man like you would know just where the most hidden paths are."

He looked at her, troubled. "Mistress, you bait me. If I say I do not know, you will think your new slave a fool; if I say I do know — you will ask me where it is."

She smiled. "I think you are clever, Jamil, far from being a fool. So clever that I would risk this Arabian stallion in a wager that you *do* know their whereabouts."

Jamil's brown eyes swept the stallion with devotion. "Such a horse is worth much — if one could live to keep it. But speaking certain information could mean death for the teller of such tales." He looked up to see her alert gaze fixed upon him. They measured each other, as though each debated the wisdom of completely trusting the other.

Helena spoke first. She must trust someone, and if not this boy, then whom?

"Vow your loyalty to me, Jamil. Help me and do as I ask, and one day I will reward you with this stallion for your service."

Jamil bit his lip and watched her intensely, then set his jaw. "Mistress, I vow my loyalty without getting the fine horse. I know the man in your chambers is not your slave. Neither is he a Byzantine — he is a fine warrior. His name is Count Tancred Redwan, a Norman lord from Sicily."

She caught her breath. "How do you know all this? You could not have learned so much from the heraldic on his scabbard."

"My ears hear much. Few pay attention to a boy. I heard Kalid and Mosul talking before you came. They were expecting Count Redwan to come for you and to try to kill Mosul. But I did not know who the man you called Bardas really was until I heard you call his name last night when he was so ill."

"It was foolish. I should have been more careful."

"It is because you love him, and you were very frightened."

"You are too wise for your age, Jamil."

"Then I saw the scabbard. The insignia of the falcon in the hunt and of the military leader William the Conqueror. I have been learning about training falcons. The art is best taught by Normans, and so I guessed his heritage. Also, he has the body of a warrior — not a eunuch."

"You must say nothing, Jamil. If you do, it will mean his death."

"Prince Kalid will kill him?"

"Prince Kalid, Mosul, even Ma'sud Khan."

"Mosul is a cruel man. I have no liking for him. He has tried to kiss my sister."

Helena shuddered, remembering the ruthless face of Mosul. How dreadful to be a slave left to the mercies of men such as he. "Then if you know the manner of man Mosul is, you will understand why he must not learn the identity of Count Redwan until he recovers his strength. Everyone must think he is the Byzantine named Bardas."

Jamil scowled as his thoughts troubled him. "Why does Mosul wish to kill him?"

"Mosul is a Moorish cousin of Tancred. Out of jealousy for a woman in Palermo, Mosul killed the half brother of Tancred and arranged to have him blamed for his death. His uncle, Walter of Sicily, is searching for him to make him stand trial in the Norman style."

"And the Norman warrior has trailed Mosul to Antioch?" he asked, obviously impressed with Tancred's determination.

"Yes . . . and if Mosul discovers that he lies helpless in my chambers, he will think nothing of putting a dagger through his heart as he sleeps upon his bed."

"No doubt he would, mistress. That is his way. I will keep your secret on pain of my death. All I can do to help the Norman warrior I will do."

"I will not forget your loyalty, Jamil. Tancred must escape the city."

The boy's eyes gleamed with excitement. "The truth is, mistress, I know of several routes from Antioch. In the palace there is a tunnel leading under the city outside the Gate of the Dog."

Her heart pounded. "Can you show me?"

"To my regret, mistress, I have never seen it. And I know of no servant who has. The entrance is said to be located somewhere in the secret chambers of the royal family."

Helena sighed. "That sounds far too dangerous. Our most secret inquiries will surely reach the emir. We could trust no one. There must be another route, perhaps through the hills."

"Aziza can be trusted. She despises Mosul and wishes also to escape Antioch. You see, we are not Seljuks but Armenians. Our father was a ruler in Antioch until he was killed defending the city. The Turks sent our mother away — we do not know where, or if she is even alive. And they made Aziza and me into slaves. They also insisted we worship Allah, though our father and mother were Christians. Sometimes I still pray to Jesus, but only in my heart. I dare not breathe His name, except to you."

"You do wisely to pray to Jesus, Jamil, for He alone is the Way, the Truth, and everlasting Life. But tell me, do you think Aziza knows a way out?"

Jamil shook his head. "She knows even less than I do. She is a girl," he said with a wave of his hand. "And she does not serve in the emir's chambers. The men who serve there have little to do with the lesser slaves. They are warriors, sworn to die to protect the emir. But there is another way out of Antioch; it leads through the far postern gate. And if I were going to have my head struck off, I could get out there. Surely, then, so could the Norman warrior."

Her excitement soared. "Let us ride there. I wish to view this gate."

"If we ride too near the gate, the guards

will spot us at once. You heard yesterday what Asad told us? No one is permitted near the Tower. It is a garrison."

"Then we will ride as near as we can. Come, the afternoon wears on. Tancred must not be left alone for long. If he awakes, he will wonder where I have gone."

As Jamil rode a little ahead of Helena, he called back over his small shoulder, "I have a goal, mistress. I want to know this warrior, to learn the art of warfare and courage from him." His brown eyes glittered. "There could be none better than he. And if I help him escape Antioch, perhaps I can escape with him. Perhaps I could even return with him to Sicily and learn the ways of the Normans!"

"Perhaps," she said with a laugh. "Perhaps we both will go to Sicily, Jamil."

"But Aziza? If I leave her in Antioch, who will protect her?"

"It may be that Aziza will marry the physician's son after all," she soothed.

The slope rose steadily toward the rugged hills. Trees and shrubs grew like a thicket, and as they continued to ascend upward, the wall of Antioch ended at the mountainous incline. Jamil drew his horse under a sycamore tree, where the afternoon shadows offered relief. He waited for her to ride up beside him. The heat was oppressive, and the silence was broken only by the drone of insects.

Helena swished a buzzing insect away from her face and stared into the distance. A small but strong gate could be made out.

"It is seldom used, mistress. It opens onto a little-known trail leading still farther into the rugged mountains. I know of it because I am Armenian," he explained quietly. "There are shepherds in the mountains. Sometimes they come down and are permitted through the gate to bring their goat cheese and olives to the market. But as you can see, mistress, while the gate is small and little used, it is strong, and to your right you can see several Seljuk guards. Once they were not there, but with the coming crusaders, Commander Yaghi-Sian stationed the guards there to watch for spies trying to get into the city."

Helena saw the guards and fought her blighted courage. "Would it be possible to pass through the gate at night?"

"There are three guards, maybe more. They are big men, warriors, and cruel," he whispered. "They killed a shepherd last month. I saw them. Even now we must not ride too close."

Helena's mind was full of plans, all reaching dead ends. There were exits from Antioch and a trail into the mountains, but one glimpse of the guards and the steep, rugged incline of the mountains convinced her that nothing could be done yet. Tancred must be strong enough to face the guards and endure the mountain trails. That would take weeks. Until then, they were trapped and must move with caution.

They rode back toward the city in silence. As they neared the incline, seeking to avoid the Tower, Helena noticed an abandoned Christian Armenian church.

"What of your people, the Armenians? Do any serve in positions of authority, or have they all been sent from Antioch to raise flocks in the hills?"

"There are some Armenians who are important. But there is much trouble between them and certain Seljuk soldiers."

She looked at him, interested at once. "What kind of trouble? Do you mean petty wrangling and jealousy?"

"Not always petty, mistress. There is dislike between the Armenians in the city and their Turkish overlords, but there is no open rebellion. Firouz once served willingly, but he is not happy now. Why do you ask, mistress?"

She noted a strange tone to his voice.

"Firouz? What about him? Why is he unhappy?"

He glanced at her as though wondering if he should tell her. "Aziza says there is gossip about his wife." Jamil looked at her from the corner of his eye.

Helena watched him intently. "Yes? Go on, Jamil. What about the wife of Firouz?"

"She spends time with another man —" He lowered his voice, even though they were on horseback and alone. "A Turkish officer close to Yaghi-Sian."

"I see. . . ." Helena was silent, thinking.

"And Firouz, the Armenian?" she asked. "Whom does he serve?"

"He is a member of Yaghi-Sian's council."

Yaghi-Sian! The Turkish commander of Antioch! Accustomed to the intrigue of the Sacred Palace, she saw that the situation could affect the security of Antioch. The seeds were there. If she could find the opportunity to germinate them, she might be able to help Tancred.

"Who is the strongest ruler? Yaghi-Sian? Emir Khan? The other emirs? Or Prince Kalid?"

"Now it is Yaghi-Sian. His military is in control. He is a great man, very wise and strong."

"And Firouz serves him." Her eyes sparkled as her thoughts raced.

"Yes, but —" he stopped. "Mistress! Look!" He pointed down into the plain surrounding Antioch.

From their position near the wall they watched, entranced by the awesome sight: a massive army was moving slowly in the direction of Antioch, a cloud of dust behind them. They spread wide across the plain as far as the eye could see, and the varied gonfanons of the feudal lords fluttered in the wind like leaves on a tree. Helena saw the blue flag of Raymond of Toulouse and the crimson banner of Bohemond and his Normans. Her heart felt a thrill.

"How many are there?" Jamil breathed, excited by the prospect of so many warriors, friendly or not. "Fifty thousand? A hundred thousand? Prince Kalid will find it impossible to enter the city with the Turkish cavalry from Aleppo, unless he is warned and returns swiftly."

Jamil looked surprised as he turned to look at her, for there was a slight smile on her lips as she stared out at the massive army of barbarians.

"I never thought the sight of barbarians could look so gallant," she breathed.

"Antioch will never surrender," Jamil offered. "The barbarians will run out of provisions."

"Yaghi-Sian will also run out of food and water if the siege continues," she said.

"For that to happen, mistress, it must last for months. Maybe an entire year. Our streams are plentiful and run down Mount Silpius. Even in the hot summer the thunderstorms in the dry hills always bring floods to fill our reservoirs. Food is also stored in great quantities in the city, and I have shown you the fields and market gardens. I do not see how the barbarians can maintain a siege."

Helena grew silent. Jamil looked troubled as he studied her face. "The thought of a long siege does not please you, mistress. I had forgotten about Count Redwan. He will be pleased the crusaders have come."

"Yes," she breathed, awed at the sight. "He will be pleased even as I am."

Jamil smiled. "Then I shall be happy too. I shall keep your secret, mistress, and his, but let no one else know how you feel. It will bring wrath upon you. Prince Kalid will surely return for you."

CHAPTER 17

Restrained

So he was trapped like a rabbit! He had been lying wounded and half dazed for the last three days in the house of his enemies — of Helena's enemies. What could he do?

The afternoon sun blazed against the drawn crimson drapes in the silent chamber. Tancred lay there, trying to reason. His sword was gone, but upon awakening, he had found his dagger near his right hand, evidently placed there by Helena. Without his weapons he felt restrained, causing his frustrations to spiral. How could he get out of this dark pit? Danger lurked on every side, and Helena was vulnerable.

His warrior-like will chafed under limitations of physical weakness, and he found it as difficult to endure as the chains that had bound him under the baron.

No! He gritted his teeth. *I refuse to think of defeat. I will survive, live to capture Mosul, and escape with the woman I love.*

Enough of this! Silken sheets! Bedridden like a hand-fed puppy! Even if it was Helena's hand, he did not want this.

Tancred struggled to his elbow, wincing. Helena was even now in danger of Kalid unexpectedly returning from Aleppo, and the days were slipping past. Every movement of his body shouted with pain. He rejected the desire to fall back to the bed. This was no time to give in to the demands of the flesh. He was a warrior who had seen many battles, felt the blow of sword and scimitar, the pain of fist and dagger. He would not give in now to a wound inflicted by a Seljuk! The bleeding had stopped and he was healing. That was sufficient. It had to be, for there was no time for anything else but survival. He must be up and planning. He needed a sword, and he must think.

Tancred grimaced as he threw the covers aside. He muzzled the protest of his flesh. *The pain is nothing,* he told himself. No one had catered to him during his past recoveries. He had managed to endure and he would do so again.

Hitching himself to one elbow, he grasped the arm of the chair and eased his feet onto the rug. For a moment his head swam dizzily, and he broke out into a sweat.

For Helena, he told himself.

With cold determination he managed to walk forward, ignoring the pain and weakness that threatened him. *The pain will not kill me,* he resolved.

Sudden anger swept over him at his uselessness. He had been no help at all to her. How many days had passed? Each day he was incapacitated meant that she must survive by her own wits. He had every confidence in her ability to match wits with Prince Kalid, but wits alone would not restrain Mosul.

Tancred's survival depended upon Mosul not knowing he was here. A scimitar through the heart while asleep would be typical of Mosul's tactics. The fact that he was wounded and defenseless would not deter an assassin. That he still lived could mean but one thing: Mosul did not yet know Tancred Redwan slept in the emir's palace, in Helena's chambers.

How long before the facts dawned upon him? Which of the soldiers had seen Helena in his arms during that precious last moment before the attack? Surely someone could eventually mention it to Mosul or Ma'sud Khan.

He made his way into the next chamber. Helena was not there. It was silent — not even the slaves were present. He was alone. The fact that she might be with Prince Kalid served to strengthen his resolve. "If the Seljuk touches her, Mosul may not be the only man to come to his end."

Hot coals still smoldered in the hearth, and the kettle of boiled meat and broth simmered on dying coals. He knelt upon the hearth cushions and warmed himself, hoping to get his blood surging. The feeling of life seeped through his body, and slowly his mind started to clear. With steady resolve he began to organize his thoughts.

The first thing he did was check his wounds. They were swollen but healing. Helena had done a thorough job, and he owed her his life. He forced himself to eat in order to gain strength. He sat staring at the embers, thinking back to the battle, pondering the whereabouts of Nicholas, Rufus, and Basil. Had they made it back through the gate into the castle? They would tell his uncle what had happened, but there was little Rolf could do to aid him. If anything, they were also trapped inside the Castle of Hohms under siege. Nothing would break that siege but the arrival of the crusading armies under Bohemond and the other princes.

He arose, struggling, and counted his steps across the bedchamber to a door that led into a private bath. Here he took time to rest, satisfied over his progress. If he could make it this far, he could go twice the distance next time, and the next. . . .

A fountain bubbled musically and the sight of greenery was refreshing. He dampened a washcloth and, with difficulty, tried to bathe without twisting and stretching his wounds. He wrapped a towel around his waist and retraced his steps to her chamber. He stopped short.

A slave girl wearing a loose-fitting burnoose stood there, startled at Tancred's appearance. He suddenly remembered who he was supposed to be.

She bowed. "A thousand pardons, Bardas. I am Aziza. Sister to Jamil, whom you shall meet. I did not realize you were up. My mistress said you must rest while your wounds are healing. It is too soon."

"And where is Lady Helena?"

"She is with Jamil. He is showing her Antioch as she tests the Arabian stallion that His Eminence gave her as a wedding gift."

"The prince is very generous."

Trusting his instincts, he tested them further. He needed help and he must take risks. "How does your master know that he can trust this Byzantine woman with his prized Arabian stallion?"

Aziza sucked in her breath. For the first time her eyes came to meet his squarely. Tancred could see that the disrespect he had shown to the woman, whose courage she must have come to admire, brought a spark to her otherwise subservient brown eyes.

"Slave Bardas! Your tongue should be cut out. You dare speak against your mistress after all she has done to save your life? You must not be thus!"

Ah! Pleased to think Helena had already won her respect, his feigned remorse was disarming. "I am repentant — perhaps my mind has been dulled by the physician's powders."

"Yes, Bardas, and you are not yet well. You must rest for your time of recovery and let your wounds heal as your mistress expects."

"I will be honest with you, Aziza. I believe that you can be trusted. I am not Bardas! But first, is it possible for you to bring me some clothes? I am not accustomed to wandering about partially garbed, especially in the women's section of the palace."

Aziza looked at him and swallowed. "You are not Bardas?"

"No —"

She stopped, as though she understood that the man before her could not possibly be a eunuch slave. She blushed, then bowed and murmured as she backed out. "At once, seigneur, at once."

She soon returned with an armload of finery. "It is not wise you dress as a lord. I brought the clothes of a common soldier. I hope they fit — and I found your boots."

"Thank you, they will do well. What of my sword?"

"I am sorry."

"So am I. Please lay the clothes on the bed. After I dress, you must return."

"Yes, seigneur." She turned and left the chamber.

Tancred managed to slip into and buckle the loose-fitting black trousers, much like Moorish finery. He reached for the silk shirt, examining it. *All too much like women's clothing,* he thought, *but it will have to do for now.*

Aziza returned a few minutes later. He saw her study him anew. "I admit you do not appear a slave," she said. "There is courage in your face. It is the confidence of a man who is free of anyone's lordship."

"Aziza, I will trust you with the truth, because I have no choice. If you betray me, it is not only I who shall suffer, but Helena."

"If anyone is aware of such things, it is I. I will say nothing."

"Do you know a certain man who goes by the name of Mosul?"

He saw her go rigid.

"I see you do. I gather you do not appreciate him."

"I hope he is not your friend."

"He is my enemy."

"He is mine also. If Mosul is your enemy too," she said quietly, "then you are my friend. I will do what I can to help you. He has frightened the man I wished to marry. Now he does not leave me in peace. He has asked Prince Kalid if he can have me. Soon I am to become his property."

"Perhaps we can do something about that. I promise Mosul will not live to enslave you."

Aziza's eyes now shone with excitement. "It may please you to know, seigneur, that the army from the West has been seen nearing the Castle of Hohms."

"It pleases me well! You are sure of this?"

"All Antioch is in an uproar. The Seljuk cavalry is on alert. Many archers are seen on the wall and in the towers. The barbarians are said to number a hundred thousand."

"A pretty sight. I will need a sword. Can you get me one?"

"I know nothing of the armory. And I dare not venture there. It is out of bounds for women. Jamil will see to your weaponry when he returns. May I go now, seigneur?"

"Wait . . . my wound makes it needful to

252

have help with my boots. Would you mind?"

Tancred eased himself to the bed and held to the cushions as he stuck out his leg.

She grabbed the boot and knelt before him. "I have read of Norman warriors."

"If you can read, my guess is that you have not always been a slave."

"You are correct. I am Armenian. Both Jamil and I were educated in many things. Before the Seljuk Turks came and ruled Antioch, my father was a prince."

"Ah . . . you bear fine blood, I see. And your movements show wit and determination. You must be very angry to be a princess and yet be treated like a slave."

"I was a child when my parents were killed. At first, I rebelled. But after a whipping and the threat that my brother Jamil would be killed, I soon learned to swallow my pride. Now I do not see myself as anyone but a woman who wishes to be free."

She looked up at him, but his eyes were on the boot of fine cordovan leather. He was scowling because it was stuck, and he could not reach with his hurting arm to pull it on.

"Is it true that Normans eat raw meat?"

His eyes left the boot.

She explained hastily. "Last year when I heard that the emperor of Constantinople had arranged for the Normans to fight the

Turks, I began to read what I could find about them." Her eyes widened. "I have read that each warrior eats one raw pig a day."

"And your historian surely finished a jug of wine before he picked up his quill. Only *one* pig? How disappointing of my brethren."

"I also read that they are ferocious fighters."

"In that, you are correct. The Seljuks would be wise to escape Antioch while they can."

The second boot was on and he stood.

She was still kneeling and looked up at him with wide eyes. "Anything else, seigneur?"

"Yes. Should you learn what the Turkish commander intends to do about the surrender of Antioch, I would like to know," he jested.

"They are prepared for a year's siege."

"That will not discourage Bohemond. He will camp around the wall for two years if need be."

"Will they take Antioch?"

"My guess is that they will. I will give you a word of advice, Aziza."

"Anything, seigneur."

"If they do take the city and soldiers come upon you, ask for Lord Bohemond. Say you are a friend of Tancred Redwan."

"Is that your name?"

"It is. Whatever happens, do not flee into the mosques. They will have no pity on a Moslem, man or woman. Rather, sew a red cross on your bodice and call for their bishop. I believe his name is Adehemar."

"Being Armenian, seigneur, I am of Christian upbringing. The red cross of the crusaders will be easy for me to wear."

She turned to leave but paused. "Forgive my boldness, and rebuke me if you will, but is Lady Helena truly the woman you love?"

Tancred smiled. "She is." His gaze hardened. "We were forced apart by the deceit of enemies. It was against her will that she was brought here to be Prince Kalid's bride. The marriage is to take place as soon as he returns from Aleppo."

"Now I would give you a word of advice, seigneur, if you would let me."

He bowed. "An honor, Princess Aziza. Say on."

She blushed. "If Mosul could manage to become the commander of the bodyguard of Prince Kalid and my mistress, he could then turn against them whenever it befitted his personal plans. A bodyguard such as yourself, loyal to Helena, would get in his way. Knowing his evil mind, he must think these things now. You must be careful."

Tancred thought the same. Mosul would

come to the chamber expecting to find a Byzantine eunuch asleep and unable to defend himself. But "Bardas" would be waiting.

He needed time to recover, but time had not been on his side. If he was to gain a fair chance to escape with Helena, he must use every moment available to outwit them.

"I must send a message to some friends of mine. They are now within the Castle of Hohms. Help me, and in return I vow to reward you when I am free. The house of Redwan is wealthy and powerful in Sicily."

"I wish no jewels. They will do me no good here as a slave. I wish for my freedom, especially from Mosul."

"Then we can help each other. Mosul, I will most gladly take care of. As for your freedom, I will do what I can."

"The friends you mention, would they be Byzantines? For I have heard that Byzantines cannot be trusted. However," she hastened, "I beg you, do not repeat my suggestion to my mistress."

Tancred's amusement touched his eyes. "Your secret is mine. But in fairness to the Byzantines, there are a few good soldiers about. And a few excellent servants of Christ as well. Bishop Nicholas Lysander for one. The friends I mentioned are at the Castle of

Hohms. Will you send the message?"

"I would go at once, but it is hopeless. I have tried before to escape. Mosul watches me. As for my brother, Jamil, he might be able to slip past the guards. But the postern gate near the slope of the city leads into the mountains. To backtrack and reach the Castle of Hohms would take five or six days."

Tancred remembered the small, seldom-used gate that he had discovered when he studied the drawing of Antioch at the Royal Library.

"The Armenian shepherds use it to bring in goats and cheese. Here, seigneur, look for yourself." She hurried across the chamber and drew aside the crimson drapes. "Do you see the upper portion of Antioch where the wall ends up near the mountains? The postern gate is behind the Great Tower. Sometimes it is guarded with fewer than six soldiers."

Tancred stared out the window, considering that half-forgotten mountain trail. By now, if Yaghi-Sian were the soldier he thought him to be, he would have guards watching that gate for spies. He also knew how steep and rugged those hills and mountains were. Escape by such a route would be impossible until he recovered.

He was more tired and weak than he had

thought, and he leaned against the wall, peering out the latticed window. Then, controlling his impatience, he turned back to Aziza. "I must send a message to the Castle of Hohms. In Sicily, messages are sent from castle to castle by pigeons or falcon. Have you anything like this here?"

"Oh yes, we use both."

"Do you have access?"

"Jamil does. He trains falcons."

"Ah . . . send for him."

"Seigneur? Is your bravery typical of the knights of the West?"

"Normans," he said distinctly and with gravity, "are not 'typical.' There are no warriors worthy to compare ourselves with." He remained straight-faced, and Aziza appeared to believe him. He went on. "But there is one thing you can do just to make certain I live through the night."

"Yes?"

"My sword," he repeated and bowed lightly. He held up his dagger. "It will be difficult to face my enemies with only this."

Her eyes widened, and she bowed and hurried out.

Wearily he sank onto the divan. If things went as he planned, a message would be sent to Nicholas to expect the caravan with Kalid coming from Aleppo. If the prince could be

258

abducted, Tancred's work here in Antioch would leave only Mosul and Kalid's indomitable uncle, Ma'sud Khan. Ma'sud was older but a rare warrior. He was the last one Tancred wished to confront. He respected him.

Hopefully, the swords of Rufus and the others would not be far away to back up his own. He thought of Cousin Leif and Hakeem. Were they safe?

Against his will, his eyes shut on their own. . . .

Startled to wakefulness by a stealthy hand on his arm, Tancred reached and grasped a wrist and whirled it aside, his dagger flashing from its invisible hiding place.

Jamil sat sprawled on the rug. His mouth was open and he blinked. He remained where he was, stunned by Tancred's swift reaction.

Tancred was on his elbow, holding the dagger, and looking down upon a slim boy. Jamil's brown eyes were wide, and the awestruck expression on his face turned suddenly to a pleased smile. "Master, that was well done!"

Tancred arched a brow and scanned him. The boy was obviously in love with soldiers and the art of war. "I am glad you approve," he said dryly.

"Oh yes, *well* done!" he repeated, and scrambled to his sandaled feet and rendered a low bow. "Jamil, at your service, master." He straightened. "Master," he ventured thoughtfully, "if I were an enemy, you would have been able to take me." He pointed to his throat.

"No — not your neck, your bottom!" Tancred declared, greatly annoyed at having been startled awake. "If you ever try anything like that again, I promise you I will put you across my knees and deliver several swift and painful raps."

The boy appeared chagrined.

"First lesson," Tancred lectured, "never sneak up on a man in his sleep."

"My humble apology, master!" Jamil scowled, his pride injured. "I only wished to test how a warrior protects himself when —"

"Secondly, never play games with a man who has a weapon and expects an assassin."

"Yes, master, I see. . . ."

Tancred relaxed and wanted to smile at the boy's earnestness, but he kept his demeanor stern. "Anything else you wish to know since you now have me awake and alert?"

Jamil took his offer seriously. "The use of the sword, and can you use a scimitar? Here

— I have one, see? It is excellent. I managed to take it from the armory this morning. Try it! See what you think —"

Tancred snatched it from his hand and laid it on the bed, eying Jamil carefully.

Seeing that look, Jamil proceeded more cautiously. "And . . . I have many questions to ask — about the training of falcons. Aziza, my sister, tells me you have sent for me?"

"Your mind is very busy," Tancred said.

"Yes, master. There is so much to learn and so little time. I am all of fourteen now. The sun hastens its setting."

"Suppose, for the moment, we get to the reason I called for you."

"As you wish." He bowed.

"Your sister told you why I sent for you?"

Jamil stepped forward and whispered, "The falcon is ready to soar. Such a falcon! The hour is now. Mosul is occupied with the Turkish commander."

Tancred rubbed his chin to hide his smile. "I see you are also adept at intrigue."

"That you would think so pleases me well."

"Good. Here is the message. I'll trust you with it. Send it to the Castle of Hohms. Should the task go ill, do not risk being caught. Destroy it."

"I will swallow it."

Jamil stuffed the bit of paper into his tunic. "It is done. But before I go, I have something for you." Jamil's eyes shone in hero worship. "Wait here, master."

"I will surely wait."

Jamil ran from the chamber and returned, proudly bearing Tancred's sword. "A warrior must not be without his sword." He smiled, pleased with himself.

"Ah! Where did you manage to get it?"

"It was easy. When they first brought you to the barracks, you were unconscious. There was much confusion. I saw the Norman insignia on the sword," he whispered. "They kept saying you were a Byzantine, but I guessed differently because of the falcon." He beamed a smile. "I have studied about the Conqueror. A valiant man, master."

"Well done, Jamil! Did anyone else see it?"

"As I told Lady Helena, I made sure no one saw it. It has been hidden behind the drape."

Tancred scanned him cautiously. "How much do you know about me and your mistress?"

"Everything," he stated proudly.

"Such a clever young warrior will undoubtedly expect me to reward him for keeping it a secret. What is your reward?"

Jamil did not hesitate. His eyes gleamed.

"If you do escape and return to Sicily, I will go with you. You will train me to be a great warrior like yourself, and when I become a man and am strong, I will be your bodyguard."

Tancred was drawn to him at once. He measured the boy. For one so young, he certainly knew what he wanted. Tancred pretended to be serious. "I will consider it. We will discuss it when we have time. Your parents may have something to say about —"

Jamil interrupted. "My parents are dead. Killed by the Seljuks. I have only Aziza, and she, too, wishes to escape. You will take me to Sicily with you? *Please,* master!"

Tancred had no wish to turn the boy into a warring soldier. "The ways of a scholar are better than the ways of a warrior."

"Nay! I shall be both," he suggested jubilantly.

Tancred pulled at Jamil's sash. "We will see at the right time. Now go. See if you can be as successful at sending the falcon as you were in retrieving my sword."

His jaw set and the brown eyes grew restless. "I will do as you wish."

Tancred scowled as though he had gotten more than he bargained for, but after a long moment he smiled. "Very well. You may come with us. But there is no guarantee, until Helena and I are free. Understand? Our success now depends on the message reaching the Castle of Hohms. I have friends there."

"My life for yours, master. I will not fail you, no matter the cost."

CHAPTER 18

Mosul

Helena ran swiftly down the wide hall toward
her chambers, anxious to tell Tancred about
the postern gate, and that with the arrival of
the western crusaders, they must be prepared to make their escape soon. When she
and Jamil had returned from their ride, Aziza
had been waiting at the stables to inform
Helena that Tancred urgently needed Jamil
to send a message. While the boy ran ahead,
Helena talked further with Aziza, wanting to
know all the details of her conversation with
Tancred.

So Tancred knew! She must hurry. They
must plan their escape. Yet how was such an
attempt even possible? Could Tancred hope
to confront the guards at the gate when he
was so weak? Not to mention the difficulty
he would have in traversing the steep mountain trail.

Reaching her chamber door, Helena sped

through it noiselessly, shutting it behind her and sliding the heavy bolt into place. She sank against it to catch her breath.

The chambers were in semidarkness, for the crimson drapes were drawn. Embers burned in the hearth, and she heard nothing but her own breathing.

Grabbing up her silk skirt, she rushed across the room to Tancred's chamber, then stopped abruptly. The empty bed stared at her. Gone! Tancred was gone!

Had Mosul found out who he was and seized him? Or . . . the unthinkable gripped her with fear . . . had he already killed him?

Her insides gave a queer little jerk. She gasped and now held a hand to her side where a sharp pain jabbed.

For a moment she remained where she was, dazed, and then a small cry slipped through her lips.

The little sob became a stilted choke, her throat cramped with pain, and her tightened fist came up against her mouth. For an endless moment Helena stood frigid, unable to move. She fought with herself, trying to control the emotion tightening inside her breast. She backed out slowly and, finding herself near the cushions by the hearth, slipped to her knees with a sob. Mosul!

"Dare I hope this emotion is spent for me?"

Her head jerked up, and Tancred stood there. His presence struck with the impact of a blow. Alive! Aside from the opening in the shirt where the bandage showed, he did not look ill. He wore the garments of the East — full black trousers and a silk shirt with wide sleeves, drawn tight at the wrist. His sword was belted on, and he appeared to be the capable warrior she remembered. He bowed low at the waist.

"As your faithful eunuch slave, I am delighted to see you again, my mistress."

She was so relieved that she forgot all else, even the suggested amusement of his greeting, and for a moment she only stared, feasting her eyes upon him. Surely he was everything any woman would want.

"Refreshment, mistress?" Exaggerating every condescending move, he waited on her with finesse. He tasted the cup first, as if checking for poison. He brought it to her where she sat on the cushions and bowed again deeply. "Your humble slave, madam. How else shall your servant please you?"

She laughed and in a few steps was in his arms. "I like you better as a Norman warrior, as long as you are mine."

He met her gaze, and the brittle blue of his

eyes melted into longing as his arms closed about her. "Have you no greeting to bestow?"

She pretended to grab a hot coal from the hearth and held it to his heart. "There! My image is now branded forever!"

He took her hand and pulled her toward him again. "Your image was branded there from the moment I first saw you. Do you know how frightening that was to a warrior who once wished no bonds, no ties?"

"And now?" she whispered.

"Now?" He leaned toward her. "I am forever bound to you, and I would have it no other way."

Her eyes were warm as they caressed his handsome face. He reached and took hold of a strand of her dark hair, then pulled softly until her face came toward his. He kissed her.

"Tancred, I am afraid. Mosul is here. How can you face him? He will kill you!"

"Nay . . . soon I will be stronger. We will escape, and if we must, we will disappear into Persia, even Cathay. Anywhere, as long as I have you."

Their lips met again and they never tired of their sweetness.

"An hour with you is but a moment," he said.

"Surely we will have many tomorrows."

"I will not risk you on the hope of tomorrow. With the arrival of the feudal lords at hand, there will be war. If we wait until the siege, it may take months to escape Antioch. We must leave soon. I've sent a message to the castle by way of Jamil's falcon. If Hakeem is there, he will bring word to Nicholas to ambush Kalid's entourage coming from Aleppo. That will leave only Mosul to deal with." He walked over to the window. "Are you sure Mosul suspects nothing?"

She was not certain. "Even if he does not, what of the soldiers? Some saw us together before the battle."

"Yes, and sooner or later one may mention it." He turned toward her, his face set. "He will come here — and I will be waiting. In the meantime you will learn all you can of what is going on in the palace. There may be something that will help us and the Normans to take the city. I never thought your Byzantine intrigue would be of advantage to me, but I was wrong."

"There may be something," she said thoughtfully. "Jamil mentioned an Armenian named Firouz. He serves Yaghi-Sian, but he is displeased."

"An Armenian? He could be a Christian. It

may be important. See what else you can learn."

Through the following days Helena kept informed of the military situation in Antioch and of the battles raging outside the walls. Each morning she sent Jamil throughout the city to spy on the Turkish command, and toward evening he would return to report all that he had learned. In turn, Helena reported to Tancred.

As Tancred listened, she told him how the Seljuks launched night attacks against the crusaders by slipping through the Bridge Gate near the Orontes River.

"I could get through that gate with them — if I had the uniform of a Seljuk."

"You must not," she pleaded. "It is too dangerous."

But he seemed not to hear her, or at least behaved as though he had not.

"They sent a barrage of arrows into the lighted tents of the crusaders and made short raids through their camps," she told him.

"What of Hakeem? Any news?"

"No. He must be with Uncle Nicholas. Perhaps they remain at the castle."

"And the Normans? How are they holding out?"

"They have run out of food, except for the

wagons of supplies the villagers and monks brought in to sell at outrageous prices. Only the wealthier knights can buy. They hope for relief from St. Symeon."

"Ah, Rainald! May his Genoese fight valiantly. What else have you learned of Firouz?"

"Nothing more, unfortunately."

"Still, he holds possibilities. If he is outraged over treatment to his wife, there is a chance he may help us. In our situation we cannot be choosy. Can you get Jamil to watch her?"

"Yes, but what do you expect to find out?"

"That remains to be seen. Tell Jamil I want to know whom she sees, when and where. He will be rewarded in Sicily."

She folded her arms. "And I thought *I* was the Byzantine."

Later that day she met with Jamil near the stables, and they rode toward the hills as was their custom. During these rides he would report to her what he had learned and receive his new orders. His winsome brown eyes were expectant.

"Learn as much about his wife as you can," Helena said, noting the boy's disappointed expression. She knew he preferred to loiter among the soldiers or cavalry to pick up bits of information on battles.

She went on. "I have learned that Firouz is busy with Yaghi-Sian at a dinner tonight. Many will be there, and I, too, am required. Do not let his wife out of your sight."

He lifted his chin bravely. "I understand, mistress."

"Report back to me or Tancred as soon as you have information. Do not be seen. If you are caught, tell no one what I asked you to do."

"I will not be seen. But what of you? Will you be at the banquet?"

"I must go. Asad requires it of me. The emir has requested my presence. Something is happening, but I do not know what."

She looked at him. Tancred had told her that Bardas was dead. It would become easy to transfer her affections to the slim boy with fine features and brown eyes. He was also clever like Bardas, though of course not as strong. He took lessons daily with the scimitar, and she felt he would one day be important to her and Tancred.

"Take care," she whispered. "You are in our hearts."

He smiled shyly. "I will, mistress."

They rode back toward the city and as they neared the incline, seeking to avoid the

Tower, Helena saw a group of soldiers. One of them recognized her and hurried to sound the news. Jamil was troubled. "I fear we will soon have company, mistress."

He was right. In a few minutes three Seljuks rode toward them. A fourth man was with them who looked to be in command. He wore the uniform of an officer and was sitting on an Arabian horse.

Jamil recognized him and hissed a warning: "Beware, it is Mosul."

Mosul! Helena prepared her emotions for the confrontation. Whatever her reaction, she must not show fear.

Mosul rode up the slope and halted his horse abruptly, causing the animal to toss back his head. Helena found her path blocked by the brutal young man. He was strong and swarthy, with sharp black eyes like a hawk and a well-trimmed beard. He bore the blood of arrogance, the insidious intentions of a man planning his climb to authority.

Dressed in light armor and wearing a dark cloak, his eyes swept Helena again. The black eyes were cold and unrelenting but glinted with an awareness of her beauty that seemed to penetrate her tunic.

Helena refused to waver.

"You are in our way, Captain. Is it customary to detain the future bride of Prince Kalid?"

Mosul bowed low in the saddle, every expression in contradiction to this polite gesture.

"Your Loveliness, I am quite aware of who you are, and I have been out searching for you since the slave admitted you had left your chambers for the stables."

Her first anxious thought was whether Mosul had been inside her chambers.

"I am under orders to guard you," he said.

Guard *her!* The news could not have been more devastating.

"And whose orders are those?"

"His Eminence, your future bridegroom."

She noted a slight tone of mockery in his voice. "He has returned, then?"

"The orders were given, Highness, before he departed. I had thought you knew of them, that Ma'sud Khan had informed you yesterday."

"He did not. Your services are not needed, Captain. I have my own bodyguard."

His mouth showed impatience. "Until the Byzantine eunuch has recovered, I am your bodyguard. From henceforth, Highness, may I suggest you go nowhere unless I am notified."

"Am I a prisoner, then?" she asked coolly.

He ignored the pert question. "It is for your safety. I am sworn to it. And now that the prince has returned with Kerbogha, he has been searching for you. Tonight there is a banquet in your honor and his."

"Kalid . . . is here . . . in Antioch?" She gripped the reins.

He smiled. "I see you are pleased, Highness."

How had Jamil failed to hear of his return?

"But how? The siege! The walls are surrounded by the crusaders —"

"There is a route from Antioch no one knows of except the royal family and military commanders. Nothing will stop Kalid."

Her heart turned cold. She must be careful not to show her dismay to Mosul.

"He is upset over your disappearance. You should not have ridden off."

She found her voice at last. "There was no need for alarm, nor for searching my chambers, as though I am some slave."

"Your chambers were not searched, Your Loveliness. But the next time you wish to ride the prized Arabian stallion, I, not Jamil, will escort you. Yet there is little time for that now. Matters have changed."

What did he mean? She felt her muscles tense. Both of Tancred's enemies were now in the city.

Mosul looked past her up the rocky slope. "What were you doing near the Tower?"

"She wished to see all of Antioch," Jamil hastened. "The view overlooked the palace."

"Are there not more worthy sights than half-starved barbarians? The coliseum built by the Byzantine emperor Justinian would surely be of more interest to the heritage of your mistress. There is nothing up the slope but dry rock . . . and a postern gate," he suggested, his eyes coming back to Helena. He measured her.

The gate Kalid and Kerbogha would come through? She said nothing and sat straight in her saddle.

"You, Jamil, know better than to ride near the Tower."

Jamil turned mute. In fear that Jamil would do something rash, she maneuvered her Arabian stallion between the boy and Mosul.

"His Eminence, the grandfather of Kalid, made it clear to me on my arrival that I am not a prisoner in Antioch. Therefore, I do not see why it is any of your affair what I do, or where I choose to ride with my slave."

Mosul's smile was unpleasant. He seemed to enjoy her resistance. "As I have explained, Prince Kalid has made me your guard. I am under orders to carry out his will until he returns. He has sent me to bring you to his chambers. There has been an unexpected change in plans."

Helena's heart pounded. What change could this be? Did they know Tancred was here?

"I dare not suggest how upset His Eminence is at your disappearance."

"Disappearance! I took my Arabian for a ride. Have you forgotten it was he who gave me the horse as a wedding gift? Am I not intended to ride him?"

Mosul's eyes were steady. "I dare not say how angry he will be when he discovers you bribed your slave boy to bring you to the postern gate leading into the mountains — he may consider making you a prisoner."

Helena felt a dart of fear where there had been none the moment before. Mosul was not an easy man to come up against. He was testing her out — she could sense that much — trying to intimidate her. Did he know about Tancred, or was he simply hoping to find a weakness he could extort for his gain?

She had her first glimpse of the nature of the man Tancred had trailed for four years — a relentless man, who had planned his brother's death in Palermo and managed to make Tancred the accused.

Mosul turned to Jamil. "This could mean

trouble for you. And for your sister, Aziza. Tell her to come to me tonight if she will save herself from punishment."

Jamil's eyes clouded. "Aziza has done nothing wrong. If there is punishment rendered, let it be mine, Commander Mosul."

Helena's anger was kindled. She had faced too long the intrigue of Lady Irene to surrender to the intimidation of Mosul's threats. Only one thing frightened her: that he would learn of Tancred. She was sure he did not know. When facing an enemy, one must never permit him to back you into a corner. Countermoves were essential, and courage came second.

"If there is any punishment to be rendered to my slaves, Captain, I will be the judge of that. You are not Jamil's master, nor Aziza's. You are not to lay a hand on either the boy or his sister. Is that clear? If you go against my wishes, I will go to His Eminence at once and plead charges against you. Do not forget that I will soon be his bride. As such, you will honor my requests. If not, I will have you replaced immediately."

Whether or not she could have him removed from his position was doubtful, but he must think she would try.

Mosul's hard face was immobile, but the black eyes glinted with temper. Helena lifted her chin and added with authority, "As for this *gate* you make so much of — are your Seljuk guards so weak that I and my slave boy could take away their weapons? Do you fear we shall flee like frightened goats into the mountains? I am here in Antioch to stay. And know this: once I become the emir's daughter-in-law, I will plot my own climb to power. Make sure, Mosul, that you do not get in my way. Not if you wish to survive, or prosper."

Mosul studied her, as though he understood she would not be as easy to intimidate as the others, including the slave girl Aziza.

Helena hoped he might think that by cooperating with her, his position in Antioch would be more secure.

She sat astride the Arabian stallion as the picture of ambition and determination. The lovely face bore the expression of authority, and the wind tossed her raven hair like the mane of a wild stallion bent on its freedom.

Mosul bowed his black head. "No threat intended, Your Loveliness. Perhaps I was too hasty in my remarks."

"Perhaps, indeed."

"His Eminence is upset; you can imagine how he feels. As I am held accountable for your safety, I was a little too harsh with Jamil.

279

If you will permit, I will now escort you to Prince Kalid."

Helena turned cold on the inside. What would she say? What if he knew? "Very well."

Mosul turned in his saddle to Jamil. "As for you, count yourself favored. His Eminence has heard of your way with falcons. He wishes to see a demonstration of the hunt this afternoon."

Jamil brightened, and there was more in his eyes than Mosul could understand. Helena guessed he wished the opportunity to use the falcon to send another message for Tancred.

"I am honored, Commander Mosul." He turned to Helena, his eyes shining. "I have long awaited such a moment, mistress. May I go to the field?"

Her throat felt dry. She feared for both Jamil and Tancred.

"You may go," she said. "But remember the banquet tonight. I expect to see you there," she said, meaning far more than simply telling him his services as a slave were expected.

"I will remember, mistress."

Mosul warned Jamil, "If I were you, I would make sure your falcon returns with the hare."

"I learned the art from the best falcon trainers in the world, the Normans. He will return with the hare."

Helena tensed. Mosul's response to the mention of the Normans caused an unexpected glint in his eyes.

"It is because of the Normans that Prince Kalid wishes to see you," said Mosul. He then gestured to the three men with him, who fell in around Helena. Mosul rode in front.

They rode slowly away from the trail, then threaded their way down the slope of the long hill. As they neared the section of the great wall that overlooked the wide plain below Antioch, Mosul lifted his hand.

Far in the distance, securely built on a rocky hill, the gray stone walls of the Castle of Hohms dominated the plain. A stab of anxiety penetrated her heart. Was her mother safe? Had she given birth yet to Sinan's child? Tancred had said that Constantine was dead. Had he been hallucinating the night he had told her so? And Nicholas — was he within the castle's wall, or had he made it back to the camp of Bohemond with the other friends of Tancred? Even so, what could they do to aid them within the city?

Helena stared off into the heated plain.

The azure sky was clear, and the distant hills were humped like resting brown camels. She gazed upon a multitude of warriors: Normans, Franks, Rhinelanders, and Italians.

Mosul's look was unpleasant. "If you hope to escape marriage to Prince Kalid by the fall of Antioch, you will be disappointed."

"What makes you think I wish to escape marriage to Prince Kalid?" she asked innocently.

He threw back his black head and laughed rudely.

"Your Loveliness, there are few who do not know about your dedication to the noble Philip Lysander and how he tried to rescue you near Athens. And Nicholas came for you in the camp of the Red Lion. Your mother was Adrianna, the wife of Sinan — and she now abides in the Castle of Hohms to give birth to his son. Do you think the family of Emir Khan does not know this, and has not made plans to take the child to his grandfather in Baghdad?"

So he knew more than she had thought. "Sinan is dead. And my mother will never surrender her child to Emir Khan."

He shrugged. "It is not my concern, Highness. I have plans of my own. I do not care if you love Philip Lysander, or how much you loathe Kalid. I simply go about my duties as his bodyguard."

"And your loyalties? Where do they rest, with Kalid or the family of Sinan?"

He smiled coolly. "Perhaps with you, Highness."

She knew he lied, and she pretended to consider. "So you know I do not love Prince Kalid?"

"When a woman is forced by guards from the Castle of Hohms to attend her wedding, what is there left to think? And your bodyguard Bardas fought fifty Turks to try to release you. He was wholeheartedly loyal and has the markings of a true warrior. A shame he will not be traveling with you to Aleppo."

For the first time she could not conceal her alarm. He was cautiously informing her of new plans. She could not go to Aleppo and leave Tancred injured and trapped in her chambers! She felt the color drain from her cheeks as she contemplated the meaning of his words. She was to be sent from Antioch! What did this mean?

"Aleppo?"

His smile was wolfish. "The siege of Antioch will be long and costly. Prince Kalid has no intention of becoming trapped here. He will leave the city to meet the sultan of Aleppo in the morning. You, of course, will accompany him. Your bodyguard is not fit for the ordeal. He will remain here under my supervision until we can join you. That is, Your Loveliness, if you still insist that I do not take his place."

Overwhelming dismay numbed her brain.

He had to have seen her consternation. His teeth flashed against his swarthy face. "Fear not, Your Loveliness. My sword will ever be ready to protect you. I will prove as faithful to you as waning Bardas. It may be I can help you."

Helena recovered her affected confidence. Now what? There was no way out. She was leaving for Aleppo in the morning. That left no time for anything. And Tancred would be left to Mosul while he was still incapacitated.

Mosul gestured toward the hot plain. "Look upon the warriors for the last time, Your Loveliness. Soon your caravan will be ready, and you will see them no more."

CHAPTER 19

Intrigue at the Banquet

Mosul escorted her through a cool garden, past a black wrought-iron gate into a courtyard where a fountain splashed. She hesitated.

"This way, Highness."

She passed through a double-arched colonnade with small inlaid lapis-lazuli-colored tiles and entered a shadowed room where there were brocaded divans and tables veined with gold. Several slaves appeared. Mosul spoke to them in low Arabic. Her tension grew.

"Where is Kalid?" she inquired when the slaves bowed toward him and left.

Mosul's smile was cool. "His Eminence has sent a message. He regrets he cannot come at this moment but will see you tonight at the banquet."

"Then I will return to my chambers."

"His Eminence has left instructions you

are to wait here until tonight."

Fear gripped her heart. "I cannot stay here! What of my wardrobe, my bodyguard —"

"You will be provided with everything you need, Highness. Simply ring the cord on the drape for a slave."

"Then I am a prisoner here, is that it?" she demanded, trying to veil her alarm. How would she get back to warn Tancred that Kalid was in Antioch? Perhaps she was being kept here under guard to hinder her from doing so. Then did Kalid know Tancred was here? Did Mosul?

"Not a prisoner, Highness — a guest, the soon-to-be bride of His Eminence."

She believed he was lying. Was Prince Kalid even here? What if he were still in Aleppo? What if this maneuver was instigated by Mosul to keep her away from Tancred while he was being arrested or assassinated?

She feared she should not have come here so meekly. What now? She must not let him know she suspected him.

"Very well. When will I be brought to the banquet?"

"Tonight. Either I or a guard will come to escort you."

She watched him leave, hearing the unmistakable clink of a key inside a lock on the wrought-iron gate in the garden.

So then. She was trapped.

Despair welled up within her. What *could* she do? Scream? Bang on the chamber door? And who would hear or pay heed? She ran to the door on the other side of the chamber and tried the latch. Locked. Of course it would be. He would have seen to that. Most likely these slaves were in submission to Mosul, or he wouldn't have brought her here. Jamil knew she had been taken away by Mosul to supposedly meet with Kalid, but how long before he returned from the hunt with the falcons? It may be hours before Tancred knew what had happened. But even so, what could he do? He dare not show himself in the palace lest he be recognized. Would she even be brought to the banquet?

A worse thought troubled her. What if Mosul told the truth about Kalid's presence? Kalid may have plans to have Mosul and his personal soldiers help them escape through the hills to bring them to Aleppo! Tancred could be attacked and she would yet become Kalid's bride!

She looked about her wildly. She must escape and warn Tancred, but *how?* She must think calmly. She'd been in equally danger-ous situations before and by the grace of God had survived. She must not sink into a pit of hopelessness. She must pray. "Ask, seek, and knock," she told herself in the gloom. If she trusted Him, if she applied herself to the task, then perhaps she would think of some way out of her dilemma. "Not for me only, but Tancred. And Jamil and Aziza!"

She paced like a trapped cat, head in hands, her heart crying out to the God she believed in, even while hopelessness assailed her soul.

First of all, Tancred was no fool. Though injured, he remained a warrior, and he had his weapons. He had already anticipated that Mosul would eventually learn who he was and would come to place a dagger in his heart. Tancred would not be taken off guard. And when she did not show, he would be wise enough to guess something had happened that she had no control over. Surely he would make plans. He would be waiting for Jamil or Aziza. They would tell him of the banquet, of the arrival of Kalid, and how she had been taken away by Mosul to meet Kalid in his chambers.

Tancred paced in Helena's chamber while Jamil stood quietly and watched him. Night had fallen on the city of Antioch and danger was closing in; he could sense it with each beat of his heart. There was little time. Jamil had succeeded in sending the message to Hakeem by falcon, but it would prove of no avail now, not if Kalid was in the city.

"You saw him?" Tancred persisted in his questioning of the boy. "You are certain?"

"I thought as you do now," Jamil replied. "I said to myself, 'Ah, Mosul lies when he tells my mistress the prince is here.' So I made certain by asking Asad, who is much upset over the banquet tonight. He affirmed it was so. Then I *saw* Kalid walking with the emir. Ma'sud joined them."

"How had he gained access to the city?"

"By the secret route in the hills known only to the royal family."

"And tonight he is at a banquet?"

"Yes, and Aziza learned my mistress will go there. All will be there. Yaghi-Sian, Commander Kerbogha, Prince Kalid — the emir himself."

What was Mosul up to? Dare Tancred risk going himself? Could he masquerade as some unexpected Turkish official sent by one of the caliphs about the security of Antioch? Not likely, for Mosul and Kalid both would be there and would recognize him at once.

"The banquet, when does it begin?"

"Soon!"

Tancred took hold of the boy's shoulders. "Your mistress is in danger. Yet if plans are in the making for the royal family to escape from Antioch with her, it is not likely they will do so tonight. That gives me a little time to think, to make plans of our own. Nevertheless, it is essential you watch her at the banquet, understood?"

"Yes, master!"

"And that goes for Aziza and the other slaves loyal to our cause. Do not let Helena out of your sight. One of you must watch her at all times." From beneath his shirt he pulled out the drawing of the palace and its environs and spread it on the table. "I want you to look at this and tell me if it is accurate. Take your time. It is very important, Jamil. Show me where Helena is being kept by Mosul. Are there any unused paths or gates or chambers nearby in which I might conceal myself?"

Jamil looked at the drawing with amazement on his face. "Where did you get this?"

"Never mind. What do you think of it? Is it accurate?"

"Well done, master. Except — we are *here*, and the chambers Mosul brought my mistress to are on the other side of the palace — *here*. And this is a path through the back garden winding by the slave quarters and the orchard. The emir's guards do not come this way often. And tonight they will be busy at the banquet. I come and go this way all the time. There are many trees and bushes to duck in and out of if someone comes. And over here — is a storage room full of wine."

"Good." Tancred folded the drawing and replaced it inside his shirt, then took the boy's arm and propelled him toward the door. "Watch your mistress. See what news you can pick up among the slaves and guests, but whatever you do, be cautious. If we lose you, we lose our best opportunity of escaping."

Jamil's eyes shone with pride. "I will not fail you, Count Redwan," he whispered. "We will yet escape to Sicily."

Tancred smiled briefly and tousled his hair. "Go, then. I will wait here until the moon sets. Be sure you return by then with whatever information you have gleaned."

Outside the palace, bright moonlight illuminated the darkness. Yet Jamil reminded himself that he must return to the Norman before the moon set. The open colonnade with its wide steps lined with trees eased down into a very large garden that was walled and guarded. Haunting music wafted on the breeze, and soft lantern light fell across the path winding through scented shrubs and vines.

Ahead, important guests from Antioch moved about with the rustle of garments; low voices and laughter floated to him. He made his way silently through the garden toward the banqueting court. He darted here and there concealed, a slim figure in his dark tunic. He went across the court, avoiding the guards on patrol. Flaring torches revealed soldiers near the gate towers and on the wall. He saw horses waiting, and he hurried on to another section of the palace grounds.

Here he entered a magical world. Dozens of colored lanterns splashed their soft light upon the scented garden like a myriad of prisms. He now heard clearly the lilting voice that sang a song of enchantment while guests talked. The spring moon shone silver in a clear sky. He hid in the trees, watching the guests move freely about the garden. The talk was cheerful, and the aroma of rich foods made his stomach growl. He remembered the crusaders, camped on the barren plain so close by. They were without supplies. Sickness and death prowled outside the walls of the city like starving dogs.

Here, in this beautiful sanctuary, war was not a reality. Here, gardens were sweet and green as slaves moved silently on bare feet.

Jamil's wide dark eyes peeped through the oleander bushes and saw his mistress. She was lovely in a shimmering dress of a Moslem princess as she strolled with Prince Kalid Khan. From her face he could not guess her fears, nor that she was unhappy with her fate. He admired her confidence, her courage to behave as though she had made peace with her destiny to become the bride of the emir's grandson.

They paused in their stroll among the guests as another man approached. Jamil recognized Yaghi-Sian, the son of the Red Lion. His physical presence belonged to that of a seasoned fighter who was hardened to suffering and death, his features bronzed by sun and weather. A fixed smile was on his lips. Several armed guards were behind him. At his side stood another official who appeared to be of Armenian blood. The Armenian's expression was one of stifled hatred; his eyes were fixed on Mosul. Jamil knew he was struggling with his own bitterness while acting out his official duties.

"I bring news from your friend, the Byzantine general Taticus," Yaghi-Sian was saying. "The words he brings are important to you as well as to Prince Kalid."

The group walked across the courtyard toward a long table where food was heaped high. Jamil crept through the garden foliage to follow.

The sight of so much food surprised him. Antioch itself was now facing a shortage of supplies. Was this a show, meant to convince Taticus of their security? There were skewers of many and various meats. Jamil recognized lamb, and there were small roasted fowl, all hot and fragrant, being spread with various sauces by the artful hands of slaves. There were many other unusual dishes as well as the finest of wine, dried fruits, nuts, and a Syrian dessert made from fruit and almonds in bite-sized morsels.

Jamil licked his lips, staring. He heard his mistress say, "General Taticus is here in Antioch? Why did you not bring him as a guest, Kalid?"

"The general cannot risk entering the city for fear that Bohemond might see him."

"He is with the Normans, then? Did the emperor send him?"

"Yes, to negotiate, even as they did with Nicaea."

"In secret?"

"How else? The Norman barbarians would kill him if they knew what he was planning. If Antioch falls, it must fall to the Byzantines. If the barbarians take the city, blood will flow in the streets. If necessary we will make a bargain with General Taticus, but we do not fear the barbarians. They will soon starve and scatter —"

Jamil's attention was drawn away. Emerging from out of the trees behind him was the Armenian named Firouz and his wife. She was in tears and looked angry. Firouz spoke in a low tone that Jamil could not hear. He watched as the Armenian took his wife by the arm and ushered her away.

Suddenly Jamil remembered what his mistress had told him to do earlier. The opportunity was ripe to overhear something important.

His eyes became slits as he pondered his actions. He glanced back at his mistress, who looked composed as she nibbled on dainties and listened to the conversation between Prince Kalid and Yaghi-Sian.

Jamil frowned. What should he do? Count Redwan had told him not to let Helena out of his sight. He looked back over his shoulder. Firouz and his wife were getting away.

But the Norman and Helena had also told him to spy on Firouz, saying it could be very important! He already knew Firouz hated the Seljuk military commanders.

Jamil made up his mind. Nothing appeared to be endangering his mistress at the moment, and so . . .

He slipped through the trees as silently as a wisp of wind and pursued the retreating footsteps of the Armenian and his weeping wife. Tonight he would be sure to hear something worthy of reporting to the Norman.

Helena watched for an opportunity. When the unguarded moment presented itself, she snatched it and was able to slip away unnoticed from the banquet and merge into the acacia trees.

She rushed through the garden toward the back of the palace and paused there to glance in all directions. Behind her, music from the *qitara* played on the warm wind. Her heart continued its pounding. Were guards on patrol ahead? Could she reach her chamber to warn Tancred?

She moved ahead, but a voice reached out to stop her. "It is good I have found you. His Eminence wonders where you have gone."

Helena looked in the direction of the voice.

Mosul stood in the shadows of some shrubs, his black eyes sharp and cold. Several soldiers were behind him. He bowed.

Helena tensed. How long had he been watching her from the shadows? Did he see her escape from the banquet?

There was something in his eyes. Suspicion?

"I was seeking my slave," Helena said. "Since you locked me in a chamber other than my own all day, I wish to inquire on the health of my bodyguard. Does that meet with your approval?" she asked coolly.

"Your thoughtfulness is noteworthy, Highness. Such concern for a eunuch slave is indeed rare."

"I think not," she quipped. "It is a matter of my own safety which concerns me. Bardas has been tested and tried in many dangers." She scanned him. "I would find it difficult to trust another bodyguard, even if he does serve the prince."

Mosul's white teeth showed in what resembled a smile.

"I assure you, Highness, by sword or scimitar, I am your faithful servant. Speaking of slaves, where is the boy Jamil?"

Her relief that he did not seek Tancred turned as quickly to concern. Kalid had said nothing, but had Mosul discovered Jamil sending the message to the Castle of Hohms?

"He is about on an errand. Why do you inquire?"

"He has disappeared."

"Surely not."

"I have guards out now looking for him."

"Guards! Seeking my slave?" she accused, as though the idea were preposterous. "For what cause?"

"He must explain curious actions to me."

"To you?" she scoffed. "Captain Mosul, you are beside yourself. Why should my slaves answer to you? And a mere boy at that!"

"Your Highness, he will either confess to me or to Prince Kalid. Which shall it be? I would not advise tempting the wrath of the prince. You will find him a hard man to soothe."

Cautiously her mind felt its way along, trying to understand. How much did Mosul know? "I left him with the chief eunuch, Asad."

"Lies are not comely for such a beautiful woman."

That he would dare say so, and also make comment of her appearance, showed him to be a dangerous man of ambitions to Kalid. She grappled for time.

"You dare accuse me of not telling the truth?" In reality, she *had* left the boy with Asad when Kalid brought her to the banquet.

"Do not pretend. Jamil was seen by another slave releasing a falcon."

So then. . . . She pressed for time. What to

say? What to do? Did this mean he knew about Tancred?

She shrugged as though bored. "Should I know what Jamil does with his falcons? Was it not you who bade him go to the field to serve His Eminence in such matters?"

The dark eyes mocked her. "Only a fool would underestimate a member of the Byzantine nobility. Your intrigue I have studied and profited from. I intend to profit still further. We both know of what I speak, Highness. Jamil sent a message to those friendly with you at the castle. I want to know to whom he sent it and why."

Mosul's ambitions could only be guessed at. Knowing his vicious nature as described by Tancred, she realized he was far more dangerous to her than Kalid.

"I do not doubt your ambitions. It is a pity that Prince Kalid does. He should never have trusted you."

"His Eminence is not as clever as you, Your Highness. His own ego demands complete loyalty from the commander of his personal bodyguard. What he does not know is that I have chosen men to guard him who are first loyal to me. They are all soldiers from Moorish descent. We owe nothing to these Seljuk Turks. In the end we will take what we want and ride free."

"You are a fool to tell me this. I could go to the prince."

"He would not believe you. And even if he did, it would do him no good, as you shall see tomorrow."

Tomorrow? "Whatever you have in mind, it will not succeed. I shall warn him of imminent betrayal."

His smile was unpleasant. "Will you? I think not."

He gestured his arm toward a path leading away from the celebration. "Shall we take a stroll, Highness? We must talk."

Helena glanced toward the silent garden and felt her skin crawl. The dark eyes were cold and mocking.

"My company will prove more congenial than the darkness of a cell."

Trapped, she turned onto the path, and Mosul walked beside her, a massive figure clothed in a black knee-length cloak. His heavy boots crunched on the gravel as the music and voices ebbed away. She shivered. She was alone with this dreadful assassin. What clever scheme did he have on his mind to advance his new cause?

"I suppose your disloyalty to Prince Kalid has something to do with the arrival of the Normans," she suggested, hoping to lure him into explaining.

Mosul gave a short, boastful laugh. "I know the warrior spirit of the Normans. I know Lord Bohemond. They are determined and fierce. They will sit out the siege of Antioch whatever length of time it takes. But I have no time to waste sitting about Antioch to satisfy the pleasure of the emir's son. The city will eventually fall, and with it, the rule of the emir's family, including Prince Kalid."

"So, of course, you have made other plans," she said coolly.

He turned his dark head and glanced down at her as she walked beside him. He leered. "Only a fool would waste his life for the sake of loyalty. What profit to me is a family soon to lose their authority to rule?"

"A better soldier would not call loyalty a waste of his life. He would call it honor."

"I have my own interpretation of honor," he scoffed. "Do not trouble yourself, Highness. Neither is the Byzantine a worthy judge of the meaning of honor. Your emperor is a master of cunning and treachery. He deals falsely behind the backs of the very warriors of the West he has summoned forth to fight his enemies."

"Never mind the emperor. What is it you intend with me?"

"Just this. Antioch will fall. I have no reason to stay in service to Kalid. There are a hundred other princes in the East, and just as many emirs and sultans. My sword is such that it will bring me into the favor of many who need protection. Why should I give my life here in Antioch while Kalid flees secretly with you to Aleppo? I prefer to further my future and protect myself."

He stopped on the path and looked down at her. In the full moonlight she saw the ruthless smile on his face and the small scar near his left eye that Tancred had put there.

"As I have already said, the falcon has not returned to its mate," he said meaningfully.

"I do not understand —"

"*Because the falcon did not return,* it has flown far. You had Jamil send a message to the Castle of Hohms."

Tancred had sent the message, but of course she could not say this.

"If Prince Kalid learns you have warned the Normans of his caravan leaving in the morning, he will be furious and — well, need I say more? The siege will be long. Perhaps a year."

A year!

"Will you spend it in a dungeon awaiting the city's fall to the Normans?"

Her muscles tensed.

"Perhaps," he said distinctly, "you will need to be rescued by me."

Helena took a step backward. He reached for her arm in a tight grip and pulled her toward him. "On the road to Aleppo, Prince Kalid will take on a new face — mine. I intend to become the new Prince Kalid and escape into Egypt."

Could he accomplish it? She believed he could. Fear seized her. "Let go of me. Do you wish me to scream? Prince Kalid will have you arrested!"

"He can do nothing. He flees Antioch like a rat to a lighted dungeon. It is your word against mine, Highness. It is Kalid who does not dare move against me. As captain of his personal bodyguard, he needs me for his protection. His head is left to my mercy."

"Then I shall enlighten him!"

"Do so, and you will see him choke on his own blood."

Did Mosul intend to kill Kalid on the road to Aleppo? Had he not said the soldiers were Moors and loyal to him? She realized suddenly that Mosul had laid his plans well. If Tancred failed, she would not be left to Prince Kalid but to Mosul. A far worse fate.

"It is too late for Prince Kalid to move against *me*," he boasted. "I have spent the last year setting my own men in place. If he is fool enough to try, we shall see who is in authority."

He released her abruptly and she stepped back, rubbing her wrists.

"Do not look so shocked, Highness. Other men have schemed to possess you, have they not? You are a woman of breathtaking beauty. It may be that I shall send word to Bishop Nicholas. If he wishes his niece back, he will pay a handsome price. And so he shall. He shall pay a royal ransom!"

"A year in a dungeon is preferred to your company! Go ahead! Bring me to Kalid! Tell him I sent a message to the Castle of Hohms if that is what you wish!"

"Then if you will not cooperate for yourself, you will for Jamil and Aziza. I have come too far and have too many ambitions to see them slip through my fingers now. You will cooperate with me to save her."

She looked into his scathing eyes. "Aziza! You have her?"

"Do you wish me to send her back to you alive? She is now being held by my guards."

Helena tried to think, but his grip was painful and his savagery frightened her.

Thus far, Mosul did not know the message sent to the Castle of Hohms had been to Nicholas and Hakeem, nor that it was his deadly enemy Tancred who had sent it. But what if Aziza were forced to talk?

"Release her unharmed and I will do what you say."

His teeth showed under his mustache. "That is better, Highness," he jeered. "But to be sure you keep your bargain, she will not be released yet."

He took hold of her again, and she struggled against his savage grip. Unexpectedly, there came the sound of a strange, sickening thud. A breath caught in his mouth, then he fell forward, knocking her down with him as he collapsed on the ground.

Helena felt the pebbles pressing and hurting her back. Half pinned beneath him, she was too stunned to move.

A harsh whisper reached her ears coming from the shrubs. "Mistress!"

Jamil! His voice was enough to send new strength racing through her veins.

Jamil threw aside the heavy stick and bent down, putting his hands under Mosul's armpit and struggling to roll him over into the dirt. Helena scrambled to her feet.

"Listen! Someone is coming!"

"Mosul's guards! Mistress, quick, away!" He grasped her wrist.

They darted and ducked through the trees until they came to an outer wall. Here, Jamil paused while she caught her breath.

"Mistress, what will you do now?"

"How much did you hear?"

"That he would escape with you to Egypt after killing Prince Kalid on the road to Aleppo."

"I must get word to Tancred. There is more at risk than our escape."

"What do you mean?" he whispered.

Helena hesitated to tell him of Aziza's plight for fear he would try to rescue his sister from the guards. Instead, she said, "Mosul knows of the message sent to the castle. He thinks I sent word to the Normans, offering to betray Prince Kalid for my freedom. Mosul's guards must not find you. They will torture you until you confess the truth."

"I will never betray you or the Norman," he insisted, his large brown eyes troubled but determined.

"You were a fine warrior just now. I shall always be in your debt. But I do not ask you to risk yourself to torture. Mosul is vicious. The best of warriors would be forced to tell him all."

"Not I, mistress, nor master Tancred!"

"You must do as I say, Jamil. Remember what you told me when we rode the stallion up the slope?"

"You mean about the postern gate and how I could escape if my head were in danger?"

"Yes, you must take my stallion now and live up to your boast. Ride to the Castle of Hohms and wait for me there."

"But, mistress! I cannot! The stallion is waiting with Prince Kalid's caravan near the Gate of the Dog. They expect to leave tomorrow. I have planted the horse so that Master Tancred can ride him when we all escape on the road to Aleppo."

"Kalid insists my bodyguard be left behind until he recovers, and Mosul's plans are to betray us. There will be no freedom, Jamil. You must take the opportunity to escape tonight."

She reached an affectionate hand to the boy's face, brushing aside the dark brown wisps of hair.

"There is no time to argue. They are looking for you. If you will not take the way of the postern gate, then you must hide."

"What of my sister?"

"I will do what I can for Aziza."

"There is other important news, mistress! It is about Firouz. I was on my way now to tell the Norman."

She had lost hope in Firouz. What good could he do her and Tancred now?

"Mistress, the moon is setting! I must go at once!"

"Go, then!"

He sprang off among the trees as nimbly and silently as a hind. She had injured her ankle and hadn't realized it until now. Slowly, she made her way toward the women's quarters in search of Asad. If anyone knew how to help Aziza, it would be the chief eunuch.

Asad stood on the lighted terrace with a scowl on his face. He paced, and every once in a while he stood on tiptoe to scan the garden. His eyes fell on Helena as she came running from the trees. He threw up his hands and came puffing down the steps.

"Your Loveliness! At last! At last! His Eminence looks for you everywhere!"

As Helena stepped into the lantern light, the chief eunuch's eyes widened.

"Ah! Ah! What has befallen you!"

"I became lost in the back garden —"

He groaned and rolled his eyes. "Back garden! What were you doing there?"

"I was looking for Aziza. When did you see her last?"

His round face scowled, showing he knew nothing of her fate.

"Aziza is not to be wandering the back garden, any more than you, fairest of women. When will you listen to my orders — you are limping!"

"It is nothing. I simply tripped over a loose stone."

His brows thundered together at the very idea of such a disgrace. "A loose stone? Here? In the emir's palace? Forbid!"

"Please, Asad, see if you can find Aziza. I fear something terrible has happened to her."

"It would be no wonder the way the damsel runs about in areas off limits to female slaves —" He stopped, and his fatherly concern overruled his anger over the impropriety of the young girls under his authority.

"Something terrible is happening to little Aziza, you say?"

She cast a glance backward to make sure none of the guards were about. "Mosul has her. She is being kept under guard. I cannot explain all that is involved. But if you can find out where she is being held and do something to release her, you may save her life."

Asad's eyes were troubled. "Mosul is a hard man. The day was bleak when His Eminence first chose to bring him to Antioch. I fear there is little I can do on my own. But I shall try."

He clapped his hands and a slave girl appeared and bowed. "When did you see Aziza last?" he asked her.

"This morning, Asad."

"Ask among the other servants and see what you can discover of her whereabouts. Be cautious."

The girl bowed and hurried out.

"Your foot worsens, Your Loveliness. The prince will never forgive me. You must rest in one of the chambers. I will send word to him to come at once."

Helena was led away with clucking noises of disapproval.

CHAPTER 20

His Eminence

A discreet knock on the chamber door brought Helena to her feet. She had been taken back to the same chambers in which Mosul had kept her locked up all day. Her garment was changed into a fresh one, and her hair was redone with jewels. She had awaited Asad's return for over an hour.

"This way, Your Eminence. She waits in here!"

Asad swept his arm wide for Prince Kalid to pass through the door, then hastened to close it behind him, leaving them alone.

Helena managed to stand, though her ankle had swollen.

Kalid faced her, no corpulent son of an emir, as Mosul liked to think of him, but a man of equal wit, and a determined warrior as fierce and as calculating as either Mosul or Tancred. It seemed to her that three warriors, each deadly and determined, vied for control of her future. If worse came to worst, she would certainly opt for the hand of Prince Kalid rather than Mosul.

Perhaps in the strength she now saw in Kalid lay the answer to part of her dilemma.

The prince's black eyes considered her coolly. "You tried to escape."

"Your Excellency," she said and gave a bow of her head. "I apologize for this inconvenience. I suppose Asad explained."

"You may dispense with formality. You came from the back garden, I understand?"

"Yes. I —"

"Then you may have seen the man who attacked my bodyguard. He was found unconscious."

She could see he was watching her response closely. Did he suspect her?

"Where is Mosul now?"

"He was taken to his chambers and the physician called. Why do you ask?"

"Because it is necessary I speak to you alone, without any of his men about."

Kalid did not appear surprised. "There are two guards waiting outside, but they are loyal."

"You must not trust any of them, Your Eminence. They are first of all loyal to Mosul. What I say now, you will reject. Yet I could not live with my conscience if I did not warn you."

He seemed surprised at her seriousness. "I am listening."

"I met Mosul in the garden. He has made plans to turn against you once we leave Antioch. The soldiers guarding your caravan to Aleppo are all loyal to him. They are Moors from Sicily. They hold no particular allegiance to the Seljuks. They intend to ambush you and take me a prisoner. If we leave Antioch in the morning without the Seljuk cavalry, I fear for your life and my captivity. He also has Aziza a prisoner and seeks the boy Jamil."

Prince Kalid stared at her. For a moment he said nothing, then his jaw tightened, and the black eyes gleamed. "Mosul told you this?"

"He did, Your Eminence. He intends to take me to Egypt and to hold me for ransom. My uncle will be asked to pay him in gold."

If Kalid believed her, he did not show it. The rugged face was immobile. After a long moment in which she heard nothing but the pounding of her heart, he walked across the chamber to where she stood and gazed long into her eyes.

Suddenly he turned his back and strode across the room toward the door. Helena darted after him, throwing herself against the door.

"I tell you the truth."

"I believe you."

He reached for the door, and she grabbed his arm. "What will you do?"

"Fear not. You will not be going with Mosul to Egypt."

"There is one thing more. There is something I wish you to do for me."

His eyes were cool and mocking. "Your favorite slave again? The bodyguard Bardas?"

She hesitated under his scrutiny. *Caution* . . . she thought. Kalid appeared to be more suspicious of her "bodyguard" than Mosul. She grappled for something to say to divert him. "With the crusaders about the walls, it will not take them long to capture the Castle of Hohms. Marriage to me will no longer give you control over it. Why not permit me to go free?"

He remained unmovable. "Within a year the barbarians will weary of their drive eastward. In laying siege to Antioch, they meet their doom. They will starve to death before the Turkish commander surrenders the city. If the barbarians are wise, they will see their mistake and return to the West, where they belong. When they do, I shall return to Antioch and lay claim to the Castle of

Hohms. There will be no army to aid your emperor."

"You are so sure. The Normans will not leave. They are as iron willed as your own people."

"You seem to know much about the Norman will, Lady Helena."

She ignored the subtle insinuation. "Then you insist I leave with you for Aleppo? In spite of Mosul's plan? In spite of defeat staring Antioch in the face?"

"I made a bargain with Lady Irene."

"My aunt is dead. So is Philip. The bargain, too, is dead."

"Ah? How do you know they are dead?"

She caught her blunder and tried desperately to shrug it off. "Bardas told me."

"News reached me at Aleppo that it was Irene's bodyguard Rufus who slew her. No one seems to know who killed Philip at the hippodrome, but Bardas could not have known."

She shrugged again and turned away as though it were nothing. "Nevertheless, the Lysander family has seen much tragedy. It is Nicholas Lysander you must deal with now. If it could be arranged to turn me over to him —"

His rude laugh silenced her from proceeding.

"Ma'sud spared the life of your bodyguard at the castle because he is a man of honor. He could see you cared for him and wished to show a kindness. But, Helena, by now you must know I will do what I must to see my plans enacted. We will speak no more of the matter. We will marry at Aleppo."

Then there was no way out, she decided. Prince Kalid would not turn back. She saw her opening and drew in a breath. "You have not yet fulfilled your part of the bargain."

"Bardas lives, does he not? What more do you wish?"

"I have warned you about Mosul. In return for my loyalty, I ask that my eunuch slave leave with me on the caravan."

He watched her so carefully that she could not stop the pink from rising in her cheeks. *I'm a fool!* she thought. *I grow exhausted and am making blunders. He knows now . . . he guesses.*

"Tell me, Helena of the Nobility, this bodyguard of yours — this heroic man who rode to contest fifty Seljuks to claim you — this 'eunuch' you concern yourself with — who sleeps as a pet in your chamber — just why does he mean so much to you?"

She tried to sound calm. "It is as I told your uncle Ma'sud Khan. Bardas served my father. He has been loyal to me since I was a child." So far she told the truth. "And I fear for his life. Mosul will try to kill him."

His smile scorned her words as though they were vain. "From what you tell me, Mosul is out to kill us both."

"He is, I tell you! And my bodyguard as well."

"Then . . . since you have warned me" — his black eyes turned cold — "your bodyguard must also be warned."

Her eyes searched his. They told her nothing.

"I will go at once," she suggested.

"Your ankle is swollen. No, it is *I* who will go warn him."

Her eyes widened. "No, you must not."

"No? Why? Because you do not wish for me to gaze upon his face? Why so?"

"Mosul will follow you there."

"Mosul is in no condition at the moment to follow me anywhere."

"But . . . but his loyal men are. They watch your every move. *Please,* Kalid, trust me."

"Trust you?" he mocked. "Why should I?"

"Because if you permit my bodyguard to come with us on the caravan, unbeknown to Mosul or his men, I will see to it that he protects you against Mosul."

Kalid's expression changed. His black eyes were suddenly cold and alert. "Indeed? In-

teresting. I wish very much to see this bodyguard of yours. He sounds like a warrior.
Could it be that we may have met before?"
He turned on his heel and headed for the
door.

"Your Eminence! Where are you going?"

"Your demands I do not appreciate."

"If you insist on seeing him, please let me
come with you. He will listen to me."

He threw open the door. "I do not need
you to beg for my life. Guards!"

"Kalid, wait —" she cried, but he strode
ahead, leaving her behind.

The two soldiers, both loyal to Mosul, appeared at once. Prince Kalid gave them a
cold appraisal, his hand on his blade.

"See to it my future princess does not leave
the chamber until the caravan leaves in the
morning."

"You make a grave mistake," she cried.

He whirled. "Silence!"

Helena had no choice; the two guards
watched her.

Kalid turned back to them. "In the morning, bring her to the caravan. I will meet you
there. There has been a change in plans. See
that Mosul rides with us from Antioch. I will
need him in Aleppo after all."

"As you wish, Eminence. Shall we send
him word of this now?"

"By all means."

When the heavy chamber door shut, Helena beat against it with her fists.

The outside bolt slid into place, and she heard the footsteps of Prince Kalid echoing down the marble hallway.

Kalid would discover Tancred. And when he did?

She fell against the door, despair welling up within her. Her body ached from bruises and her ankle seemed worse. She hobbled to the cushions and sank down, wincing as she removed her slipper from her swollen foot.

Outside in the hall it was quiet. The night held the threat of danger for them all. And come morning, only the strongest warrior, and the most clever, would be alive.

CHAPTER 21

Firouz's Revenge

The moon had set. Where was Jamil?

Tancred anxiously paced the chamber, dressed all in black in order to melt into the shadows of the trees should it be forced upon him to seek Helena and Jamil. He would not wait. Anything could have gone wrong. He belted on his scabbard and moved toward the door. It opened and Jamil darted in, out of breath, his eyes wide.

"News of great importance, master!"

Tancred caught him and ushered him away from the door, setting him down on an ottoman. "Speak!"

"Mosul plans to kill Kalid on the road to Aleppo and bring my mistress to Egypt!"

Tancred's handsome jaw set with anger. "Where is he now?"

Jamil grinned. "I knocked him unconscious."

"Well done! Where is Helena now?"

"She bid me come quickly to warn you. Kalid's caravan leaves tomorrow to escape the city. And there is more — the Armenian named Firouz suspects evil done to his wife by none other than Mosul! And Firouz is furious over this dishonor. It is good news, yes? Surely you will make something of it, master!"

Tancred restrained his anxiety over Helena long enough to grasp the importance of Firouz. "You are sure of this? How do you know?"

"I overheard. His wife was crying and blaming Mosul. She confessed that he treated her with disrespect, then scorned her. I heard every word. Firouz spoke bitterly of the Seljuk Turks despoiling their women and vowed that he would avenge her."

"Ah!" He had thought it might be so, but he had not suspected Mosul. "Did Firouz say how he might avenge her?"

Jamil's eyes gleamed like lighted pools. He whispered, "He has heard of Bohemond. He seeks a contact with him. He may betray the Turks into the hands of Bohemond."

Tancred grew still. Then, grabbing the boy, he hugged him. "Brilliant spy work. I will adopt you in Sicily as my son."

"Master!"

"I must speak with Firouz tonight."

"I . . . I will hide in the bushes near . . . near his quarters," he quavered, tears welling in his eyes, though he blinked hard. "Tonight when h-he returns, I will tell him you wish to see him."

Tancred gave him a comforting squeeze. Jamil swallowed his emotions and said more calmly, "There is a trail winding up Mount Silpius, near the great Citadel. We can meet there unnoticed. I often go there."

"Well done. Tell him to come alone."

"Yes, master."

"You will call me Tancred now."

"Yes . . . Tancred." He smiled shyly, drew in a breath, then slipped away again as cautiously as a falcon.

Tancred looked after him and smiled.

The gray stone wall, thirty feet high, stood above him, hardly visible in the darkness. On the southern section of the city, the far half of the wall was situated up among the hills and had only small postern gates, which opened onto narrow footpaths. It was too treacherous for an army to station itself within these ravines to attack Antioch. Normans, under the control of Bohemond's nephew, also patrolled the hills, cutting off supplies being brought through these gates by Syrians. Meanwhile, the armies of the feudal lords were camped on the plain north of the city.

The silence was interrupted by the faint stir of the wind rustling the laurel trees near the mosque. As soon as darkness fell there came a flurry of movement among the guards in the city. If anything went wrong and Firouz was discovered to be a betrayer, none of their lives would be worth anything come morning.

As Tancred walked toward the mosque, he heard a rush of commands coming from the Turkish captains on the street, followed by running feet of soldiers hasting to obey orders. He saw the flash of torches and the Turks mounting swift horses to ride in the direction of Mount Silpius.

Farther ahead in the darkness at the end of the street was a dome-covered building and several tombs. Tancred neared to meet with Firouz. A few white-turbaned hadjis were in the galleries. Tancred caught the smell of burnt-out candles. He paused and waited.

Firouz came from the shadows, his round face intense. They walked through the court while Firouz talked in hoarse whispers.

"You serve the Norman Bohemond?" he asked Tancred.

"I have an audience with him."

"Then listen well. You will never take

Antioch by siege. And though the Byzantine emperor sends his artillery to destroy the walls, Antioch will stand impregnable. There is only one way for your massive army to get inside Antioch."

"I am listening eagerly."

"Did you pass the sixty-foot Tower of the Two Sisters?"

"I did. The Tower is impregnable."

"Yes, but nothing remains impregnable to him who has the key to the gate. I," he said firmly, his voice shaking with rage, "will see that Bohemond is let in."

Astounded, Tancred remained silent for a moment. He could see by the offended man's face that he was serious and determined.

"What do you expect in return for this deed?"

"Vengeance!"

Tancred imagined what it would mean for unsuspecting Antioch to suddenly have the gate opened and nearly a hundred thousand swords turned loose.

"You shall indeed see the blood of vengeance," he warned.

"I wish to see it!" His voice shook.

"Your wife —"

"Do not speak of my wife! They have shamed her! I want Mosul killed as well!

Do you understand?"

"When the fighting begins, there will be few, if any, who escape. Bohemond will need surety that you speak the truth."

Firouz was undaunted. "He may hold my son as hostage."

"How shall I get out of the city?"

"It is all arranged. Horses wait. I will bring you there myself tonight. We must move swiftly. You must meet with Bohemond and return by tomorrow night to take the city. Will you bring word to your Norman lord?"

He would need to leave Helena to Kalid until they took the city. Dare he wait? Anything could happen before he reached her again. Suppose Kalid moved her to another location? Suppose the rabble following the crusaders reached her before he did? Once the men stormed the gate, he had no doubt in his mind what would happen — a massacre. He wanted no part of it. And Helena could be mistaken for a Moslem princess.

"I will deliver your message, but Helena Lysander must come with me tonight. And I have the boy to think of. I cannot leave without them. Can you arrange it?"

"No, impossible! There is no time for that! I will see the boy is safe. But Lady Helena is under guard by Kalid. His soldiers surround her. If you go there now it will mean the end of our plan and your death."

"Never," said Tancred. "I cannot leave her to him."

"Kalid has no plans to leave Antioch now. Kerbogha comes with a Turkish cavalry, and so he will wait."

"No, anything could go wrong."

"Then I will see to it that spies watch her chamber until your return. If anyone should seek to move her, I will use the power of intrigue to thwart them."

"Thwart them?" Tancred scoffed. "How?"

"I can thwart Kalid," he said with contempt. "There are ways. But if you wish Antioch — you must go tonight."

Tancred gritted, weighing the outcome of his choice. If he stayed, there was little chance he could get Helena out of the palace and away from the guard, whereas access to the Norman camp might mean that he would locate Nicholas, Hakeem, or Leif. Their swords added to his own would better ensure his success in rescuing her. He could also confirm the need for an ambush on the road to Aleppo, just in case something went wrong and either Kalid or Mosul managed to escape.

"All right. What we do, we do tonight.

Firouz, your name will go down in history."

"Let history record my deed — and the defeat of the Turks. Let Bohemond ride into Antioch!"

"He shall. And the result will long be remembered. What plans do you have for Bohemond?"

"Tomorrow let Bohemond sound his trumpets of war to gather his forces, then ride off to the east as if marching to confront Kerbogha. As soon as night falls, he is to double back. Have him gather his knights silently under the Tower of the Two Sisters. Wait until the patrol of Turks make their round of the wall with torches. When the torches are out" — he paused — "a rope ladder will be hanging over the wall. I will be in the Tower. The invincible Bohemond must come up first with the Normans.

"After the first three towers are conquered, the gate can be opened for the host. The city of Antioch," he stated with venom, "will belong to the Normans."

True to his promise, Firouz had horses waiting in the hills. He scanned Tancred uneasily. "You are strong enough to do this? Jamil says you were near death."

"I've recovered," Tancred claimed, but he

would not say how weak he felt. "How do you expect to get me through the gate?"

"There is a trail along Mount Silpius that leads to a shepherd's gate."

Tancred was not sure he knew what he was doing. "There are many gates. Why is this one different? Surely it is guarded."

"It is guarded. But it opens each morning to permit shepherds to leave with their goats. While an army of crusaders would easily be spotted nearing the gate, one shepherd coming and going is a customary sight. The shepherds are deemed of little threat to the Seljuk guards. Often the shepherds bring them gifts of wine, cheese, and figs from the small Armenian villages in the hills. Your clothes are waiting."

"And the shepherd I replace?"

"He is well and privy to our plan. He's an Armenian Christian who also welcomes the arrival of the crusaders. All is arranged. You have but to follow my orders."

Within two hours they had come to the place near the gate, and while it was yet dark, the simple but clever ruse was carried out under the nose of the Turkish guards who walked the wall, watching the distant hills for signs of an advancing army.

Tancred found a horse tied and waiting a mile from the wall and a satchel containing more weapons. Before the sun arose in the east he was riding toward the crusaders' camp to meet with Bohemond.

CHAPTER 22

Norman Conflict

The sun was hot and the Norman camp astir with activity by the time Tancred rode among the thousands of tents. They had noticed him coming from a distance and the word spread. Immediately he asked for Bohemond. Several Normans came forward to greet him.

"Any news from Nicholas and Leif?"

"We have sent Ordic to the Castle of Hohms to learn what happened."

Did he imagine a guarded glance between them?

Tancred, more weary in body than he would admit to himself, remained astride the horse as they led him forward to a large tent where the Norman standard fluttered on a pole.

The tent floor was spread with Moslem prayer rugs captured in battles. The red-haired lord was awake and armed, a massive warrior with muscles bulging in his arms, chest, and back. Tancred explained about Firouz and his wife. "The Armenian is prepared to let the Normans into the city. To prove his sincerity, his son will be sent as a hostage."

The cold blue eyes of the Norman glinted. He was silent. Then he responded as Tancred had known he would. "I accept."

The news was to be kept from the other feudal lords. Bohemond wanted to be ruler of the city and had a plan. With boldness he called for a council.

Tancred sat beside him. Without mentioning the Armenian or his offer, Bohemond suggested, "Whoever among us manages to break through and take Antioch should become lord of the city."

At first they refused indignantly. "Have we not all endured this siege? No single lord should be given Antioch!"

One of the chief knights was bidden into the command tent to bring important news.

"Kerbogha is within three days of the city. He has raised a new army of Moslems from the East and comes to bolster Yaghi-Sian. The fresh army of cursed infidels outnumbers us greatly."

Tense silence held the lords.

"If you intend to take Antioch, you must

do so now," said Tancred. "Soon it will be too late."

While the news of Kerbogha's relief army was ill news for the crusaders, it was favorable to Tancred. Kalid would not choose to leave Antioch now, not until Kerbogha arrived. He had three days in which to rescue Helena. And if the Normans took the city, he would have her safely away even sooner.

The desert wind sent the tent flaps shaking, like an omen of calamity riding quickly from the East. The princes looked at one another with grim determination.

"Kerbogha's cavalry will be well fed and their horses fresh," said Tancred. "Your knights and fighting men will be trapped between the walls of Antioch and the river. Supplies will not reach us from St. Symeon; we will be worse off than we are now. I suggest to the lords and princes that they accept Bohemond's offer while there is time."

"Tancred is right. If Bohemond and his Normans can win the city, let us bestow it upon him willingly," agreed Duke Godfrey. "I wish Antioch behind me. Let us get on to the holy city of Jerusalem!"

Tancred went to the tent of his cousin Leif. Adele made much ado over his injuries, bidding him rest while she rushed for the physician Thomas of Aguilers. She returned, bringing the famed medical man, and set about to prepare nourishing food. When they were alone again he inquired about Leif.

"A message arrived a week ago," she said in a low voice, glancing toward the tent opening. "He remains with Nicholas. They received your message sent by falcon. A return message was sent by falcon to Hakeem. He came late one night a week ago, searching for news of you, but I had none to give him."

"Hakeem! He is here?"

"He stayed only long enough to leave the warning from Nicholas and Leif."

"What warning?"

"Uncle Walter and members of the clan had visited the Castle of Hohms only a week before you arrived to confront the Turks over Lady Helena. Nicholas and Leif now ride secretly toward Aleppo as you bade in your message. And Seigneur Rolf Redwan and Rufus also ride with Nicholas. Rolf is anxious to see you — and to confront Walter."

That his adoptive father would be resentful enough toward Walter's avenging spirit to leave the castle and ride with Nicholas surprised Tancred. He suddenly longed to see him again. He was growing weary of battle and conflict and yearned for rest of soul and warm conversation with family and friends, especially Rolf and Nicholas.

"Where is Uncle Walter now?"

Adele stiffened. Tancred saw the direction of her gaze and turned his head just as a brusque voice he remembered well ordered, "Do not reach for your sword, Tancred."

Members of the Redwan clan moved into the tent, encircling him. Tancred despised his folly.

Adele gasped. "You have no right to come in here! If Leif were here he'd draw blade against Walter!"

"Stay out of this, Adele. If Leif were here, he, too, would answer for treachery."

Tancred's eyes met with several of his stalwart cousins, then confronted his uncle Walter Redwan, now head of the clan.

Walter was in his forties, ruggedly handsome, with a red glint to his hair. A deep scar ran across his cheek. He was garbed in ringed leather armor, a long Viking sword strapped to his lean hip.

Walter, in seeing his nephew for the first time since his respectable and scholarly studies at the Salerno medical school near Rome, appeared faintly surprised as Tancred stood from the cushions — as though the warrior before him could not be his nephew. Then Walter's countenance on the deeply bronzed face hardened.

Tancred carefully revealed nothing of his own thoughts or feelings at seeing his blood kin again. His uncle's lack of trust in his honor had hurt him deeply, but in facing him now Tancred affected immobility, certain he would not plead with him for leniency. Tancred often wondered if Walter may not have desired the guilt for Derek's death to be placed on him. He remembered what the old one, Odo, had said that night in the Redwan castle while Tancred escaped: *"Walter may be my son, but pride does not blind me to his ambitions. It is not the loss of young Derek that prompts him to see you pass through the ordeal of craven, but the knowledge that you are the future heir of the Redwan legacy."*

Was it true? In many ways Walter was an honorable warrior.

Count Walter strode boldly forward until he came within feet of Tancred. "Bind him," Walter ordered.

"He is injured from battle. Can you not see?" insisted Adele. "Have you no pity?"

"I do not want his pity," stated Tancred.

Walter's cheek flinched. "I had no intention of offering you any."

Tancred's lean, wolfish cousins came toward him, yet they moved uncertainly, and he believed he saw divided wills. They would not meet his level gaze, as though they did

335

not enjoy what they were doing.

Cousin Cervon warned, "Do not try to draw blade against us, Tancred. Not even you can take fifteen Redwans."

Tancred looked at the lean, savage man in his thirties. "There can be no trial until Rolf is present as my adoptive father. He is with Nicholas on the road to Aleppo. Will you ride with me there? Is Walter willing to bring me on my way? Matters can be settled there fairly and according to custom."

"Rolf believes you are innocent," said Cervon.

It was also true that Rolf was in line to succeed Tancred's blood father, Dreux, as head of the family, but Rolf had left Sicily for reasons no one talked about. It was readily understood by the clan that should Rolf step forth to claim his birthright, Walter must step down.

Walter's blue eyes were brittle, the strong jawline stubbornly set. "To kill your brother was not enough? You will duel your uncle as well?"

Tancred ignored the charge. "Mosul assassinated Derek. He is in Antioch serving Prince Kalid. I would soon now have caught him, had I not been betrayed."

"Do you still insult me with this lying tale of Mosul?" Walter demanded shortly.

"If you had spent these near three years hounding Mosul instead of me, you would have learned my vow to be truth."

His uncle did not speak, nothing moving but the twitch of a muscle in his face. Then, unwillingly, his eyes swept Tancred. He sighed. "Sight of the younger son of Dreux conjures blood affection, I confess. I loved my brother Dreux, whose skills as a warrior I respected. And alas! You look much like him. There are times, Tancred, when late at night before the campfire I tell myself you could not have killed Derek. Not *you*, the one son of Dreux who respected life and wished to be a physician. But" — and he sighed again — "it was your dagger. Slaves reported having seen you flee the courtyard where Derek met with Kamila. Everyone knows how you were to marry her, but she loved Derek. Jealousy can cause a man to do things he would at other times loathe in someone else."

"I did not kill him. I did not love Kamila. The slaves lie. And Mosul is the answer to all things between us."

"Neither your silken tongue nor your way with the sword will save you, Tancred. You demand the presence of Rolf? Impossible. It is said he is not at the castle but setting up an ambush on the road toward Aleppo. Do I not know that you are friendly with the Moslems? And should we behave the fools in riding with you to Aleppo? It is said Commander Kerbogha rides from that direction with a cavalry of Turks. Or is it that you wish to turn us over to him?" He turned away. "Take his weapon, Cervon. We will hold fair and just trial among the Normans."

Tancred turned and looked at his cousin.

Uneasily, Cervon gestured. "Unbelt your scabbard."

Tancred did so. Another kinsman scowled, as though he thought the whole business of the morning rather nasty.

"Bind him strongly," said Cervon Redwan. "If you don't," he said smoothly, "we may lose our long-lost cousin before we ever take Antioch."

Something in his voice caused Tancred to look at him. Cervon only smiled.

"I remember well how he used to escape us in the woods," said Cousin Olin. "He always was a —"

"Silence!" commanded Count Walter. "We will not discuss the past. There is to be no mention of family! Not here, not now, not ever!"

"If you hold me prisoner, Antioch will not be taken," said Tancred. "I have come from inside the city with a message for Bohemond.

Send for him. Let him speak. He will tell you it is so."

Cervon grinned at Olin. "First he lures Norris and Leif away to his side, now he tells us the fate of Antioch was of his brilliant making. Next he will have us riding with him to trap Mosul."

Then they did not know Norris was dead, Tancred realized. If he told them, they would surely believe him guilty of his death also.

An hour later a tense, hushed silence held the Redwan clan, for they had long sought this time.

Tancred had been tied hand and foot, spread-eagled to two posts.

The thirty Redwans, astride their Great Horses, detached themselves in groups of six, swinging themselves in a wide circle and closing in about him.

The lords, Tancred's uncles, had debated with Walter over the wisdom of pursuing the custom of craven at this time. "It is true what Adele said. He has taken serious wounds in battle," said Cervon to Walter. "It is not good to go through with the trial now."

If *craven* were used to determine guilt, the accused, by surviving the prescribed ordeal, was declared not guilty. The Norman punishment, however, was so severe that few survived the hours, or sometimes days, of endurance.

"He is not strong," argued Olin. "The trial cannot be fair to him. Is it not best to wait?"

Walter held the reins of his horse in mute silence. It troubled him that Tancred had not once pleaded to be released. He knew that some had begun to doubt his guilt, and in a private meeting they had tried unsuccessfully to have him released.

"Why not abide by the rules and wait for Rolf?" offered Richard. He was a stalwart man, and more just than any of his brothers. He was able to read and write, and it had been from Richard that Tancred, when a boy, had received his own love for knowledge and books. Richard's fair hair, tipped lightly with silver, was clipped short at his neck Norman style, and he was clean-shaven, another Norman custom. The green eyes looked down upon Tancred with gravity.

"Come, my nephew Tancred, confess. It will be better so. We both know your uncle Walter to be a relentless and stubborn man." He gestured a scowl toward Walter. "He is not easily appeased, as you know. But as the eldest of your uncles, it is in my power to see you spared the ordeal of craven, if you will confess bloodguiltiness."

"As I already swore to you at Sicily, I am innocent of my brother's death," Tancred declared.

Walter could not keep silent. His stark blue eyes thundered down upon him. "Then why did you flee!"

"Did I not swear to you I was innocent that very night in the castle?" Tancred returned. "Yet I could see you did not know my heart, nor would you trust my vow. I knew I had to work alone to find Mosul."

Count Walter flushed angrily. "I know you much better than even you think."

"Do you, my uncle? Then how is it you have hounded me these years? Why did you not trust me to bring Mosul back to Sicily to stand before you?"

Count Walter's hand gripped the reins until his knuckles showed white. His lips were tightly sealed in silence. "It is because Derek's Norman mother swore to me that it was you who assassinated her son."

"Is not the reason obvious?" said Tancred with weariness.

Walter's eyes faltered momentarily. He had once been in love with Derek's mother until she had married Dreux. Had he too easily believed her words that night? Walter's iron gaze flickered, then swerved away from Tancred's.

"There are servants who back up her witness."

"Are the servants not loyal to her? Their witness is worthless. You yourself have many enemies among the Moors. It is my belief Mosul was hired to assassinate Derek, and then leave my dagger. I will prove it. But not while tied up here like a slave."

Count Walter's eyes glinted. He, too, had been tortured by these very thoughts as he traveled across Europe in relentless search of Tancred. Little by little he had begun to wrestle with his troubled conscience. How many nights he had wrestled with the memory of that last night in the castle when he had confronted Tancred over the death of Derek.

On that night over two years ago, Tancred's dagger had been produced, along with witnesses. The ordeal between them had been so emotionally violent that it had destroyed their relationship. Tancred had implored him to trust his honor and his loyalty to the family, yet Walter had reacted too hastily, and in bitterness of soul swore that Tancred would die.

Tancred escaped the Redwan castle through the help of Walter's father, Odo. Walter, though regretting his temper, had never seen Tancred again, until now.

He needed this nephew in Sicily far more than he needed the others, yet he could not humble himself to admit it. Now after seeing Tancred, Walter was more distraught, yet outwardly he refused to show his family pride in this magnificent warrior before him. One glimpse of the young man had pierced his heart. Tancred was truly a Norman in all the aspects that Count Walter gloried in. His own son Norris had come to his side. Yes, he knew Norris was dead; word had reached his brother Rolf at the Castle of Hohms, but he would not let Tancred know that he knew. Not yet.

"I am bound by duty to see that justice is paid for the death of Derek," said Walter stubbornly.

Tancred did not waver before the hard, measuring look Walter gave him.

"No one of us wants justice for his death more than I. He was *my* brother!"

Walter winced before he could halt the whiplash of the stinging rebuke. The others glanced at him. Was it not the honor of Tancred that was on trial? Neither Erich, Leif, or Norris had believed him guilty. They had come to know him too well.

"Release me to go to Antioch," Tancred pressed. "I will find Mosul and I will bring him to you alive." His eyes hardened as they

scanned his uncle. "If it is craven you wish —
then I accept your judgment."

Walter tensed slightly, and the others
scowled. They had been working against craven.

"I only ask that it be fairly done in the sight
of all of you. Let craven become the duel
fought between Mosul and myself. The man
who survives, let him go free."

"And if he loses?"

"He shall be hanged," said Tancred.

Uncle Richard scowled. "But if it is true
that Mosul is guilty, and you are not —"

Tancred interrupted, his eyes riveted on
Walter. "Nay. I will defend my honor according to Norman values. Naught else will
please the head of our clan, nor will it please
me. Only then can I ride on in peace."

Ride on? Did this mean Tancred had no
desire to resume his family position in Sicily?
Walter had not only lost his firstborn, Norris,
but his nephew Erich was dead, and maybe
even Leif too — and now Tancred appeared
willing to walk away.

Count Walter masked any emotion. He refused to soften his stand, even though he
could feel the eyes of Richard, Cervon, Olin,
and the others warning him to release the
matter as one would release a falcon to its
freedom.

"It will be as you ask, Tancred. You must prove your innocence by craven. And craven will be a duel between you and Mosul. Your honor is at stake." Then he added roughly, wheeling his horse, "Find Mosul. And if not, you will yet stand trial."

"I will find him," gritted Tancred.

"You have my ruling. We will speak no more until you bring him to me!" Walter turned his horse and rode back toward the camp.

Richard gestured to Cervon. "Cut your cousin Tancred free and restore his weapons and armor."

Cervon rode up to the stakes and, drawing his dagger from his belt, leaned his horse to cut the ropes at Tancred's wrists.

Tancred looked after Walter, rubbing his wrists where the rope had pressed. His action in releasing him to find Mosul surprised him. Why the change in his uncle?

"He is afraid to show his feelings," said Cervon.

Tancred remained unmoved. "Walter fears nothing."

"He has remembered you with bitter regrets."

Tancred gave a bitter laugh, showing his doubt.

Cervon frowned at his unbelief. "He

wishes your vindication and your return to Sicily. But he will not say so."

"Does he?" asked Tancred dryly.

Cervon shrugged lazily and turned his horse to ride, waiting for his cousin Tancred.

Tancred belted on his sword and mounted his horse, refusing to comment on his own mixed feelings. His eyes glinted as they met Cervon's. Making no further comment, Tancred rode away from them and did not look back. Adele was waiting for him with Bishop Adehemar and, seeing he was free, came running toward him.

CHAPTER 23

Tower of the Two Sisters

The stars gleamed in the black sky as Tancred and Bohemond moved silently toward the wall. The Normans kept a safe distance among the ravines until they came to the Tower of the Two Sisters. They dismounted and waited. The hours crept by with slow agony. Then, at last, the torches on the summit of the wall appeared, and as the Turks made their rounds for the night, silence followed their passing. Bohemond was now in the ditch with some of his Normans, Tancred with them. As they felt their way along the wall, their hands perspiring with tension, Tancred found the ladder of twisted rope hanging from an open window in the Tower. Firouz had done his work!

"Go up quietly," ordered Bohemond.

Tancred was forced to wait, reserving his strength for the escape with Helena and the confrontation with Mosul, a strong warrior.

He worried about his weakness, yet he would not relent. He had come too far in the long journey to turn back now.

One by one some sixty knights crawled up the ladder; Tancred followed after. Firouz saw him and came quickly, yet his face showed that the sight of the knights in armor did little to relieve his agitation.

"Where is your lord Bohemond? There are too few of you! There must be more knights!"

"The Normans will not disappoint you," said Tancred with irony.

The knights took little notice of Firouz and were running along the wall. One by one the towers were seized as the surprised Seljuks fell to the slash of the long swords. More ladders were thrown from the tower windows, and still more knights scaled the wall. Voices shouted in the darkness; Bohemond sounded the trumpet. The blast stabbed throughout the city as the first flashes of dawn spread over the hills, and the knights threw open the Gate of the Two Sisters. Normans, Franks, Rhinelanders, Lombards, Provençals, and the rabble on foot streamed through the gate with shouting and clashing blades. Some rushed up the steps of the towers, their blades striking everyone in sight; others ran down in the direction of the populous city, which was awaking to the terror of dawn.

Tancred, armed with weapons and chain mesh, moved away from the Tower to begin his own mission.

At the golden palace, a wild and weird cry awoke Prince Kalid Khan. What was this? It was not the first morning call to the mosque but the summons to war! But how? Kerbogha was still a day's journey from Antioch. He listened, his heart thundering as he heard the distant shouts of fighting men, followed by the alarm sounding in Yaghi-Sian's palace.

"Guards!" Prince Kalid jumped to his feet and threw on his clothes, grabbing his scimitar, but no guards came.

Below in the hall of the great house, the slaves were scattering in panic. One shouted to him, "Your horse is waiting, Eminence! The barbarians are in the city!"

"How?" Kalid shouted wrathfully. "How did they get in? How?"

"Yaghi-Sian is trying to escape, master! Run for the Bridge Gate. They do not yet hold it."

"Do not run!" shouted Kalid. "Make for the Citadel! We will hole up there."

"But the crimson standard of Bohemond

is already planted on the hill below the Citadel!"

Kalid cursed between his teeth. Treachery! How could this happen when Kerbogha was but a day's journey with fresh troops? They could have slaughtered the barbarians!

"Get my horse! Meet me in the court. I will get Helena."

Outside in the hall Tancred heard a familiar voice shouting orders. Swiftly he took his place in the shadows and lifted his sword. He listened. The chamber door opened and a man came bounding through, a sword in his hand.

Kalid.

Tancred stepped out of the shadows and his distant cousin stood staring at him with astonishment.

"So . . . it is *you*, Tancred. I might have guessed you were the beloved bodyguard. Only when I learned of the death of Bardas did I realize. I went to the chamber to find you, but you had escaped."

"I came back. I am not one to disappoint."

Kalid measured him with bitter humor. "A eunuch bodyguard!"

"Where is she?"

Prince Kalid's lean smile hardened. "Helena?"

"As if you need ask. I shall take her from you. For her sake we must get out of here lest they mistake her for a Moslem princess."

"She is safely locked within her chamber until I leave with her. I am afraid, my Norman cousin, you will not be on the caravan. You were a fool to come here alone. It was never my wish to fight you and see you die. After all, there is Moorish blood that yet unites us, though thinly."

"As you once said, Your Excellency, there are few women worth risking one's head for. Now and then, one comes along to try a warrior's folly."

"Yes. I see what you mean. We have the same astute tastes for the finer things of life," he sighed. "Wine, a good breed of stallion, a beautiful woman."

"Only one woman."

Kalid took in the chain mesh that reflected beneath the leather tunic. "I see you are recovering well enough. You can thank her for that — and Ma'sud. The other captains would have killed you outside the Castle of Hohms. Your distant uncle and I have spared your life. And now you betray the blood of al-Kareem to allow these vile barbarian dogs to devour the city."

"I did not come on crusade. I came for Mosul. You know that. It would be enough if you will let Helena go with me. It is her choice. You do not love her. There are other women for you. Let us make peace!"

Kalid's eyes dropped to Tancred's sword.

"Perhaps there is no need for that."

He lowered the point of his blade.

"Go in peace. You have my word."

"Your word I will accept, but only if she comes with me."

Kalid's face hardened. "I cannot oblige you. This is one woman I will not share with another."

"Again, we understand each other."

"She will never belong to you."

"I do not wish to kill you, my cousin. We have enjoyed a few pleasures together. That is why I allowed you and the Red Lion to ride away when we met in battle near Dorylaeum."

"And Adrianna, she is well? She has given birth to Sinan's child?"

"I do not know. But Nicholas will not allow the child to be sent to Cairo."

"That is not our argument. We have our own differences."

"So we have. And I must insist you release Helena."

Kalid's smile was mocking. "Ah? After I paid gold to Lady Irene? She is a difficult woman to satisfy."

"No doubt. You have my sympathy. She is dead now, having met the wrath of Rufus."

"So I have heard. No sorrow is lost."

"But better to lose a satchel of gold than your head."

"When a man pays the amount of gold I have, the bargain stands."

For a moment a muscle did not flinch in Tancred's face. He stood perfectly still, then his eyes narrowed. "I would not be a fool if I were you, Kalid. You know I am a better swordsman than you. If you force me to kill you this night, your blood is upon your own soul."

Kalid's eyes flashed with sudden wrath, yet he was confident. "You are no match for me now." He came at him with contempt. "It is you who will die."

Tancred met him with caution, for he knew the prince was a notable swordsman, and Tancred was unsure of his own strength. This he had not expected, and he was saving the last of his strength for Mosul.

Kalid's blade smashed against his, turning it, and he lunged, hoping to ram it through his heart, but Tancred reacted swiftly and swerved his blow, and Kalid lost position. At once Tancred could have yielded a deadly blow, but instead, he used his boot against him, sending the prince sprawling backward to the floor.

"Think again, Kalid."

Kalid was on his feet, his eyes cold. The door flew open and a guard appeared. Seeing what was happening, he lifted his scimitar.

"Kill him," Kalid ordered coldly.

"Will you not fight for the woman you want?" Tancred mocked. "Are you then a coward? Your long boast was full of the wind!"

There was only this moment. In his best physical condition it would have been nearly impossible to take them both. And now?

"Kill him!" Prince Kalid commanded again.

In a flash, Tancred's dagger slipped from his wrist sheath and struck with accuracy. The guard's weapon clattered to the tile floor, both hands grasping the handle of the dagger protruding from his chest. Kalid came with a rush. Tancred hurled the table into him and he tumbled over it, his breath knocked from him.

Tancred was wearying quickly. His legs were trembling and his arm felt numb. Only the thought of Helena kept him on his feet.

Kalid was white, trying to inhale, and per-spiring. "Go!" he gasped bitterly, his blade lowered.

Tancred could do little but lean there,

fighting dizziness. Then he wiped his forehead on his sleeve and retrieved his dagger.

"Your life for mine," he said breathlessly. "We are even again."

Finding the key to the chamber on the wounded guard, he took it and then stood beside Kalid. He removed Kalid's cloak and also took his dagger. "I shall borrow these. When you come to Palermo to see al-Kareem you may have them back."

Kalid smirked.

Tancred crossed the hall to Helena's chambers. He entered, shut the door, and slid the bolt into place.

Helena, where was she?

The Turks were fleeing in any way they could, on horseback or on foot, stumbling over the dead as they did. Some fought madly, others fled into the mosque, only to find it a tomb instead of a sanctuary.

Yaghi-Sian, with a few of his prized bodyguards on thoroughbreds, raced like the wind to escape through the gate, their scimitars swinging and striking down the Franks on foot who tried to haul them from their saddles. The Turkish commander swept through the gate and out of the city, galloping toward the hills to Kerbogha.

"Yaghi-Sian," someone shouted after him.

A group of Armenians and Syrians from the city heard it. Hating their Turkish overlord, they took out after him.

Unexpectedly, Yaghi-Sian was thrown from his horse on the mountain trail and lay stunned. Unable to move, he was overtaken. An angry Armenian was the first to reach him. Without hesitation he struck him dead.

The others rode up. "Take his head and bring it to Bohemond. He will pay handsomely for such a trophy."

Within Antioch the rampage continued. Knights fought their way down from the slopes toward the Bridge Gate. It was seized, and the army of the Provençals stormed in. Bohemond and the Normans were assailing the walls of the Citadel, while the rabble followers began the slaughter and looting of private residences.

Outside in the sunlight the ravages of war heightened. Bodies littered the streets. The Syrians and Armenians in the city now joined the rabble on foot, turning against the Seljuks.

Tancred fought his way through the crowd, striking hard blows to several frenzied men who could not distinguish Turk from Norman. He reached the women's quarters, which had not yet been broken into by the soldiers.

He threw open the gilded doors and entered, sword in hand, and the chief eunuch, Asad, protested vigorously as he followed Tancred down the hall. Asad's rounded belly was heaving as he expostulated. "Whoever you are, I have told you, there are no women here! They have taken Lady Helena away!"

Tancred pushed him to one side and threw open the chamber door where Helena had been kept. The room was empty. In one corner near a bed of cushions he saw one slipper.

"She twisted her foot in the back garden," Asad explained as Tancred picked it up. "I intended to bring hot water for her to soak the injury, but when I came he was here. She was quite upset, for he told her that her bodyguard had been slain by one of his soldiers."

Tancred grabbed him by the front of his tunic, lifting him to his tiptoes. Asad's short arms flailed wildly, and fright twisted his face as he stared up into the scathing blue-gray eyes.

"Auspicious one! Please —"

"Who was *he?* Who took her away?"

"Commander" — he choked — "Mosul . . . and his guards!"

"Mosul!" He dropped the front of his tunic so quickly that Asad lost his balance and fell onto the cushions. "He told her I was dead?"

"O Great One! Who was I to stop such a man? He was very angry when he learned that Prince Kalid discovered his treachery against him!"

"What treachery? Be swift!"

"His Eminence, Prince Kalid, expected Mosul to ambush him on the road to Aleppo. Kalid gave orders that Mosul's men were to be replaced. Mosul discovered this and came here for Lady Helena."

"When? How long ago?"

"Not long, a few hours ago, before the barbarians entered the city. He was furious and was wearing a bandage about his head. There had been a mishap earlier in the garden. Someone struck him —"

"Master! I knew you would come here! I have been waiting!"

Tancred turned to see Jamil beckoning wildly. "News, master, very bad!"

Asad wrung his hands. "If something is wrong, should His Eminence not be summoned?" he suggested timidly.

"Wrong! Look out your window, Asad. And if you have a place to hide, do so! You'll be dead in an hour if you do not."

Asad paled and looked as though he would faint, but he soon recovered. "O Great One! Yes! Yes!"

"The wine storage, Asad!" said Jamil. "Hide among the empty barrels!"

His eyes widened with hope. "The wine storage!" He turned and fled.

Tancred drew the door shut and slid the bolt into place. Jamil had run ahead to the steps leading into the garden. "Over here, master!" He darted into the trees. Seeing the way clear, Tancred followed.

The boy was agitated, tugging at Tancred's arm.

"I was hiding among the baggage when I heard the sound of horses. I looked out and saw Mosul and three guards. They were swiftly joined by twenty soldiers. Mosul had Helena with him on his horse. And — and —" Tears filled his eyes. "Aziza is dead. She tried to stop him — to defend her mistress, and he killed her."

Tancred gritted his rage. *Dead.* He gripped the boy in a comforting grasp, but there was no time now to grieve. Jamil, too, seemed to know it and conducted himself bravely. "Helena — Mosul rode away with her!"

"What!" His rage sent Jamil jumping backward.

"I would have killed him but —"

Tancred could hardly control his wrath. Mosul! The vile assassin! He had Helena

. . . what would it be? Murder? A forced marriage? Or worse?

Jamil was still shaken by the rage on his master's face. "Take him alive, master! Then make him sweat your sword! You will overtake him. The stallion runs like lightning and your sword will take his head!"

Tancred clamped his jaw to force himself to think clearly. "Where did they go, which way? Did you hear?"

"They changed plans. They will not go to Aleppo, nor yet to Egypt, but Baghdad. Mosul mentioned an emir he once served there. The mistress will be held for ransom. He will ask much gold of Nicholas for her release."

Then Mosul did not know who he was, or what Helena meant to him. When he did know —

"Come! Horses wait!"

They ran ahead, staying close to the shadows of the trees. Nearing the Gate of the Dog, Jamil stopped, crouching in the darkness.

"It is clear, master, quick. Ahead is the caravan that Kalid was preparing — and there are horses!"

Tancred followed Jamil among the kneeling camels and the piles of baggage to where two horses were saddled, still untouched by the fleeing mobs.

Tancred mounted the Arabian stallion, who pranced with nervous excitement. He snatched the reins of the second horse from Jamil.

"I am sorry, my little friend. I will need both horses to overtake them. I will ride all night until I pick up Mosul's trail."

But the expression on Jamil's face broke his heart.

"All right," he relented. "We go to the stables to see if you can get another horse."

Jamil's face brightened. "Yes, master! But wait — this is for you!"

Jamil jumped on top of the baggage and grabbed a light chain-mail vest, a damascened helmet, gloves, and a black riding cloak.

He ran back to the side of the stallion and handed them up to Tancred. His brown eyes shone.

They rode to the stables, and Jamil ran inside to saddle a horse. Tancred feared there would be none left. He waited impatiently. The Arabian stallion also seemed impatient, and he kept bobbing his head and tasting the bit, then rolled his eyes at his new master, as if he were satisfied.

Tancred waited until he feared something had gone awry. He rode through the wide doors and glanced about. It did not take long before those seeking horses caught sight of him.

"You! Infidel Turk! Come down!"

Jamil spoke not a word as he crouched on the beam.

"Set the stables on fire. That will bring him down!"

"No! The horse feed will be lost. Go up after him."

One of the rabble started upward. Jamil drew his yataghan, a curved dagger.

"Make one move toward my son and you will be minus your head!" came Tancred's voice behind them.

They whirled, confused. "You are a Norman — one of us. Do you defend an infidel?"

Tancred lifted his curved blade. The two men lowered their sword and ax, backing toward the stable door.

"You fools — he is Christian Armenian. If you are in sight when we ride out, your bodies will join those you have slaughtered."

Jamil shimmied down from the rafters as fast as he had gone up. A young black horse he had long wanted was saddled, and he swung himself up.

Tancred rode out into the sunlight, Jamil behind, his young face telling that he was under no illusion of the difficulty before them. The roar of battle was like distant thunder.

Tancred handed him a sword. "Be ready for anything. If anyone tries to pull you from the saddle, use it."

Jamil bravely latched hold of the blade. "I am ready," he said.

Tancred gripped his blade, his left hand holding the reins, and looked at him. The glance between them said far more than any spoken words.

They rode toward the street.

Antioch was now in the hands of the crusaders. There were so many dead in the streets that the horses could hardly keep from stumbling. Jamil had gotten rid of his Turkish dress and was covered with Tancred's cloak. A foot soldier grabbed at his reins, but Jamil struck him. The others backed away. "Keep moving," Tancred told him. "Do not stop."

Up on the hill the massive Citadel was besieged by the Normans. The Turks inside held out, waiting for Kerbogha. At last Tancred reached the Bridge Gate where the Provençal knights held their position. Here, they were now safe. Without a glance back, Tancred rode aside and waited for Jamil to ride through.

The river Orontes was ahead, blue in the

warm sun. The battle for Antioch was far from over, for the cavalry of Kerbogha was only a day away. The two forces would again clash on the plain before the city finally rested in the hands of Bohemond. Then there would follow the battles for Jerusalem and Bethlehem. Tancred's own battle was not over. He and Jamil would search for Helena. As for Sicily and what awaited him if he took possession of his father's wealthy heritage, he did not know. That would also wait for another day.

They galloped down the Fortified Bridge, then turned toward the Gate of the Dog. Neither of them looked back. The tension eased, and the memory of death was released as the wind blew against them, warm and free. Their thoroughbreds raced over the road as though borne upon wings.

Far behind them a distant shout reached Tancred. He looked over his shoulder and saw one horse fast on their trail, a warrior waving his arm wildly, the scimitar flashing in the hot sun. A second look at the horse and the falcon that was released to soar toward him, and Tancred knew who the warrior was. The falcon flew past him, its shrill cry piercing the wind. His loyal friend — Hakeem!

★ ★ ★

The Gate of the Dog was behind them and the road stretched ahead. Tancred admired the Arabian beneath him as the desert wind rushed past free and wild. The stallion's wide nostrils flared, the shiny mane floated, and its breath came like a ballad of ecstasy: *For this I was born, for this I was trained, for this I live!*

The sand flew by beneath him, and beside him rode Jamil and Hakeem and the extra horse. Helena's image burned in his heart like a torch leading him onward; the rhythm of hoofbeats skimming the road echoed with the beat of his heart. Helena, Helena. He would find her in time, he must! Mosul! The assassin! He had killed his brother Derek, he had murdered his lovely cousin Kamila, and now, Aziza! Mosul had eluded him like a slimy serpent for too long! And now he had Helena in his control!

CHAPTER 24

On the Desert

Mosul and his Moors draped themselves in black hoods, their only protection from the harsh desert surroundings. Helena had only a cloak that she kept tightly wrapped about her burnoose, but it did little to stop the wind and stinging sand.

Tancred . . . dead. The stabbing words repeated themselves in her mind without mercy. Scalding tears stung her eyelids as the wind blasted her face. Bitter, rebellious toward her captors, she refused to talk or eat and kept her head turned away whenever Mosul walked up to her.

They camped beneath the stars, a day's journey from Antioch, and several Moorish soldiers made a fire in a windbreak. Helena sat sullenly by the fire. Her ankle was still swollen, and to make her misery worse, she had no shoes. Mosul had forced her from the chamber without any personal provisions.

Grieved by Tancred's death and in discomfort, the possibility of escape did not enter her mind. She felt dazed, nauseated. She was left to Mosul's selfish appetites and to a fate in Baghdad that she dare not think of. Where was her God? Had He forsaken her at last? Did He not love her any longer?

I have failed Him, she thought. *The ruin of all things dear and precious to me is my just reward!*

She kept her head bent to avoid the eyes of the other thirty soldiers loitering about. None of them dared speak to her, for Mosul's intentions were clearly known.

A Moor squatted by the small fire roasting a desert bird he had taken with an arrow, and Helena stared blankly at the flames sputtering up from the dripping juices. The odor was horrid. She felt nauseated at its sight, for the head and claws were still in place. She turned her face to avoid the smoke drifting in her direction.

"You are not hungry?" the soldier asked quietly.

She shook her head.

He started to say something more but lapsed into silence when Mosul saw them speaking. He walked up to the fire with his mulled wine and stared down at Helena. Her stomach muscles tightened.

"You are cold?" Mosul asked.

Trying to cease her trembling, Helena shook her head no.

"Your foot is yet swollen. Let me see it."

"No! Do not touch me!"

Heads shifted in their direction. In the darkness the soldiers' expressions could not be seen. Did they feel pity for her, or simply indifference?

Mosul's black brows thundered together. "Can you do nothing but squall like a child? Drink this!" He handed her the mug.

With a sob Helena flung it into the fire. The flames sputtered.

Mosul muttered under his breath and jerked her to her feet, and for a moment she thought he would strike her. It was suddenly silent as every eye riveted upon them. Helena tried to pull away.

"You whine like a child," he mocked. "This bodyguard for whom you weep so much must have been your adopted papa!"

"You ordered him killed! I despise you!"

His grip bruised her arms. "You best learn to please me. You have no one now but me. Remember that!" When she responded only by lapsing into genuine dismay, Mosul's hands dropped from her and he strode away angrily.

The Moors turned away and continued

their preoccupation.

Dead. . . . Helena sank to the ground near the fire. *He* was dead, the one man she loved and wanted, and she whispered into the night, expecting no listeners but the Great Creator. "Tancred, oh, Tancred. . . ." But at once she saw her mistake, for the Moor attending the roasting bird looked up.

He stared across the flames at her. His eyes narrowed as if the name had to detach itself from some unpleasant memory in order to find its proper place. Then slowly, he put the bird aside and was on his feet. He glanced over at Mosul, who had his back turned toward them. He walked over to him.

Helena watched him talking. Mosul tensed. His head jerked toward her.

He knew who the bodyguard was! What if he did? What did it matter? Tancred was dead. If anything, the fact that she had managed to keep it a secret in Antioch would only make him angry. If he became disgusted with her, perhaps he would leave her alone.

Mosul left the Moor and strode toward her, his face tense. For a long moment he did not speak but stared down at her intently.

"What name is this that you lament?"

Helena kept silent. *Please, Lord, help me,* she prayed.

He grasped her arm and roughly pulled her

to her feet, ignoring her as she winced on her swollen ankle. "Tancred?" he nearly spat the word as if it were bitter on his tongue. "Redwan? Tancred Redwan?"

Her eyes collided with his, showing his hatred. "Yes," she spat back and managed to jerk free of his grasp. She hobbled back a step and looked among the Moorish soldiers, shouting, "Tancred Redwan from Sicily. He was a ruling lord, was he not? From the house of al-Kareem! You have betrayed him. And had he lived he would soon have been on your trail. He would have killed your commander." She turned back to Mosul and cried, "Assassin! You murdered Derek Redwan!"

Mosul appeared too stunned to react to her accusation.

She wondered at the change that came over him. His expression was twisted with unbelief, then fear, at the thought of the man who had hunted him for so long.

Helena wondered, surprised at his change. He was now concerned only with information.

"Tancred Jehan Redwan would not be your slave," he suggested. "He traveled alone; he fought alone. You lie to me."

"Are you frightened of a dead man?" she mocked. "Does your vile conscience rise to torment you? You assassinated his brother. And now you had a guard kill Tancred while he slept. How cowardly!"

Still he did not react to her words. He turned from the fire to stare off into the desert darkness behind them, as though listening to the whine of the Arabian winds. Swiftly Mosul kicked sand on the fire, putting them in darkness. A swirl of smoke curled upward and was carried off with a gust of wind. Helena clasped her arms about her, staring at him, alert. Why . . . he was afraid, she thought, bemused by the realization.

"There will be no camp tonight. Get the horses," he ordered. "We will ride through the night to reach the ruin."

Helena watched him as he swiftly walked off. She turned to the Moor, who was trying to retrieve his half-cooked bird from the ashes. "Does your commander fear ghosts?" she mocked bitterly.

"No, he fears the man."

She looked down on him as he poked in the ashes. She was still hurting and dazed. "Why should he fear Tancred when he —" She stopped short. Sudden understanding leaped through her heart. Her eyes brightened and great joy filled her with praise. "Thank you, heavenly Father, for protecting him!" She turned quickly and gazed into the darkness toward the direction of Antioch.

"You are right," said the Moor. "Jehan is not dead."

Tancred would come, she thought. Even now he may be out there in the desert trailing after them. The thought brought comfort, and new strength steeled her emotions. She looked up toward the stars. *Thank you, most merciful God,* she prayed. *You have not abandoned me.*

The soldiers, all from Sicily, knew well that Tancred had been searching for Mosul for years. As they mounted their horses, no one spoke, but the looks exchanged between them said that Mosul was a worried man.

"He should be worried," Helena stated boldly, seated astride the horse. Now she felt giddy with new hope. "Tancred will come! Mosul not only murdered his brother, but now he has stolen his wife!"

Astonishment spread across many a face. This beautiful woman was the *wife* of Jehan?

She did not understand her blunder until Mosul whirled and stared up at her. At the look on his face she froze in horror.

The silence was broken as he threw back his head and laughed loudly.

Helena cringed at his glee.

"You are his wife? Then let him come!

When he does, I shall have him at my mercy. So you are his woman, are you?" he repeated, astounded. He turned to the soldiers and gestured to Helena. "The woman of Jehan!"

He laughed again, but his soldiers were sober.

Mosul walked up to where she sat astride the horse and snatched the reins from her hands. His eyes moved over her.

"So that is why he risked the blades of fifty Seljuks. And to think I was fool enough to not guess it. He was within my sword at that moment and I knew it not. And Kalid, what a fool you made of him. It could not be better! I shall not merely have gold from Nicholas — I shall have the wolf who has trailed me all these years! Now let us see what he can do."

Helena stared down at him, sickened by her blunder.

One of the Moors who had been riding behind as a scout now rode into the camp. "Mosul, we are being followed," he warned.

Mosul was alert. "Kalid's men?"

"Three men. They soon separated. Now there is but one man who trails us. He has a black stallion and a spare horse, but I long ago lost sight of him."

My stallion. It is Tancred. It has to be, Helena thought.

"This one who trails us knows what he is doing. I would not have known he followed except he deliberately sent this horse ahead. With a message." He handed Mosul a note. "It was attached to the saddle."

Mosul read the words written in the Moorish tongue, and his face turned deathly pale.

Tancred was not far behind! Helena wanted to laugh with joy. A gust of warm wind came against her, and it seemed her beloved's presence reached with the wind to embrace her. His presence was so strongly felt that she actually looked about in the darkness for him, her heart beating heavily, sensing in some way the nearness of the man she loved, and from it she took courage. She could endure anything now — Tancred was coming! He was out there, not far away, and she was sure that he had sent the note to not only undermine Mosul's confidence, but to bolster hers.

Mosul crushed the note in his hand and looked up at her, his eyes blazing. Helena smiled and lifted her chin bravely.

"You do well to be afraid," she warned. "Tancred's way with the sword is respected and feared by his enemies. Your men know this too."

Helena called over to the Moorish soldiers. "Take heed. Does not the name Redwan mean anything to you? If you wish to live, slip away into the night. For he will surely come, and who is to say he will come alone?"

Mosul seized her roughly from the saddle, and she thought his strong hands would snap her in two.

"Speak thus again and he will find you with a dagger in your heart."

He let her go and Helena crumpled to the sand. Unable to move for a moment, she lay there, dazed.

She heard the Moorish guard speaking in a low voice to Mosul. "Why not leave the woman here? No amount of gold from Nicholas is worth facing Jehan and the Redwans. Let us divide into three groups. He will not know which set of hoofprints to follow."

"No," Mosul growled. "We will not run like a pack of sheep. We are twenty soldiers; Tancred is alone. Let him come." He gazed down at Helena with a hard look. "Set an ambush for him. I want him alive!"

At dawn they approached what Helena guessed was some old abandoned castle keep. The walls were breached; large and small stones were scattered on the slope or piled in mounds, and they were covered with dried summer grasses. Wide steps, like those belonging to a Greek pavilion, led upward to a hall surrounded with a high but crumbling wall. In one corner Helena saw steep inner steps leading onto a crumbling terrace. From the terrace, there was a wide view of the desert. No one could approach without being seen.

Mosul's remaining men were on guard and waited throughout the day for those in charge of the ambush to return with their prey. Helena was kept in an ancient banqueting hall, now open to the sky and the desert elements, where Mosul could watch her closely.

"Have you no pity?" she pleaded. "I can hardly escape with a swollen ankle. Is there any reason why I must be tied to this pillar?"

Mosul stood behind a broken section of the wall, staring out across the plain. He looked over at her and scanned her. Then taking out his dagger he came up behind the pillar and cut the rope binding her wrists.

"This warrior you crave will yet be bound," he warned.

Helena forced herself to remain outwardly composed.

"All the Redwans are the same," he said bitterly. "Lords! Demanding! I have but one good thing to say of the man you want: he is a warrior equal to me. He has survived these years on his own merit, his own sword, even as I have. Did you know we are related?"

"Yes. How could two boys raised together in the house of al-Kareem turn so violently against each other?"

"I learned to hate him. He bested me in everything I did. When he stole the heart of Kamila from me —"

Mosul must have decided he had said too much, for he stopped.

"You will not catch him like some hungry beast in a trap," she challenged. "And he will not bargain with you on my account."

He laughed shortly. "Oh yes he will, *Your Highness*."

"Tancred does not die so easily," she retorted, remembering what he had often jested. "He will elude any snare you set in order to bring you to justice."

Her suggestion that the ambush could fail, leaving Mosul still hunted by the wolf, kindled a spark of fear in his face that turned swiftly to bitter hatred.

"Then if he comes I will see he dies a thousand deaths before my sword finally takes him!"

Helena hid a shudder of fear and, as if very cold, drew her soiled cloak about her. Mosul retook his position by the broken wall, his eyes once again riveting on the plain. The sun beat upon it, and the rocks reflected the heat.

"He will come for you," he murmured. "I know him that well. And in this he shall find his doom."

Helena would choose death for herself rather than become Tancred's reason for defeat.

The noon sun rose high in the blue sky and beat down into the roofless hall. She was thirsty but refused to taste Mosul's mulled wine.

Tancred is too wise to be taken in an ambush, she repeated to herself for the hundredth time that day. If she knew him as she thought she did, he would expect Mosul to set a trap.

CHAPTER 25

The Castle Ruin

The sun was now low behind the hills of Asia. When darkness fell like a mantle over the plain, Tancred would emerge from his place of hiding, Helena consoled herself. Somehow he would pursue the trail they had ridden to the ruin, and he would be near. She struggled to keep her fears from growing worse in the darkness.

Mosul leaned his shoulder against the wall and stared at her. Helena refused to look at him.

Above her head the sky was growing ever darker; stars began to emerge white and glittering. The wind picked up and sang sharply about the corners of the ruin. She could only see Mosul's darkened silhouette now. He remained where he had been for most of the day, at the wall staring into the plain. Helena shuddered. There was no sound, no movement but the wind playing among the fallen stones and rocks, rustling the dried grasses like the shaking of a serpent's tail.

She had to speak to break the silence. "Where are the soldiers you left behind to set the ambush?" she taunted. "Why have they not returned with your captive?"

Mosul did not move. His silhouette now merged into the darkness and she could hardly see him.

"I shall tell you," she went on. "The ambush failed. Even now Tancred is astride a fine Arabian stallion and soon will be here."

Mosul tensed and looked out across the wall. He heard unexpected horse hooves approaching . . . then galloping across the stone courtyard below, echoing in the shadowed ruins.

Mosul drew his sword, every muscle in his strong body ready, alert for action as the sound of running feet came bounding up into the open hall.

A dark figure came toward them and announced, "Mosul, the men you ordered to set the ambush have left. They have turned back toward Aleppo."

In the darkness, Mosul's swarthy face was hidden, but his voice reeked with disgust, and something else . . . fear?

"The whimpering cowards. So they have run out on me? Well, it will do Jehan no good. How many men are on watch below?"

"Twelve."

"It is enough. Spread out. Keep watch."

When the Moorish soldier left, Helena said gleefully, "Did I not tell you? Tancred will not be trapped so easily."

Mosul was beside her, his fingers biting into her arm. He propelled her across the stone floor, toward the steps circling up to the terrace. Helena struggled on her throbbing ankle, wincing as he pushed her ahead of him up the steps.

Without a protective wall about the terrace, the wind blasted against her as they stepped onto the stone floor. In some places the stone was caving in and he led her cautiously toward the other end.

"If he is fool enough to come to the ruins tonight, he will find taking you from me impossible. One move from him and you will go over the side. Not a thought even I wish to contemplate. So sit down there and be still."

Helena clenched her teeth to keep them from chattering, not wanting Mosul to know how terrified she was of heights. She shut her eyes tightly and tried not to picture the steep drop below, or the crumbling terrace deck without a raised boundary. She drew her cloak tightly around her and huddled with her arms about her knees, her face pressed hard against them, trembling, a feeling of panic seizing her.

"I will not think about it," she kept repeating. Tiny droplets of moisture ran down her ribs. She would see something else in her mind. Tancred! She agonized to bring up his image, for it sent courage to her soul.

His eyes, she thought, as stormy as the bluish gray of a turbulent sea, then as quiet as an early morn when the dew was wet beneath one's bare feet. His hair, curling at the nape of his neck, glinting with light and dark browns, and just a tinge of auburn where it caught the sun. . . . Tancred, the *barbarian*. Tancred, the suave and gallant *Knight*. Tancred, the overpowering but tender warrior who would one day be her husband. Tancred, the knave who had deliberately overheard her conversation with Philip that night so long ago in Philip's chamber. She could smile at the memory now. Whoever he was, or whether he were all of these images and more, she loved him. He was *there* with her on that high and precarious terrace, so close in her memory that she could almost feel the heat of his arms about her and hear the spoken words in her ear.

Helena raised her head with a jerk and looked about in the deep night's darkness, the wind touching her face and pulling her hair.

Tancred *was* there!

No, she must be mad, or so half crazed with fear that she imagined it. Yet she could sense his nearness, and a strange calmness stole over her. He was somewhere very near the ruins — he had to be. Helena groped her way to her feet and stood there. Their very hearts came together to beat as one, as if their love was carried by the warm winds to unite, to touch.

"Tancred?" she whispered.

"Silence," said Mosul. "Sit down!"

She looked across the stone floor at Mosul. The spell was shattered. She sank to the cold stone, where she was once again on the dreaded heights of that frightening floor in the darkness, alone with Mosul. Yet she could not dismiss the conviction that Tancred, too, was somewhere near the ruins. She closed her eyes and let the wind play about her.

When her lashes fluttered open, the dimness of a pale yellow dawn painted the eastern sky. Shadows were still deep in the low places of the purplish hills, and a lonely shriek from a bird heralded a new day. With wings unfurled, it soared overhead, and she shaded her eyes to watch its graceful flight.

Oh, that she had wings to fly! The bird flew across the plain behind some rocks and landed.

That bird. Was it a falcon? Her hopes soared.

There came the rush of feet up the steps, and once again a soldier appeared to report to Mosul. Helena was not supposed to hear, but she did.

"The men exchanged watches through the night, but he has slipped among us and away again."

Mosul scrambled to his feet. "Impossible."

The guard's expression was troubled. "This was left on the steps below."

Mosul was reluctant to reach for the note. He stared as though it could not exist. At last he snatched it from the soldier, then glanced over at Helena. She was afraid to smile.

As he read, his face paled, then deepened to an ugly flush at whatever insult was written in the Moorish tongue.

He whirled to face the barren wilderness. "Even now he watches us."

"He must have wings," said the soldier.

"So he is here, is he?" Mosul strode over to Helena and, grabbing her by the arm, hauled her to the edge of the terrace.

"No!" Helena screamed before she could stifle her agony.

The soldier looked upon her with a hint of pity. He took a step toward her, then halted, perhaps thinking better of it. He said to Mosul, as if to ease his commander's rage, "Jehan may have gone back for more men."

"And leave the woman for whom he risks everything in order to rescue? I tell you, he is here!"

Helena stared below her. The ground teetered and convulsed under her dimmed vision, and her spine tingled. "No! No!" Her eyes closed tightly, the tears rolled down her face, her dark hair sticking — she started to scream, clutching at Mosul wildly.

Mosul was stunned at her reaction, but he was just as quickly delighted with her fear. Thinking of Tancred watching, he burst out with a chilling laugh. "Jehan! You are out there! I know you are!"

Mosul's shout echoed through the ruin. "Hear her scream? Curse yourself for not coming to her aid. Come for her if you dare!"

There was no answer from the ruins below. Mosul's dark eyes scanned the distant rocks for the slightest movement. The wind shook the grass and whined around the corners of the keep. Seeing nothing below, Mosul stepped back, releasing Helena to fall into the arms of the guard. The soldier quickly led her away from the precarious edge and lowered her to the floor, a look of pity on his rugged face.

"I am a soldier, not a fiend," he whispered to Helena. "What has gotten into Mosul to make him act this way? He seems crazed with fear and vengeance. No wonder half the men serving him have stolen away. Who wishes to follow a commander like this?"

He looked over at Mosul with a scowl. Mosul was staring at the rocks, his eyes darting here and there.

Morning, then afternoon, passed slowly, and when night descended like a cloak over the ruins, another of the soldiers approached Mosul. Without a word he produced another note.

Mosul gritted, "Where was it found?"

"On your horse," the guard said flatly. "The men are growing tense. They do not care for this invisible wolf hunt. He could put a dagger in any one of us and we would never know it!"

"If he is here, why have we not seen him?" Mosul demanded, infuriated.

"The men are nervous. We are only twelve now. They begin to question the wisdom of holding the Byzantine woman."

"Who are they to question me? I am in command."

"They think Jehan has the powers of a magician."

Mosul spat. "What manner of men are these who sit about in the dark conjuring up tales? He is a man with flesh that cuts and bleeds. He cannot be in two places at once. He is here in the ruins! Find him!"

"We have looked. There is no flesh and blood, only notes that promise a fate worse than death if you touch the woman. I tell you the men wish to ride out of here now, tonight. Leave her to him, Mosul! Let us go now while we have our lives. It is not worth the risk."

Mosul read the warning contained in the note. His brow glinted with perspiration; he cursed under his breath and hurled his container of wine.

"He mocks us. He takes us for fools." He began to pace. "So he is bold enough to think he can get past the guards into this hall tonight?"

Helena was on her feet. "I told you he would come!"

He whirled and pointed a warning with his drawn blade. "Silence your tongue, woman."

The guard's face was troubled. "That he was able to get past is proven by the two messages he left you, Mosul."

"Impossible, I tell you. It is a trick. He seeks to sow the seeds of fear and panic. It will not work. Does he take me for a fool?" He walked over to the crumbling wall and peered off into the darkness. Not a sound was heard from the empty plain but the scuttling of dry brush in the wind.

"If Tancred thinks to get past the watch tonight, then let him try. I shall be ready for him. Alert the men — take your watch!"

Helena's heart pounded. Tancred was wise to trouble Mosul's peace of mind. What was the old saying? *"Whom the gods would destroy, they first drive to madness."*

Helena watched him. Even now Mosul was tense. His gaze was riveted on the steps leading down into the hall. Her lips turned into a slight smile. Tancred's warning that he would come tonight had already put Mosul on the defensive.

Deeper darkness descended upon the plain, a sliver of moon giving only a hint of light. The ruin stood etched like a skeleton of the past against the backdrop of shadowy hills. Mosul did not sleep. He dare not if Tancred was coming tonight.

With every sudden gust of wind whining past the crevices and making eerie soblike sounds, Mosul lifted his sword, expectant, waiting.

The lonely hours of night inched toward dawn; faint glimmers of morning light began to chase the shadows where Helena hovered between restless sleep and wakefulness. She, too, waited, but with quiet confidence. Tancred knew exactly what he was doing.

Mosul did not know. He was still awake as the eastern sunrise lightened the horizon. The shadows fled before the bursting sun. Suddenly he shouted his rage. "Tancred! I will kill you!"

Helena bolted upright, heart pounding. But Tancred was not on the terrace. Mosul was gazing out across the breached wall of the ruin to the plain below.

"Warriors!" he gasped. "How did they arrive without the guards hearing?"

Mosul rushed to count them, even as Helena did — twenty, thirty, forty men astride Great horses, their Norman armor glinting in the bright morning sun. The flag was boldly planted before them to greet the eyes of Mosul in the morning light. The Redwan falcon! The insignia immediately identified them as Normans, men in liege to Walter of Sicily, Tancred's uncle.

She looked at Mosul. Sweat dotted his furrowed brow, a twisted look of horror on his face. What must he be thinking?

★ ★ ★

Mosul's mind took the unpleasant route back to Sicily, where once he had served the Redwan family, back to the Redwan castle, and to the Moorish section of Palermo. With assistance from Redwan enemies among the Moors, witnesses had been paid in gold to vow that they had seen Tancred kill his brother in a fit of jealous rage, then flee.

Mosul had left Sicily, taking a ship to the Golden Horn in Constantinople. One day he discovered that Tancred had followed him and was asking questions. Thereafter, wherever Mosul fled, Tancred remained close on his trail. He had followed him from Sicily to Constantinople to the camp of the Red Lion and then to Antioch.

Mosul's dark eyes squinted, riveting on the Redwan gonfanon with the emblem of the falcon. And now it had come to this moment. Tancred was here.

Then above, in the morning sky, Mosul's eyes caught sight of a magnificent falcon swooping low to land on the shoulder of a warrior on an Arabian stallion who came from the rocks and rode toward the ruin. Mosul swore under his breath. So! That was it! That was how the messages were delivered! A falcon!

He gritted his teeth.

A guard appeared. "There are forty Norman warriors. We are trapped."

"Not as long as I possess the woman he wants," Mosul hissed.

A distant voice from below was shouting up in their direction.

That voice! Mosul knew it well. His eyes fixed on the warrior astride the horse. Tancred broke rank from the others and rode forward alone. The horse's prancing hooves beat time on the stone court, then stopped, followed by silence.

A gust of wind sent Tancred's challenge bouncing among the ruins.

"Mosul!"

"I hear you, Jehan! One word from me and the arrows of my men will cut you down."

"Your men have deserted you. You are alone!"

"He speaks truth," the guard whispered to Mosul. "I was next to the last watch. When I awoke they had slipped away. There are only two of us."

Mosul's jaw set. He wiped his face on his sleeve. "So be it." Then he shouted down from the portico, "I have my sword, Redwan — that and the woman! It is enough!"

Below, Tancred held his mount steady,

but the stallion was impatient for action and bobbed his head under the bit. Tancred stared up at the terrace. He could only guess Mosul's hidden position. Somehow he must get Mosul to come alone to meet him. He dared make no move with Helena at his mercy.

"In the name of Norman justice I challenge you, Mosul! Come, defend your claim to innocence in Derek Redwan's murder!"

"Why should I? You killed him," Mosul shouted back. "All the rulers of Sicily know it to be so. They have not left Sicily to fight the Turks but to find you. Will you deceive them now by trapping me? Hear me!" Mosul shouted toward the main body of warriors. "Tancred killed Derek Redwan! There are witnesses!"

Tancred looked over at Walter of Sicily, who remained immobile astride his Great Horse, but his knuckles showed white as he gripped his reins. Tancred's other uncles, William and Robert, moved restlessly on their mounts. His cousins, including Leif, exchanged glances with the other five young Redwan warriors. Leif was scowling, and Tancred believed he knew what he was thinking, that Tancred was making a mistake, that his strength was not in keeping with the ordeal ahead.

On the way from Antioch with Hakeem and Jamil, Tancred had been surprised to meet up with Nicholas. He had been waiting to bring him to meet his father and the Redwan clan that had accompanied him from the Castle of Hohms. Had it not been for the intervention of his adoptive father, Rolf, and of Nicholas, the clan would have imprisoned him by now. But at the Castle of Hohms, Rolf and Nicholas had convinced Walter to grant Tancred this final opportunity to prove himself. Leif, too, had convinced Walter that the death of Norris had been the fault of Philip.

Tancred looked up at the ruins and goaded Mosul's ego. "You are a warrior, are you not?" he challenged. "Come, show your sword! Will you hide behind the shield of a woman? Will you send her forth to contest me?"

"I could take you, Tancred! As for the woman, she is worth her beauty in Lysander's gold. She stays with me!"

"Let us meet at last, Mosul. Here . . . now! The rulers of Sicily look on as judges. They have agreed to render guilt or innocence upon the warrior who survives. Where is, then, the justification for your refusal to face me? Kill me, and you will be free! Defend your claim to innocence! Unless you admit to the deed of an assassin. Come, swine! Murderer of women!"

Mosul's black eyes flared with rage. He was trapped and he knew it. Tancred had left him no room to maneuver. Either he would die trying to escape, or he would kill Tancred in a duel. The latter would be difficult, but not impossible. His reputation as a Moorish swordsman was known and respected. But if he tried to escape — he would be run down by the Redwans and forced to walk the red-hot coals.

He licked his lips. "If I take you, does your father Rolf give the Norman vow to let me depart in peace?"

"You have not only his vow, but the vow of all the lords here gathered."

"What of the woman?" Mosul shouted.

"If I fail, the lords have sworn not to intervene. But Nicholas will pay a satchel of gold for her release. Think, Mosul! Your freedom and the gold! Come forth! Defend your innocence! Will it be on foot or with horse?"

"Horse," Mosul shouted down, "and let it be to the death!"

In reply, Tancred threw down the gauntlet and, turning the stallion, rode backward a few paces and waited.

Soon, a Norman led another horse across the court toward the steps and held the reins, waiting for Mosul.

The moments were prolonged with tense silence as Tancred waited. Mosul would come. There was no other hope of his escape. Tancred's eyes were riveted on the wide stone steps leading to the pavilion. A slight movement behind a broken pillar — then a warrior stood in the shadows. He stepped forward into the sunlight.

Mosul. The wind rustled his black hood. His tunic was belted and reached to his upper thighs. He came slowly down the steps, his boots against the loose stone, a deadly, determined expression on his swarthy face. His hand rested on his sheathed sword.

One glimpse of the man he had sought for so long and Tancred's strong jaw clenched. At last.

Nicholas and another Norman soldier came with pieces of armor: the customary chain mesh that went over the tunics, the helmets with face shields to protect the bridge of the nose, and leggings.

As Tancred put on his helmet, his eyes suddenly caught sight of Helena being forced across the pavilion by Mosul's remaining guard. She wore an ankle-length hooded cloak, but the strong wind blew it back, showing her hair being tossed about. One glimpse of her, and his arms ached to embrace her. Did she know how much he loved her, and that he had every intention of taking Mosul?

As the guard pushed her forward to view the spectacle, Tancred could see the fear on her face. His temper surged. He rode forward shouting, "Take her away!"

The Moor hastened to oblige, but Helena jerked free. She stared down at Tancred, weak with a torrent of emotions: fear, dismay, pain, and love. As their eyes met and briefly held, there leaped up within her heart a breathtaking certainty. He would be victorious. And Tancred, as warrior, was utterly confident of his ability to take Mosul!

She wanted to cry out to him that she loved him, but the words never left her lips, for a Norman lord on horseback shouted for the ordeal to begin at once.

Tancred called up, "Wait for me inside."

Wait for him . . . he said, because he would return to her.

She watched him lower his face shield, then turn to trot ahead. The Normans had formed two lines, and as he rode through them, followed by Mosul, Helena's stomach flinched.

"Please," she demanded of the Moorish guard, "turn me loose. I will not leave your side. I must watch!"

The Moorish soldier was in no mood to contest anyone, for several Normans stood by watching to make sure he did not use the opportunity to escape. Helena could not bear to let her eyes stray from Tancred. She watched, perspiring but scarcely breathing.

CHAPTER 26

Confrontation

Mosul was a powerful warrior, adept with sword and scimitar, and seated tall on his horse he gave every appearance of a seasoned fighter. Tancred knew that he was not to be treated lightly. Mosul had served the Redwan castle in Sicily before Derek's death, and Tancred had jousted with him and the other castle defenders in rigorous training. He knew what Mosul was capable of.

Yet Tancred was confident. There had never been a warrior who could unseat him. Mosul would not be the first. For too long Tancred had sought this moment.

He touched his face shield and drew his blade, then looked across the field to his uncle and adoptive father, Seigneur Rolf Redwan, awaiting the signal. Rolf, a flaxen-haired soldier with the body of a Viking, had already confronted his younger brother Walter with anger over the injustice he believed had been done to Tancred.

"I have a mind to return to Sicily and take over as head of the clan," he had roared at Walter.

"Then come!" countered Walter. "There are enemies enough among the Moslem Moors to keep both our blades occupied!"

Nicholas had hinted to Tancred earlier that Rolf would not return, explaining that a warm friendship had flared between him and Adrianna.

Tancred shook these family thoughts from his mind and looked across at Mosul. The duel would demand all of his mental and physical strength. He must not be distracted. Absently, he touched the chain mesh beneath his leather tunic where the bandages from his injury were tightly bound. He prayed for strength to endure.

Faithful Hakeem was there too, the one Moor among the Normans, the falcon with him, its feathers ruffling in the breeze. Hakeem had come to him alone before Tancred rode to meet Mosul. *"It is a battle between two Moors, master. Remember the treacherous use of his sword when the two of you were boys? Always he would go for the scimitar when you knocked the blade from his right! He has not changed."*

Jamil was tight faced and in prayer as he

sat back upon a pile of stones. Tancred had given him his cloak as a reminder of his promise to adopt him. Though the morning was hot, Jamil had securely wrapped himself in it.

Tancred looked over at the line of Redwans and saw Leif with Cervon and Olin. Leif gave him a confident raise of his hand in salute.

Uncle Walter was there too, watching in stoic silence, his stark blue eyes riveted on Tancred, but there was evidence of turmoil in the movement of his gloved hands as he flipped the reins. Cousin Cervon had again mentioned that their uncle Walter was somewhat of a changed man since the heartrending news had reached him of the death of his only son, Norris.

"He now has cause to think he was wrong in pronouncing you guilty of Derek's death. Pain has opened his conscience to his own sins."

Rolf prepared to signal that the duel should begin at once.

The moment came. Mosul, with face shield in place, sword ready, galloped toward Tancred, and Tancred rode swiftly to confront him, the sleek Arabian gaining speed. Mosul's sword came with the force of a strong right arm, but Tancred deflected his blade, redirecting its energy.

Turning the Arabian with ease, he struck a quick, vicious blow against Mosul's helmet.

The ringing blow dimmed Mosul's wit, and for a moment he lost balance in his saddle. Tancred turned to ram the yard of steel through his chest, but a shout reached his ears: "Alive! Alive!"

Nicholas's warning voice sent a flash of cold reason through Tancred's senses. He did not want Mosul dead — not yet.

Tancred eased the stallion in a half circle around Mosul.

Too easy! Having tailed him from Sicily to Antioch, was his enemy to crumble in defeat in a fight easily won? Mosul must pay! He must fear!

"You have grown fat and lazy," Tancred mocked. "The trophy of your head must not come in one blow. I am used to fighting warriors, not palace guards!"

In a rage Mosul drove at him with the heavy Norman horse, thinking to run him down, but Tancred swerved the stallion, which seemed to flow to the side smoothly as Mosul's horse thundered past. The Arabian shook its mane and its nostrils flared as though insulted by the Great Horse.

Mosul thrust his sword, trying desperately to reopen Tancred's wound. Aware of the danger, Tancred foiled the attack and merely moved out of reach, opting to keep his vulnerable side away from Mosul's attack.

The Moors were expert in the use of swords. If Tancred had not deliberately drilled himself in becoming adept to every ploy, Mosul could gain the upper hand. Tancred met and challenged Mosul's display of dueling steel. Their swords flashed, touching, jumping, at times seeming to caress. They engaged, detached, each man seeking a brief second of weakness in the other. Mosul sought the ultimate moment to bring home the thrust of death, but Tancred fought to unnerve him.

The duel proceeded, requiring every skill and intense concentration. Despite his weakened condition, Tancred remained confident, aware that Mosul should be afflicted by both conscience and lack of sleep.

"Come, assassin! You must do better! Face-to-face you fail! Is that why you struck my brother in his back?"

Mosul strove to fend off Tancred's sword. Though he did not speak, Tancred knew it was because he feared he would lose concentration. But he heard every gibe, and they cut as deeply as any point of steel.

Tancred was tiring but dared not show it. "You disappoint me! Is this all you can do?"

He shoved Mosul's blade back with contempt.

For a moment they paused, swords crossed, and Mosul's ragged breathing came to his ears.

"After these years I expected more of a challenge than this!"

Tancred pressed him all the harder. Mosul was frightened. Desperately he lunged at him, striking viciously but also growing careless. Tancred saw the muscles in his arms trembling with the prolonged intensity of struggle. As his blade sought to come down, Tancred's blade came up sharply and Mosul's slid off. Again, he sent a deliberate blow ringing against Mosul's helmet, dazing him. Seizing the moment, Tancred followed through with another, beating against his helmet savagely. Mosul was slipping from the saddle. Tancred unleashed a final blow of fury, knocking Mosul to the ground.

Tancred wheeled the stallion to circle him. In any other situation he would have leaned down to strike the death blow, or trample him into the ground with the horse's hooves. The death of his enemy was at last easily within his control. But again the distant shout, this time from Cousin Leif: "Stay your hand! You want him alive!"

Tancred swung low in the saddle and

caught up Mosul's sword, the final act of victory. He held it up to catch the sun's rays, then hurled it at him with contempt.

It was over.

Helena stood on the steps of the castle ruin waiting for Tancred. Her dark eyes flashed as she watched him ride across the court toward the wide stairs. She started down the steps before he ever reached her, trying to run the remaining distance that kept them apart. She had forgotten her ankle and gave a little cry as she nearly collapsed.

He dismounted and ran toward her, sweeping her up into his arms. Their adoring gaze held, speaking silent words of love. Determined that nothing should ever part them again, they clung to each other, their lips meeting in tender, enduring passion while the whining wind played among the stone ruins of a thousand yesterdays. Tomorrow bid them enter their dreams as one, their hope and confidence bound up together in the Christ who sits supreme over time and circumstance.

Jamil, watching the pair, could not restrain his jubilation and tried to break away, but Nicholas caught him by the back of his tunic.

"Master Nicholas," Jamil protested, "I

only wish to tell him that it was well done! Oh, I could see it again, sevenfold!"

"You bloodthirsty cub."

Jamil grinned. "The cub wishes only to learn from the tiger!"

"You deserve serious watching," Nicholas told him, a subdued twinkle in his eye. "A warrior fights when he must. But only in honor, and then reluctantly. A cub who sniffs with pleasure at the smell of battle is likely to find himself running off to lick his wounds."

"I shall try to remember that," Jamil stated with a serious tone.

Nicholas forced a scowl. "You *will* remember if you are turned over to me as Tancred wishes."

"Turned . . . over to you?"

Nicholas covered a smile. "You will first become a scholar. A disciple of the Scriptures. When you master these, then you will be ready to handle the sword wisely. For you will then know who your True Master is."

Jamil moved uneasily. "I wish to be like Tancred."

"Then you will learn to read and write, to speak Greek and Latin as well."

Nicholas threw back his dark head and laughed at the expression on Jamil's young face. He tousled his head. "Be of good cheer, Jamil. Tancred will also teach you the use of the sword. And even I have a few warrior lessons worthy of passing on!"

Tancred left Helena with Nicholas and rode to the center of the line, where Walter sat astride his Great Horse like a monument to William the Conqueror, looking down on Mosul.

"Here is the assassin of Derek Redwan," stated Tancred.

Mosul raised his black head in defiance. His eyes refused to yield to Count Walter's stare. "Killing Derek was a mistake. I meant my dagger to enter the heart of Tancred Jehan."

Tight-lipped, Walter demanded, "Why Jehan?"

"Kamila. I thought she loved Tancred. I did not know it was Derek."

"But the dagger was Tancred's."

"Your enemies planned it so. It suited me well enough."

"My enemies?" breathed Walter. "And their reason?"

Mosul shrugged disdainfully. "Greed, hate, ambition — what other reasons do men kill for?"

"Are you saying there was no other reason for my enemies to plot against us?" he asked in fury, gripping his sword.

Mosul's black eyes mocked him. "Were not greed and jealousy the reasons you believed Tancred killed his brother? Are they suddenly not sufficient to satisfy you? Nay, there was no great reason. Tancred was simply in the way."

Rebuked by the very man who had murdered Derek, Walter lifted his weapon, but Rolf swiftly stayed his arm. "Nay, brother."

Tancred broke the bitter silence. "These enemies in Palermo who paid you to blame Derek's death on me — who are they?" At one time, Tancred had believed Walter himself had been the mind behind it. He no longer believed it and was relieved.

Mosul turned and looked up at him. For a moment he said nothing. A slight, grudging glimmer of respect showed in his eyes as he scanned him. Tancred had fought well and honorably.

"Ibn-Rushid."

Tancred remembered the name but not the man. He exchanged glances with his father Rolf, then Walter. Did they know who he was?

Rolf shook his head and shifted in his saddle, the leather squeaking. "You have heard of him, Walter?"

Walter showed surprise. "A hundred enemies and I am taken off guard by ibn-Rushid."

"Who is he?" Tancred asked.

"A scholar," Walter said with contempt. "A philosopher. It was he who first wished to take your mother to be his wife. I did not know he harbored bitterness against your father Dreux, or you as the offspring. Ibn-Rushid loved the daughter of al-Kareem. That she was given to a Norman lord like Dreux blinded him with bitterness. I should have known . . . but I did not," he said with self-incrimination. "I have not thought of him since you were born."

"Never underestimate an Arab philosopher," said Mosul, his voice contemptuous.

"Next time, I will be wiser," Count Walter retorted. "But that will not bring Derek back, nor will it save you, assassin!"

He gestured for Mosul to be taken from his sight. "Hang him." The others rode off and left Tancred and Walter alone.

Jamil jumped down from Nicholas's horse and was about to run after them to watch the hanging, but Tancred spurred his horse forward and, leaning down, caught him up to the front of his saddle.

"Tancred, I was only going to —"

"I know well what is on your mind. See that rock over there in the shade?"

"Yes. . . ."

"Go sit and contemplate justice. And," he warned, "be there the next time I look."

A minute later Tancred rode back to Count Walter. They rode together to where the stone ruins were scattered below on a sloping mound of earth. Here they stopped and dismounted.

The dry wind rustled the seasonal grasses of browns and golds.

Tancred felt the silence between them. For a long moment neither spoke, then his uncle sighed.

"What will you do now?"

Tancred's answer was swift. "Return to Sicily. This ibn-Rushid must answer."

"I doubt not you will succeed." The blue eyes glinted with subdued pride as they took him in. "You fought well."

Tancred said nothing. Uncomfortable, he turned to see if Jamil was still seated on the rock.

"And after ibn-Rushid?" Walter asked. "Rolf wishes you to stay at the Castle of Hohms."

"I will stay in Sicily," Tancred replied.

Walter's hard eyes softened. "I hoped I would hear you say that."

"I am not asking for sentiment."

"I do not offer sentiment. I speak the truth. Even Rolf was a father to you only legally. It was Nicholas who taught you as a youth to be inwardly strong, to be a warrior. And so you have survived where others would have failed."

He turned his head and looked ahead. "Derek would have failed had he been in your position. He was tender, oft a fool. But you" — he looked at him again — "I knew your courage would drive you on. But to reclaim your honor and to find the true guilty one? I confess I did not know you so well, Tancred. Nicholas did. In truth, he is your father."

"Yes, in that you speak the truth."

"I have something to confess to you —"

"It is not necessary."

Walter looked at him sharply. "Do you fear I will at last show a droplet of tenderness? Is that too much for you to accept?"

"I have learned these years to live with your hate."

"Then I want you to understand what I would never tell another. There was never hate — anything but that. Ask your uncles. They know. I drove myself the more rigorously to find you, not for retribution alone — though I told myself it was so — but for the need to lay eyes on you again. I knew I was wrong but could not humble myself before the clan or you to admit it. I hoped you would humble yourself before me, giving me face to yield, to offer you forgiveness for a crime you did not commit, but you would not relent your integrity, and I would not be the first to admit error in judgment."

"Was it not you who taught me from boyhood never to surrender if my cause was just?"

"Hah! So I did . . . but I have not lived up to my own standard."

"We all fail. That you admit your pride is a consolation to me."

Walter spoke quietly, the tone of his voice strange to Tancred. "Then . . . you *do* understand?"

"I do not fully understand myself. You expect me to understand you? I knew you only as the head of the clan, with the responsibility of being a Norman lord, kin to William the Conqueror. If there is a kinder man within you, I do not know him, nor do I understand him."

"Then you will forgive me if I did not fully understand you. For you also, even as a youth, hid your heart behind armor."

"I was a Moor before you received me as a

Norman son of Dreux. To shield my heart was safer."

"Much safer. I hid mine as well. Do not all men?"

"Then we do understand each other." Tancred looked at him and was able to smile.

Walter, too, showed a brief grin. "Then perhaps we can both understand better in the future. . . . This woman Helena, the niece of Nicholas —" Walter gestured his head back toward where she waited with her uncle. "She is to be congratulated for reaching beyond your armor to your heart." He gave Tancred a hard appraisal. "Where did you find her?"

"Constantinople."

Walter arched his brow. "A spoiled damsel, is she?"

"She improves with time," he said with a glint of amusement in his eyes. "She is well worth the trouble. She was the daughter of General Lysander. Her courage is indomitable. I am exceedingly proud of her."

The tension had eased, yet the constraint between them remained. Words were few; much was left unsaid. Tancred turned to walk back.

"Wait," Walter said.

Tancred paused and followed Walter's gaze to where the Redwans lounged near their horses, watching them.

"You know what they expect, do you not?" said Walter. "Though they would never admit it, they expect a show of peace."

Tancred looked at him and saw the quiet flame of hunger in his uncle's eyes. It would have been easy to walk away. It was difficult to come to grips with the need that he, too, felt. Suddenly he laughed. "Peace, my uncle!" He threw his arms around him.

Count Walter Redwan grasped him tightly. "My son! Everything is yours. The galleons, the merchant shops, the castle — with your strong hand and wit it will survive in my absence. The enemy, like hungry wolves, wait to snatch it up while I am gone."

"What is this? You are not returning?"

"I will go on with Bohemond. We have Antioch. And now? Jerusalem!"

"I have no heart for the crusade," confessed Tancred.

"It is good that you do not."

"We have much to say to each other. But first, there is one more thing I must do before we leave this place." Tancred turned and looked toward the ruins, scanning the area. He rode forward alone.

CHAPTER 27

God Is Good

Tancred found what he was looking for tied some distance away behind the old ruins. He gave a familiar whistle. Alzira pricked up her ears, gave a low whinny, and stood on her hind legs, pawing the air. He came up to untie the rope as the mare turned her soft nose and nuzzled his neck.

"Well, girl, you look none the worse for our long separation. I cannot say the same for your owner." And he searched through Mosul's saddlebags until he found his father's sword with the Redwan heraldic engraved on the handle and sheath. He wondered that Mosul had not destroyed it, but perhaps it gave him reason to gloat each time he saw it, thinking of his cruel victory. At last his precious possessions were his again — the sword of Count Dreux Redwan and Alzira.

He mounted her and rode back through

the ruins to rejoin Helena. The mare's hooves echoed from the ancient stones as she pranced forward, tossing her head and swishing her tail.

Helena, sitting astride the stallion, waited with Nicholas and Jamil to return to the Castle of Hohms.

As Tancred reached them, his eyes on Helena, Jamil's smile was wistful. He turned to Nicholas. "They are happy, are they not, Master Nicholas?"

"They are, Jamil," he agreed. "Such a warrior and so beautiful a lady match well together — especially when she is my niece. Like the wind to the wings of the falcon, and the legs of the Arabian in a race across the desert."

"Come," said Tancred. "Let us leave this forsaken place at once."

Seigneur Rolf Redwan had been disappointed to learn that Tancred would not remain at the castle long. However, his pleasure over the upcoming marriage to Helena and the expectation of visiting many grandchildren in Sicily appeased him. After all, Adrianna would now be staying at the castle instead of returning to Constantinople. He had fallen in love with her while protecting her from Constantine during these past months. As far as Rolf was concerned, it was a miracle, a gift from God. Adrianna had told him she felt the same way. She wanted to remain with him at the Castle of Hohms with her son, now several months old, and eventually they would marry.

Helena had been overjoyed at seeing her mother again and her new baby brother. And now the news that Rolf and Adrianna were to be married! Tancred's and her happiness was complete.

Hakeem, too, had ridden with them to the castle. Now he snored below in the great hall, content to have his head in place, knowing he was returning to the Moorish section of Palermo, where he could once again visit al-Kareem.

And Nicholas, too, had reason for celebration. Adrianna had named her son "Nicholas." Nicholas was pleased over his sister's wish to marry Rolf Redwan. The boy would have a strong father and would be raised to worship Christ. Thereafter, Nicholas had made the surprising decision to go on with the crusader knights to liberate Jerusalem.

"You are sure you will not return to Sicily with us?" asked Tancred.

"In time perhaps. First I wish to see Jerusalem freed, then there is the Lysander inheritance and summer palace in Constantinople to deal with. It belongs to me, Adrianna, and Helena. Who knows whether one day you and Helena might not wish to live there, or your sons and daughters?"

"Then if you will be going on to Jerusalem with the crusader knights, I would ask that you return the relic," Tancred told him, reaching into his tunic and pulling out a small cloth bundle. Wrapped inside the aged material was the ancient lance head that Odo Redwan, the family priest at the Redwan castle in Palermo, had so long ago entrusted to him to return to its place at the Holy Sepulcher in Jerusalem. It was purported to have belonged to the Roman soldier who pierced Christ's side at His crucifixion.

Tancred handed the sacred object to Nicholas and said, "I entrust this to your safekeeping now. May God go with you."

"And with you, my son," said Nicholas. "Do not fear for me. I will live through this crusade, and you will one day greet me in Sicily and introduce me to your children!"

After darkness fell, Tancred stood on the castle steps with Helena in his arms. How silent the desert night! How warm the wind coming down from the rocky hills! How delicate the pale yellow of the moon in the ebony sky! Tomorrow they would leave for St.

Symeon to catch a boat to Cyprus, and from there to the Norman kingdom of Sicily.

"I have great reason to express my gratefulness to God. I now possess what I have wanted since the first time I saw you. Like a vision you had vanished. And now you are here, and you are mine. As God is gracious, I shall marry you in Sicily."

Her eyes looked directly into his. His hands were warm and strong as they drew her against him.

"I am yours," she whispered. "I will always be yours."

The Redwan castle, Helena thought with excitement. *Sicily . . . Palermo . . . what will life be like with Tancred?*

Jamil approached from the courtyard. He sported a fancy hat with a feather, which Nicholas had given him. He stopped when he saw Tancred and Helena locked in each other's arms. The smile on his handsome young face showed his own satisfaction. Life in the West was going to be good, he told himself. He sensed it in his heart. He could feel it in the warm westerly wind that had risen like a blessing from God, softly touching his face. He remembered his sister, Aziza, with sadness and yet hope. He looked up at the silvery stars and knew that as a

Christian with faith in the Savior Jesus, she had a new home with Him, where she was forever safe. He silently retraced his steps to find Nicholas.

God is good, he thought, and he left his new parents in their joyful embrace.

Glossary

craven: a Norman trial to establish guilt or innocence.

gonfanon: a banner that hangs directly from the shaft of a lance, just below the lance head.

Great Horse: a specially bred war horse of the western knights that could endure heavy weight and the clash of battle. It responded to leg commands so the knight could fight with both hands.

heraldic: a family insignia worn on the helmet, gonfanon, or shield.

keep: the stronghold of the castle, used as a watchtower and arsenal. The thick walls were laced with arrow loops. Usually there was a well beneath. The storage and eating rooms were above, and sleeping quarters were on the top level.

mace: a favorite weapon of warrior-priests; was sanctified and carried in ceremonial processions, slung on a loop on the right wrist. It was made of wood with quatrefoil-shaped head.

morning star: a type of mace; a round ball studded with spikes and attached to a handle by a chain.

scimitar: a curved single-edged sword of eastern origin.

seigneur: the trusted commander of a castle, a term of respect.

LINDA CHAIKIN is a full-time, best-selling author. She is a graduate of Multnomah School of the Bible in Portland, Oregon. She and her husband, Steve, are involved with a church-planting mission among Hindus in Kerala, India. They make their home in California.

All our Large Print titles are designed for easy reading, and all our books are made to last. Other Thorndike Press Large Print books are available at your library, through selected bookstores, or directly from us.

For information about titles, please call:

(800) 223-1244

or visit our Web site at: www.gale.com/thorndike

To share your comments, please write:

Publisher
Thorndike Press
P.O. Box 159
Thorndike, Maine 04986

F   22.95
Chai   Thorndike
Chaikin, Linda. <u>LARGE PRINT</u>
Behind the Veil.